With Devils Dwell

Anne Reeve

First published in Great Britain in 2013 by Anne Reeve

Typeset by A M Graphics,
240 Bloomfield Road, Blackpool. FY1 6QG

Printed and bound by Moulton Printing,
132 Highfield Road, Blackpool. FY4 2HH

WITH DEVILS DWELL

When Alyce Wilson suffers a blow to her head with Doctor Owen Rathlin's hansom cab, she is taken inside his house to recover. She is unable to remember anything. Owen decides to 'christen' her with a new name, Rhoda Lambay, 'Lambay Street so you won't forget where I live will you Rhoda Lambay?' With his departure Rhoda becomes aware of something sinister in the house. Her decision to leave early next morning puts Rhoda's life in jeopardy. She has been caught like a fish in a net, with no way of escape. Danger, terror and fear of not knowing her past produces a dread of the future. Her only friend is Molly a convict girl. It is with Molly's help she has to learn to play the 'deadly games' that will test her own sanity and strength. Can she capture the 'devil serpent' in its own trap and set free the elusive butterfly which remains deeply hidden within the 'tangled terrors' securely locked behind her own 'secret door'?

Dedicated to the memory of John, a devoted father and a loving husband.

There is a dreadful Hell
And everlasting pains
There sinners must with devils dwell
In darkness, fire and chains
　　　Song 11 (Heaven and Hell)
　　　Doctor Isaac Watts

I

Alyce opened her eyes aware of dark hair and a frowning face looking down at her. 'She's coming round,' the man's voice said. She tried to get up but strong hands stopped her. 'Where am I?' she asked. She felt dampness seeping into her clothing. Soft mist blended into hazy faces.

'Stay where you are. You're quite safe. I'm Doctor Owen Rathlin.'

The handsome face peered closer. Dark brown eyes stared intently into hers. He spoke softly and held her hand.

'I'm so sorry. My hansom cab knocked you down. You...'

She vaguely heard what he said. The next thing she remembered was waking up between crisp white cotton sheets, with a faint waft of lavender, tucked up in a warm bed.

'Is this a hospital?' she asked, growing frightened. 'Where am I?'

'Bless you no love. This is Doctor Rathlin's house.'

The voice belonged to a plump smiling woman who moved around the room making sure everything was in its place. She came over to the bed, arms folded across her stiff, white apron.

'Now, don't you worry none,' she smiled down at her, 'Doctor Rathlin will look after you. I'm Martha, the Doctor's housekeeper.'

Martha stooped to pick up a worn brown leather bag.

'You had this valise with you Miss...I'll leave it here beside you.'

'A valise?' Alyce echoed. 'I don't recognise it. Are you sure it's mine?'

'You can open it later Miss...Err...umm...What name shall I call you Miss?' Martha paused with her hand on the brass doorknob. Alyce felt the air in the room almost choke her. Fear pushed ajar the secret door, deep down in her inner soul. It created a cold draught.

'I DON'T KNOW,' she cried. 'I DON'T REMEMBER MY NAME!'

'You had a nasty bang on the head. Try and rest now.'

Martha nodded her head and closed the door quietly.

Later when Doctor Rathlin entered the room, he looked concerned. He took hold of her hand gently. The warmth of his hand helped reassure her.

'Martha tells me you can't remember your name', he said.

'I can't remember anything doctor,' replied Alyce.

'It will come back to you soon. This sometimes happens when you receive a blow to the head. You were lucky you weren't killed,' said Doctor Rathlin. He held her face between strong lean fingers.

'You have bruises to your face and neck', he observed. He held out her arms. 'And here too. It looks as if you've had a beating of some sort.'

When he stood up he towered over her.

'Can you remember how you got them?' he asked. 'They're certainly not from your accident.'

She shook her head. A salty tear ran down her cheek. She caught it deftly with her tongue, so that he wouldn't notice.

'You must stay here until you are well enough.'

He crossed to the window and pulled aside the heavy velvet curtain. 'It was this damned fog that caused your accident', he said.

Alyce could see fingers of fog beckoning her. She shuddered and was suddenly glad of the safety and warmth of the strange bed. She heard him give a deep sigh. He closed the curtain, turned and walked towards her smiling.

'Now, a temporary name for you,' he said, smiling.

He snapped his long fingers as if he were plucking something from the air.

'Let's see… What about....Rhoda Lambay?' he suggested.

'Rhoda Lambay?' she whispered softly. 'Yes I like Rhoda.'

'And ...Lambay Street, London, is where I live here', he said.

They laughed together.

'Now you won't forget that will you?' he asked.

'No...I'll never forget it.'

Accepting her new name Rhoda felt her face growing warmer. She felt the secret door inside her open ever so slightly, letting in soft gossamer wings that fluttered, something she hadn't experienced before.

When he left the room her head started to throb. She rested against the perfumed lavender pillow. Then she remembered the valise. She hadn't opened it. Reaching for it Rhoda threw the contents onto the bed. A purple striped cotton dress, handkerchiefs, five gold sovereigns, a silver mirror and silver hair brush embossed with swirling leaves of ivy and flowers. Rhoda studied herself in the mirror. A pale face with large sea green eyes stared back at her. There were a few bruises on her face. How on earth did they get there, she wondered.

Lifting the hairbrush she brushed her shimmering red gold hair, and as she did so a golden dart of memory struck her........soft mewling kittens in a box.... She smiled at the memory of it. Then like a magician's sleight of hand she saw....BLOOD...red like popping bursting berries, holly berry red, running down her fingers. She threw the mirror. It crashed against the wooden washstand. Rhoda stared at it, unable to understand what was happening to her.

Carefully climbing out of the bed she crossed the room. Hands shaking, holding a blue flowered jug, she poured warm water into the china wash bowl. After washing, she was surprised to see no sign of any blood in the water or on her fingers.

Martha appeared with a tray of hot chicken soup and soft bread rolls. The smell of food made Rhoda realise how hungry she was. She flopped down on the patchwork quilt. Her heart bumped like a collie's tail hitting a cold larder door.

'Found anything to help you remember Miss?'

Martha set the tray down and eyed the contents on the bed. Rhoda shook her head.

'No nothing. I don't recognise any of it as belonging to me.'

'Never you mind. It will all come back to you, never fear. Now eat this while it's hot Miss Rhoda. It will do you good it will.'

Rhoda smiled faintly at her new name. At least she had been given some identity. Martha's keen eyes spotted the silver mirror. She picked up all the pieces and carried them carefully across the room to show Rhoda.

'Oh dear, look at this Miss Rhoda!' Martha cried. 'The mirror's broken. Now that means seven years bad luck if ever there was.'

II

Rhoda felt much better the next morning. The suffocating mist that had hovered outside her bedroom window was slowly whisping its way into soft lighter swathes. Her head continued to throb and try as she may she couldn't remember anything about herself. She had eaten a good breakfast of lightly boiled egg and toasted muffins, muffled in butter. She had just finished her tea when Martha came bursting into the room.

'Doctor Rathlin would like you to come down to the drawing room, please Miss Rhoda, to meet Mrs Rathlin.'

Rhoda pulled at the thin cotton dress and looked worried.

'Do you feel alright Miss....?' Martha looked concerned. 'I mean I can tell them you don't feel up to it if.....'

'No...No...It's just this dress. It's not at all suitable is it Martha?'

'Well in the circumstances you look fine. Don't you worry now.'

On the way down stairs Martha told her that her grey woollen dress was being cleaned and that it should be ready later.

Martha opened the door to the drawing room. Rhoda took a deep breath and stepped inside. She was surprised at the gloom. The heavy blue drapes were partly open, allowing the only light in the room together with the fire, which burned steadily in the hearth. Fringed crimson pelmets stretched across the mantelpiece, like long arms greeting each other. Rhoda became fascinated with the gleaming brass fender. It guarded the ornate fireplace like a walled fortress. The brass fire irons glowed in the firelight like hundreds of staring unblinking eyes. Rhoda turned her head away from their hypnotic gaze. A hand stretched out to greet her.

'Rhoda, come and meet Mrs Rathlin.'

Doctor Rathlin caught hold of her arm and steered her gently through small tables laden with all kinds of objects. A strong perfume of musk filled the air. With the heat from the fire Rhoda felt as if she were about to faint. Doctor Rathlin must have sensed her fear. His strong hand tightened on her arm. He bent his head close to her warm face.

'Don't be afraid Rhoda,' he said.

As he pressed his hand firmly against the back of her waist she could feel the warmth of it through her thin cotton dress. Now that her eyes had become accustomed to the gloom she saw a figure seated in the corner, close to a large Chinese vase that held long feathered grasses. Mrs Rathlin sat in a high backed mahogany chair, a grey fringed shawl draped across her lap. She held out a long, thin hand towards Rhoda.

'You look well my dear,' she said in a tired voice.

Rhoda tried not to stare at her too much, but she couldn't help it. The red of the fire seared scarlet, the heat more intense. Rhoda could see sunken eyes, surrounded by pock marked skin. Thin yellow hair sprouted out from a white lace cap. Mrs Rathlin was hideously disfigured. Rhoda thought her age to be around sixty years. Rhoda immediately felt sorry for her. She placed her feet on one of the large cabbage roses on the green carpet and bent closer towards her.

'I feel much better today thank you,' she said.

There was a long silence in the room. Rhoda had the feeling she should not be there. A clock struck the half hour. Doctor Rathlin spoke.

'Goodness me! I must be away.' He turned to Rhoda. 'I'm afraid I have to go away for several weeks.' He squeezed Rhoda's hand. 'But you are welcome to stay here for as long as you wish.' Rhoda knew her cheeks were burning. How she wished he could stay. She felt so safe with him near to her. He seemed loathe to let go of her hand. 'And don't worry about your memory. It will return I promise you.'

He gazed down at her, his brown eyes appearing to tell her something, but she didn't know what it was. The more she looked into his eyes it was as though she was drawn to them. Rhoda thought she could see a sadness there, something lurking in their hidden depths. He dropped her hand quickly, running his hand across his dark brow.

'I'll just have a word with Martha, before I leave,' he said.

Rhoda watched his tall frame leave the room. It was as if part of her soul had gone with him. She became confused by her emotions, thinking they could be accounted for by the blow to her head.

'Strange you cannot remember who you are,' said Mrs Rathlin. She peered more closely at her. Rhoda touched her own face. It was burning. Suddenly the atmosphere in the room had changed. The tone of Mrs Rathlin's voice had changed... it had become menacing.

'No...I can't remember who I am.'

Rhoda watched as the hundreds of glowing eyes of the brass irons winked knowingly in the fierce firelight.

'How...old...are...you?' Mrs Rathlin snarled the words at her.

She suddenly felt afraid of this woman, wanting to run from her and the stifling room.

'I don't know. I'm sorry I........'

'Can't remember...is that it? How fortunate for you to have Doctor Rathlin bring you here.' She stopped and tapped her thin fingers on the shawl.

'Let me see, you must be seventeen or eighteen years of age I'd say.'

'I'm really sorry. I wish I knew.'

'What about parents..... Do you have a mother, father, sister, brother or … A LOVER maybe?'

Rhoda shook her head. Why was Mrs Rathlin questioning her like this?

'Come now...Don't tell me you're an orphan child.'

Before Rhoda could give an answer Mrs Rathlin had waved her hand.

'Don't tell me. I can guess what YOU are!'

She started to rise from her chair, her long thin hand raised as if to strike Rhoda.

'Look at the way you're dressed. Do you want money? Is that what you want? I know what you are, a common slut.'

Rhoda protested hotly. 'I'm sorry about the way I'm dressed, but this is all I had in my valise. My other dress is being cleaned by Martha. As for me wanting money Mrs Rathlin, I have money in my valise...'

'So what do you want then?'

Mrs Rathlin walked towards her. Rhoda backed away in fear. Why was Mrs Rathlin behaving in this way?

'Nothing, but I object to you calling me a slut. I am....'

'Leaving here as soon as......' Mrs Rathlin added to her words but Rhoda didn't hear the rest. The room swallowed her. A high black wave swelled over her. Rhoda let herself drown in the black inkwell.

When she opened her eyes she was looking up at Doctor Rathlin.

'Do you feel better now?' he asked.

She was lying on the bed. Martha came in with a tumbler of cool water for her to sip. Rhoda was alarmed at what had happened. She clasped his hand. He mistook her fear for the sudden fainting spell she had experienced. She was afraid to tell him what had happened between her and Mrs Rathlin when he had left the room. For one moment she thought she had imagined it all. Perhaps it was from the blow to her head. She gripped his hand tighter. He looked concerned.

'It's alright. You're fine now. Try and rest. I've arranged for a Doctor Roberts to see you while I'm away.'

'Thank you for being so kind to me,' she whispered.

He squeezed her shoulder. 'Has something frightened you? Have you remembered something?'

She shook her head, fighting back tears that welled into her green eyes stinging them like soap bubbles. The lump in her throat was painful.

'I'm sorry that I have to go away. But it is important.'

Again he appeared loathe to let go of her hand. She continued to cling to him as if her very life depended on him. He frowned at her again.

'Are you sure you will be alright, Rhoda Lambay?'

She smiled when he said her name. He said it as if he had always known her. It was difficult to break the invisible thread that drew their gazes together. She looked down at her hands breaking the invisible bond.

'Remember, if you ever want my assistance at any time.....well, what I mean is...err...will you let me know when your memory returns?'

As he left the room he paused by the door.

'I would like to know your real name...You can't keep the name of Rhoda Lambay forever can you?' he said.

She sat up, folding her hands in her lap. They felt warm from his grip.

'I might have to keep it if I can't remember my real name. After all you christened me with it, Doctor Rathlin.'

'Yes I did. And my real name is Owen Rathlin. Will you remember?'

'I will always remember. And thank you again.....Owen Rathlin.'

'I don't make a habit of giving beautiful women new names. But be good Rhoda Lambay.'

He winked at her and she flushed. Oh why did he have to go? He touched his forehead, as if in a salute to her. Then he was gone.

She pressed her hot face into the lavender scented pillow and let her tears soak into the white linen. He didn't say how long he would be away. But Rhoda knew in that moment, she could not stay in the house much longer. Mrs Rathlin had made her feelings very clear. His mother was obviously an extremely possessive person where her son Owen was concerned.

It was later when Martha came into her room to see if she was feeling better. She carried a tray of dainty sandwiches, some fruit and a silver pot of tea.

'A pity there wasn't anything in your valise to help you remember Miss Rhoda.'

She put the tray down on the bed.

'Now have some nice hot tea and sandwiches. This will make you feel better.'

She decided not to tell Martha what had been said when she met Mrs Rathlin that morning in the drawing room. Martha fussed about the room. It was obvious to Rhoda that Doctor Rathlin's mother was old and infirm. Perhaps if she tried to open some conversation with Martha about Mrs Rathlin she might be able to understand her hostile attitude towards her. The strange woman had disturbed her and made her feel afraid. But then Rhoda felt some pity for Mrs Rathlin. It might not have been her intention to hurt with such barbed remarks. Rhoda wondered how she had become so disfigured. But why on earth should Mrs Rathlin hate her so? She couldn't help having the accident with the hansom cab. Mrs Rathlin wanted to keep her son solely to herself for some reason or other.

Rhoda sipped the hot tea.

'Doctor Rathlin's mother looks quite ill. I fear she is suffering from a dreadful disease of some kind poor woman. I do so pity her.'

Martha stopped plumping up the pillows on the bed, turned round and stared at Rhoda with a look of astonishment on her face.

'Did you say 'MOTHER?' Martha asked.

Rhoda put down the delicate, blue flowered china cup carefully.

'Yes. I said Doctor Rathlin's mother looks quite ill I…..'

'Isabella Rathlin is Doctor Rathlin's ......WIFE........NOT... his mother.' Martha bent down to continue making the bed.

'She can hardly walk or talk at all now.'

Martha stood up and rubbed her back.

'Yet she is so sweet and good natured for all of it. Never a cross word from her. Never.'

Were they talking about the same woman? Rhoda began to wonder if the blow to her head had made her insane. She could never tell Martha what had happened when she met Isabella Rathlin that morning. Who would believe her? She became afraid again. A small secret door deep within her opened slightly letting in a cold draught of terror. She thought about the holly berry blood on her hands earlier. She glanced down at her clenched hands showing white knuckles, then turned them over slowly. Yes, there it was again, drops of red blood. Why? Why did she keep seeing them? She knew then she had to get away from the house. Something was about to happen to her. She could smell the fear of it.

III

Rhoda had spent a restless night. Now that Owen Rathlin had gone away she didn't feel safe in the house. Isabella Rathlin had made it quite clear that she didn't want her there. Martha had been loathe to talk about her mistress. She was loyal to them both. She had just shaken her head and murmured 'poor soul'

Rhoda made a quick plan. Her valise was already packed . Martha had put the contents back neatly for her. She dressed herself quickly then sat down to write a letter to Doctor and Mrs Rathlin, thanking them both for their kindness to her. She sealed the envelope and put it on the dressing table. She could be away and out of the house before anyone knew she was gone. Rhoda picked up her valise.

Her hand was on the door knob when a loud knocking stopped her.

'Open up in the name of the law!' a voice shouted.

Rhoda was startled. What on earth could be wrong at this hour of the morning. She opened her door. A constable stood in the doorway.

'Aha! Just about to leave were you Miss?'

He stared down at Rhoda and the valise she was carrying.

'Yes I was. Why what's happening?'

The constable entered the room closely followed by Mrs Rathlin. She pushed herself past Rhoda as the constable caught hold of the valise.

'Oh dear I must sit down. Oh my poor old heart!'

Mrs Rathlin flopped down into an armchair, clutching her chest.

'This is all too much for me constable.'

'Open up your valise, please Miss,' the constable ordered.

There on top of the contents was a white cotton petticoat. Rhoda knew immediately that it didn't belong to her. The constable picked it up and handed it to Mrs Rathlin.

'This your petticoat Madam?' he asked the shocked Mrs Rathlin.

'Yes, it's mine. Look it has my name on it, 'Isabella Rathlin' see here.'

She showed the name to the constable.

'There… I knew she was a thief the moment I saw her.'

Mrs Rathlin's face was red with anger.

'This is what comes of my husband taking someone in off the streets constable. You get no thanks for showing kindness and Christian service.'

Rhoda was only half listening. Her eyes were on the white petticoat. How on earth had it got there? Who would have put it in her valise? It could only be a mistake. Her thoughts were interrupted as she heard Mrs

Rathlin say her name wasn't really Rhoda Lambay.

'Is that right Miss? Using an alias are you then?' The constable looked serious.

At last Rhoda found her voice. She had been so taken aback at what had happened.

'I didn't take the petticoat constable. I don't know how it got into my valise. It must be some dreadful mistake.'

Rhoda felt her face getting hot.

'Dreadful it is...taking you in off the.....'

Before Mrs Rathlin could finish, Rhoda stopped her.

'I can say with all honesty I didn't take the petticoat constable.'

'Honesty doesn't seem to suit you Miss. Now what's your real name?' The constable was getting impatient.

'I don't know constable. I've lost my memory,' said Rhoda.

The constable checked the rest of the contents of the valise.

'A funny assortment I must say.' He held up the gold sovereigns. Mrs Rathlin's eyes glittered with hatred.

'Well I can honestly say they are not mine constable. But they could well be stolen from someone else.'

Mrs Rathlin gave Rhoda a sly look.

It was only much later after she had been arrested and flung into a cell that Rhoda could think clearly. She had kept protesting her innocence and now to find herself imprisoned for stealing made her feel angry. She tried to remember what had happened before the accident with Owen Rathlin's hansom cab. Where could she have been going to or coming from? Mrs Rathlin had said about her parents, but no matter how she tried she couldn't remember a thing about them. Everything appeared like twisting, tantalising mists. Then other thoughts played a goading game with her. Perhaps she was a thief. There was certainly a strange assortment of things in her valise. Rhoda could not recognise any of them as hers. She knew she hadn't stolen the white petticoat. Her memory was clear after the accident. She could swear on the holy bible she did not steal it.

Her situation was now desperate. No one knew where she was and wouldn't think of looking in a prison cell for her. Fear softly pushed ajar the secret door again. She felt the cold rush of air. She wanted to cry out against it but it held her. She rocked backwards and forwards on the hard bench willing herself not to see the blood on her hands.

There had to be a way out of her predicament. She sat still. She would write a letter. She would write to Owen Rathlin. She wiped her tears on the hem of her dress. But he had gone away. For how long? And Isabella Rathlin would only see it and open it. It wouldn't do. There had to be another way. She rocked to and fro again. Tomorrow she would remember everything. Tomorrow.....

Rhoda stared down at her hands...holly berry, blood red, drops...Why was she seeing them again? Where did they come from? Was it a sly trick of her imagination playing a game of guilt? If only she could remember.

Rhoda felt faint again. Her head ached and the stifling situation engulfed her like an unseen force. It surrounded her, like a serpent's coils crushing her cold body. Was it a form of madness that had taken hold of her? Was she going insane? She felt as if she couldn't breathe.

She stood up screaming, pushing clammy fingers hard against her forehead willing herself not to see the blood. Cautiously she looked down at her hands again, turned them over palms upwards and stretched the trembling fingers wide apart... the blood had gone. Vanished....like a magician's sleight of hand.

IV

Rhoda spent a terrible night locked up in the cell. The sounds of women's screams and curses seemed like a living nightmare from which she would never wake up. She had screamed out herself, protested her innocence and even cursed the white petticoat. But no one heard her. The gaoler had kicked the door with some force and called out to her.

'Make less noise or you'll have the stick.'

The next morning she heard the rattle of the bolts being drawn back. She sat up. For one moment she thought it might be for her freedom. The door swung open. A young girl was shoved through, almost losing her footing until Rhoda caught hold of her to save her fall. The young girl, with dark brown hair and shining eyes as black as blackberries, stared down at her. She looked to be the same age as herself but taller. She stood before Rhoda, her hands on her hips.

'Hello I'm Molly. Thanks for catching me.'

Rhoda made some room for her on the cold bench. Molly continued to stare.

'You look like a lady...or something. What are you in for?'

Rhoda shook her head. Tears filled her eyes again.

'No...I'm no lady. I don't think I'm a 'something' either?'

Rhoda felt herself go hot with anger.

'I didn't steal any rotten white petticoat. It's all a mistake. I didn't steal anything.'

Molly put her arm around Rhoda's shoulders. She laughed softly.

'Well I did,' Molly whispered to her. 'I took a cheese! Well, stole it I suppose.'

'A cheese?' Rhoda gasped in surprise. 'You mean a whole cheese?'

'Well yes... I was blumin' hungry,' Molly shouted out.

Rhoda started to giggle. The thought of Molly eating a whole cheese was too much for her. Molly screwed her nose up and down like a mouse. Then she laughed too. They could both see the funny side of it.

'Well I was going to sell it, not eat it all. Why are you in here then?' Rhoda told her whole story, from the time of her accident until her arrest for stealing the white petticoat belonging to Isabella Rathlin.

'So this Doctor gave you a new name then. It sounds very posh I must say. I wish I had a posh name instead of plain Molly Williams, one time dairy maid.'

'Well the name Rhoda Lambay is only until I remember my real name. Owen Rathlin thinks my memory will come back soon.'

'God love us all!' exclaimed Molly. Her eyes shining like blackberries widened even larger. 'What are you going to do about it?'

'What am I going to do about what?'

'About getting out of here, that's what. This Isabella Rathlin sounds very sinister to me. Why would she be against you, for being in her house?'

It all seemed so unreal. She had to agree with Molly.

Molly stood up and faced her with arms folded.

'It seems as if Isabella Rathlin wanted you out of the house forever.' She bent closer to Rhoda and whispered, 'Jealousy I shouldn't wonder.'

'Jealousy?'

'She might have thought you were going to steal her husband.'

Rhoda flushed as she remembered the strong, lean hands, the kind, brown eyes that looked like deep, fathomless pools gazing down at her.

'That's absolute nonsense,' Rhoda protested.

'Why? ...Was he handsome then, this old Doctor Rathlin?'

Rhoda's heart fluttered like a rare and undiscovered butterfly, waiting to be named. She could only stop its movements by pressing her hand firmly against her heart. She was afraid of the sensations it gave her yet at the same time experienced a warmth from it. It became a living thing, a part of her, primitive in form. Even in that moment she knew it would remain deep within her, hidden, secret, until the time came when it could be named. A christening, like her new name...Rhoda Lambay.

'Old?...He's not old...he's...ummm...a good doctor. Yes he's a very good Doctor...Owen Rathlin.'

'Oooh Owen is it? ... and...?'

'And yes, I suppose he is handsome... in a way.'

'Well there you are then. It should be staring you in the face Rhoda. You being very pretty she thought you would steal his heart away!'

'That's preposterous Molly. It never entered my head!'"

'Well post pret us or not. It certainly entered HER head!' declared Molly.

Rhoda and Molly laughed together. As they laughed Rhoda wondered had she shared such laughter like this with someone in her past? The last person had been Owen Rathlin. Would she ever see him again?

As time passed Molly became a dear and close friend. She would never have got through the dark, miserable days without her company. The headaches were painful each day. Rhoda prayed she would get some relief. The warders took no notice of her complaint. The sickness was the worst part. It was as if the whole of her insides were being drawn with an invisible hook up into her red-raw throat. Every minute, in every hour, each bleak day passed like grey, silk strands of strangling fear.

The chilled voices of the gaolers and the tormented cries of the women prisoners who cursed their way through the barriers of contempt and suffering, echoed through the gaol and, trying to push their futile way through these barriers, were the soft sobs of hollow-faced, wide-eyed children.

Rhoda could no longer eat.

'You must keep your strength up Rhoda. You have to face the Magistrate,' Molly implored her, as she forced her to eat with small mouthfuls of food.

'I can't Molly. I would rather die I feel so wretched.'

'You're not going to die Rhoda. You must be strong.'

When the dreaded day of her trial arrived, Rhoda was so sick and petrified she could hardly stand. Molly sponged her face with a torn piece of her own white petticoat. Rhoda clutched the damp cloth close to her breast. Her head was throbbing with so much pain. She tried to cling to Molly but they were roughly shoved apart. Her legs felt weak as she was pulled along by a brutal gaoler. What was going to happen to her now? Then it was her turn to enter the dimly lit court room.

Everything was spinning in the room, faces whirling around her, strangers to her, every one of them. Not one friendly face. There was so much being said she only vaguely heard the words. She could see faces leering at her, heard voices as if from far away. Her head was swimming in a downward spiral, in a whirlpool of vapour, like a stealthy serpent dragging her down to its lair. She could hear some muffled words...'petticoat stolen' 'Isabella Rathlin took her in'...'she took advantage of a good Christian woman.' Rhoda protested and tried to protect her innocence.

The Magistrate asked her what her real name was. He looked impatient waiting for her to reply.

'I'm sorry but I don't remember my real name...'

'You've got nothing to say, unless the Court hears your real name.'

The Magistrate was nodding his head towards Isabella Rathlin who sat fanning her face in the heat of the courtroom. In the haze Rhoda could see her gloating at his words. But where was Owen Rathlin? Why did she imagine he would be there to rescue her from this terrifying ordeal? He had gone away. If only there was some way for him to find her. If only... as she thought about it she knew it was impossible. She gripped the wooden rail in one last effort to remain on her feet, looking around the court room for the last time, in case he might be there in the turmoil of faces.

Then more accusations against her, more words... 'Five gold sovereigns'... 'other items must have been stolen.'

Finally Rhoda screamed out that her name was not Rhoda Lambay. She didn't know what it was. The irate Magistrate muttered something she could not hear. He was oblivious to her pleas. Her sweating hands, which had so desperately clung to the slippery wooden rail, lost their grip. Rhoda slumped to the hard scrubbed floor in a faint. She had missed what the Magistrate had said to her. She had missed out on her last plea for mercy.

She had missed hearing her sentence.

When she woke again Molly was leaning over her looking anxious.

'You're quite safe. Stay where you are...'

In her agitated state of mind, she thought it was Owen Rathlin, come to help her. Molly had unknowingly used the same words as he had done.

This confused her.

'What's happened?' she asked struggling to sit up.

Molly forced her to lie back down.

'You've been ill for days. Thank God you've come round.'

'What do you mean 'for days'? Have I been ill so long? I don't remember. Molly what's happening? I have to get back into the Court Room. I have to plead for....'

'That was days ago. You fainted and they carried you back here. You've already been sentenced...'

Rhoda tried to sit up. 'What do you mean sentenced? What sentence?'

'It's alright Rhoda, I'm with you but you must rest now before we leave for Millbank. We'll be held there for a while.'

'MILLBANK! What's that?'

'It's a prison on the banks of the River Thames. Don't worry Rhoda. We're together. No matter what happens I'll look after you. You've become my dearest friend. Don't worry.'

Rhoda sipped some of the water Molly had brought her. She squeezed the scrap of white petticoat drenched with cold water on to her face.

'Molly please, don't let me faint again. I feel as if I'm dying when I do. Talk to me Molly. Just keep talking to me.'

Rhoda trembled. What was Molly talking about...prison...being held there? Why were they being held? What for and where was Owen?...He must come to help her. She clung on to the memory of his face as she fell back on to the hard bunk. Tiredness overwhelmed her.

'Someone will come to get me you'll see, someone will come.'

'Get some rest now,' Molly said gently. 'Try and sleep. We have a long voyage ahead of us.' But Rhoda never heard. She was asleep.

V

Rhoda stared down at the heavy irons that constricted her ankles.

'Why do we have to wear these, we're not going anywhere?'

'You're all wearing them because you are about to be transported to Millbank,' the warder announced in a loud voice. 'It's a clearing house for female transportees. You'll be given new clothing. Now line up!'

Rhoda managed to catch Molly's hand, she could hardly stand up. The warder pushed some of the older women roughly into line. Some of the children were crying noisily as they clung to their mothers' skirts.

The coach they were travelling in lurched violently, rocking from side to side with its weighted cargo of female prisoners. It was a clear night. A few stars were shining. She could feel the fresh, cold night air on her face. It gave her a glimmer of hope that someone would find her at last. Perhaps here at Millbank she would be able to contact Owen Rathlin. If only her memory would return. If she could find out her real identity that would give her some hope of gaining her freedom.

As Rhoda entered Millbank, she could see towering walls and turrets which resembled a castle. A wall with high pointed railings surrounded it.

A few solitary bushes guarded the arched gateway while overhead a yellow lamp gave out a feeble light. The place looked formidable but once inside it appeared to buzz with cleanliness and efficiency.

'Discipline and order are carried out here,' said a buxom warder. 'Newgate Prison is a filthy place with no order. Here any misconduct will be noted. Warders will make a report on your character.'

Rhoda tried to stay close to Molly as they were all ushered into a freezing room. Cries of horror went up from the women assembled there. Rhoda was soon to know the reason why. Their hair was to be shorn.

When it was her turn, Rhoda tried to resist but she was over-powered by two heavy handed warders. The scissors sheared through her long golden hair. This was the utmost degradation. She was powerless to overcome the horror of it all. She watched an old lady forcibly held down. The woman recoiled in horror at what was about to happen to her. She spat and scratched her captors, kicking and screaming abuse at them.

'You won't take my hair. You can beat me, but don't cut my hair!'

One of the warders knocked her on the jaw. She fell silent as her head lolled to one side of the chair. Rhoda squeezed her fists hard. Why didn't she rebel against it like the old lady. Her head started to hurt again with the rough handling of the shears. She looked down at the stone floor littered with locks of hair. It was a carpet of hair - brown, black, soft children's hair, chestnut. Her own crowning glory of tresses mingled as in a blaze of colour they fell. Their last vestige of womanliness had gone, disappeared under fresh tangled heaps, fluttered and blended with the thin, frail strands of grey. Brushed, curled, straight, even, unkempt hair alive with lice. All had fallen there… like hopes, dreams, all sheared away.

In that vulnerable situation she remembered…other hands, soft white hands that had brushed her hair with a silver brush. 'One hundred strokes for beautiful hair.' It was her mother's voice that came to her, she knew. It startled her, that wisp of a memory. It had appeared to her in all its softness, downy, like a baby's first curl…Then it was gone. The sobs of the women added to her own.

After a tepid bath a change of dress. Brown serge, a blue check apron and muslin cap. Rhoda was glad of the cap. She pulled it down well over her forehead to hide her shorn hair. After supper of bread, gruel and salt, the hard board was raised up on her bench to serve as a pillow. Rhoda slept soundly for the first time since her arrest.

The next morning she saw Molly when someone read them the scriptures. They were put into groups of twelve. A thin girl who looked about their own age called Lizzie smiled at them as she was put into their group.

'Cor blimey, we're like the twelve disciples,' Lizzie sighed.

Rhoda caught the eye of one small boy with large blue eyes. She managed to give him a smile. He clutched his mother's hand tightly.

'How long will we be here?' he asked his mother. She shook her head and looked sadly at Rhoda.

That night Rhoda couldn't sleep. There were so many questions she wanted to ask Molly. She opened her mouth to talk to her then decided against it. Molly looked worried and tired. She tried hard to sleep but the noise was terrible. The shouts of the warders, the curses of the women and sudden screams in the night made them both start up shaking with fright. Rhoda closed her eyes and tried to shut out her surroundings. Then suddenly leaping, tumbling thoughts came hurtling towards her. Her head ached constantly. Thoughts, flying, whirling, spinning, came cart-wheeling into her mind like a mad troupe of unrehearsed acrobats, who, when finally tiring of their unpolished performance, left her breathless, anxious for the next act to begin. Rhoda wondered if she was going mad. The place was like Bedlam….

VI

The days seemed to fly by at Millbank. Rhoda had surprised herself by knowing so much about the scriptures. She was given a group of female convicts to read to them each day religious tracts and scripture from the bible.

One foggy day, when they finished their daily exercise in the yard, a middle aged visitor came to see Rhoda. Mrs Rebecca Evans. She was a gentle lady with a small face and cheeks that looked like shrivelled rosy apples. Mrs Evans was from the Ladies Committee and was surprised when Rhoda told her she knew most of the scriptures stories and read to the convict women...

'Well my dear, you appear to have good manners, dignity and decorum,' said Mrs Evans with a warm smile. Then her face became serious. 'But tell me, what manner of sin brought you to this shocking place?'

Rhoda knew she would be able to confide in her. Mrs Evans listened, intent on every word that Rhoda said.

'Well... If I can help you in any way my dear, of course I will.'

Mrs Evans looked concerned. 'It does seem very strange indeed that Mrs Rathlin was so rude to you, especially a lady in her position. As to why she planted the white petticoat in your valise....well. It may be that the poor lady might well be losing her mind.' Mrs Evans sat down again on the wooden benches.

'But you will help me, please Mrs Evans. You are my only hope left now.' Rhoda caught at her gloved hand. 'Say you will.'

'But if Doctor Rathlin is away from home I will have to see him when he returns. I will do that for you my dear.'

Rhoda's eyes filled with tears of hope. This was the first time since her arrest, apart from Molly, that anyone had volunteered to help her. How many times had she pleaded her innocence only to be answered with blank stares and disapproving harsh words. No one had believed her and now this elderly lady gave her some form of hope, a way out of her jeopardy.

'I could write a letter.' Rhoda felt her hopes rising with every word. 'Then you could give it to him...couldn't you?'

Mrs Rebecca Evans didn't hesitate.

'Of course I will deliver it for you...but, it may take some time. But rest assured it will get to him.' She squeezed Rhoda's hand.

'I have no pen or paper.' Rhoda shook her head.

From her bag Mrs Evans produced a sheet of folded paper and a pencil.'

'Will this do? I'm afraid I have nothing else.'

Rhoda couldn't believe it. This helpful lady must be some kind of angel. She kept the letter brief. It was more of a note than a letter. She didn't want any trouble for Mrs Evans. If she was caught carrying the letter the warders might confiscate it. Rhoda took the pencil.

'You are so kind to do this for me.'

'Well be quick as you can and write it before someone sees you. I have an envelope here you can have.'

Millbank Penitentiary
11th November 1850
Dear Doctor Rathlin,

Please help me. I am being held here, found guilty of a crime I did not commit. I can assure you I am innocent of any wrongdoing. You did say that if I ever needed your assistance you would help me. If you would try to arrange to get here as speedily as possible I can explain everything to you.

Yours in haste,
Rhoda Lambay

Rhoda showed the letter to Mrs Evans, so that she knew the contents of it. Then she closed the envelope and handed it to Mrs Evans.

'You must put the address on it my dear and I'll be off.'

She handed the envelope back to Rhoda.

'BUT I DON'T KNOW THE ADDRESS!' Rhoda started to panic.

'All I can remember is Doctor Owen Rathlin, Lambay Street.'

'But where abouts in London?' Mrs Evans frowned. 'London is a big place, my dear. I must know what part of London it is?' she insisted.

'I don't know.. I only know the name he gave me, Rhoda Lambay, was because he lived in Lambay Street.'

She hadn't thought to ask where the house was situated in London. Mrs Evans put a hand on her shoulder and smiled softly.

'Don't give up - try and remember where you were before the hansom cab knocked you down.'

'I can't remember anything before the accident.'

It was time for Mrs Evans to leave. She took hold of Rhoda's hand.

'Look....I'll keep the letter safe. Goodness knows, but I'll try and find out where Lambay Street is. Meanwhile try and think of any landmark you might have seen...it may help.'

Rhoda watched her leave. Mrs Evans patted her bag that contained the special letter. She gave Rhoda a knowing look. Then she was gone. With Mrs Evans went her last and only chance of help and hope. She prayed the letter would get to him. He would come to help her.

It was later when she told Molly about the letter - she thought Molly would have been pleased for her, instead she looked dejected.

'He won't find you.' Molly's eyes were filled with tears. 'Not in here he won't.' Molly's lower lip trembled. She chewed on it.

'What do you mean...NOT IN HERE?' Rhoda felt the secret door deep down in her inner soul slowly open ... letting in a cold draught of air.

'He won't find you, we're being transported again that's why.'

Rhoda grabbed hold of Molly's arms and shook her.

'Transported again... we've already been transported to here. We can't be transported again for heaven's sake.'

'Yes we can. And we are. I just heard about it.'

Molly hissed the words and broke herself free of Rhoda's hold. She rubbed at her sore arms. Rhoda caught hold of Molly's arm again, gentler this time.

'Where on earth are we going to Molly?'

'By ship to VAN DIEMAN'S LAND!'

'What Van Dieman's Land? Where is that?'

'It's at the bottom of the world...that's where?'

'But there is still time for Owen to find me Molly...still time.'

Molly took a strong hold of Rhoda's shoulder. Her eyes glittered with the tears she tried to hide from her friend.

'Listen to me. We sail tonight on the Sea Duchess.'

'NO...No...It can't be true! He'll get my letter. I know he'll come for me. I can't go there Molly. ......I'll die if I do... Oh God! What am I going to do? How much time do we have? When are we going?'

Rhoda became more breathless. Molly shook her furiously, only letting her go when she gasped for breath and tears stemmed her fear.

'We are being transported for seven years to Van Dieman's Land.'

Molly said the words slowly and carefully. 'You must have forgotten I told you. Your sentence and mine is for seven years Rhoda.'

Rhoda felt her secret inner door swing wide open. She let out a gasp of terror as the cold air threatened to freeze and stop her heart for ever. Molly caught hold of her. Together their tears mingled, their arms entwined each other, moulded, sculpted, locked like lovers. Heads buried on damp shoulders until Rhoda pulled away from her friend and wiped her tears, which stung her salty face, with the frill of her white petticoat.

Rhoda stood beside Molly as their new clothing was given out. The bundles of clothes were to be their only source of equipment for their voyage to Van Dieman's Land. Rhoda stared down at the quantity, astounded at the growing pile, turning them over and holding them up to inspect each item.

'Look at these Molly. Three shifts, shoes, three pairs of worsted stockings, a cotton jacket, linen cap, two cotton petti..........'

A harsh voice interrupted her.

'Be quick and get dressed,' the Matron called out to the subdued women. The convict women stood, in awe of the clothing. Never had they seen so much. They had stolen, thieved, lied, even prostituted themselves to get such items and here it was, almost thrown at them freely. Rhoda picked up two flannel petticoats and two cotton ones. Tears stung her eyes. Here she stood, about to be transported for a crime she did not commit...stealing a white petticoat and now she was given four of them. In her anger she wanted to tear them apart.

'What's the matter with you? Never seen a petticoat before?'

The Matron walked on past Rhoda, stopped, and then turned.

'You CONVICTS should get down on your knees and be thankful for what you have been issued with.'

It was the word 'CONVICTS' that struck Rhoda. She had never thought she would be branded a convict. A thief, maybe, but hearing the word said aloud sounded harsh, cruel, and unreal. She felt as if she didn't know herself any longer. Her real identity eluded her. Perhaps it always would. Only the name Rhoda Lambay belonged to her and with that name she belonged to Owen Rathlin. She would always keep it, always be known by it. He had given her the name she cherished. She dressed quickly then sat quietly...waiting. The smell and coarseness of the strange new clothing almost suffocated her.

She glanced around at the other women convicts. Suddenly everything was quiet: even the children seemed calm, speaking in whispered voices... waiting. Her heart thudded high up in her chest. She put a trembling hand against her throat, pressing it, almost squeezing it, to still the surge of fear. Rhoda caught sight of the young boy staring at her, with enormous tear-filled eyes. Rhoda gave him a fleeting smile, somehow it helped her to try and fight the sinewy coils of terror slowly constricting her.

Rhoda was sick again. Molly stood over her and wiped her mouth.

When she had finished she clutched the piece of torn white petticoat tightly in her hand.

'You'll feel better when we embark on the Sea Duchess,' Molly said, trying to comfort her friend.

'When do we...embark ?' Rhoda asked. The very sound of the word 'embark' held terror for her. Never had she known such fear.

'Tonight...now...we're leaving soon,' Molly's voice wavered. She didn't look at Rhoda, but Rhoda could sense Molly's fear. She took hold of her friend's hand and squeezed it tightly.

'Thank God you are with me Molly. I'm sure I'd die without you.'

'And thank God you are here with me. We must always remain friends Rhoda, no matter what happens....promise me.'

'I have no need to promise you, Molly. You will always be my dearest friend no matter what happens to us.'

'Here listen to us going on like we were going to meet our end or something. Things could be worse, I suppose. Let's look on this as an adventure. At least we'll have more freedom on the ship.'

Rhoda smiled to hide her heartache. What Molly said was true. Things could be worse. But it was the total disbelief that engulfed her. It seemed to feed upon her. There was nothing she could do now. It was too late for anyone to help her. She was going to be transported for a crime she didn't commit. And, worst of all, she didn't know who she was or where she had come from. Someone must be worrying and wondering about her. She had tried all ways to remember but couldn't remember anything.

'It might be that you don't want to remember,' Molly said to her.

But Molly was wrong. She did want to remember. More than anything she wanted to find out who she really was. She tried to think back to when her hair was being cut...soft, white hands that had brushed her red gold hair with the silver hairbrush... 'One hundred strokes for your beautiful hair.' It was her mother's voice, she knew that, and then the memory of it had gone. Only the bitterness remained of the loss of her beautiful hair. The only adornment she treasured. Her long, living, golden hair - gone forever.

Something was happening now. Leg irons were being fastened onto the women convicts. Rhoda became angry. Another degradation to suffer. Some of the women protested, but they were held down and forced.

'What next I wonder? First they cut off our hair, now we have to wear leg irons,' Rhoda muttered to Molly.

One of the women warders heard her, as she bent down to check they were fastened properly.

'You have to be shackled to embark on the ship. They'll take them off when you get on board.'

The warder pushed them all into lines. Rhoda looked at their terrified white faces. The irons on her ankles were so heavy for her. She wondered if she would fall down. Rhoda imagined how an animal would behave caught in a trap. It would try all ways to free itself. But she was a human being. It would be useless to rant and rage against it. Better to forget the shame, the indignity of the chains.

It was night time so no one could see them being led out, except snooping stars. There were a few bright ones. Rhoda looked up for a few brief moments. It looked as if someone had thrown a handful of diamonds up into the black crepe sky. There were some tiny glimmers as stars tried to claw their way through the thick, black swathe. This was the last time her feet would be on English soil for many years, unless some miracle happened. But she knew in her heart it wasn't to be.

'Goodbye England...Farewell Doctor Owen Rathlin. I will always keep you locked up in my heart.'

One of the warders shoved her violently. She stumbled and almost fell forward. Molly threw out her hand to stop her.

'Gerra move on can't you? We 'aven't got all night,' the warder shrilled.

VII

It was late night time when they were taken to the point of embarkation. They filed across the road, shuffling slowly, down steps to a waiting steam tug...then on to the 'Nore'. Rhoda looked up at three giant crosses stretching their arms across the starlit sky. The sheer wooden strength of them held her in awe and wonder.

'God the father, God the son and God the Holy Ghost,' Rhoda whispered at the sight of the three towering masts of the Man-o-War, the 'Sea Duchess'. Why she said it she didn't know, it was just the sight of the magnificence of it. This was to be her home for months on end. It would take her to a strange land to begin her sentence. A part of her wanted to end it there and then. She could jump over the side of the tug but the shackles on her leg stopped her. Then strangely the other part of her filled her with some unexplained excitement, an unexpectedness tinged with exhilaration. It was like looking at a painting, but she was part of it...and now she was going to enter it, belong to it, for the long voyage that would take her down under the world.

'They're taking us down to HELL!' one convict woman shouted.

Once on board, the shackles were taken off. Rhoda rubbed her ankles; in that short time they were chaffed and bleeding. Two young ladies introduced themselves as 'Ladies of the Committee'. They were carrying on the work of one Mrs Elizabeth Fry, who was concerned about the conditions of prisoners. They set about putting the women into groups of twelve, separated from the hardened core that shouted abuse and cursed the ladies who tried to help alleviate their fears. A young lady with fair hair who looked the same age as Rhoda smiled at her.

'Take these,' she said, handing her a bundle. 'They will help you pass the time on your voyage.'

Rhoda looked at the bundle she had been given of pieces of cloth, pins, needles, a thimble and bodkins, all inside a workbag.

'Thank you,' Rhoda said, 'I'm a good seamstress.'

'Good, then you will always be in demand.' The young lady smiled at her. 'You can make patchwork quilts to make some money for yourself. They'll fetch a guinea each, when you get to Rio.'

'Yes,' Rhoda suddenly remembered, 'I can do very fine needlework. I've just remembered.'

'There you are then...keep on sewing, that way the time will fly by.'

The lady smiled again and left them with their bundles.

'You remembered you can sew then,' said Molly.

'It just came to me all of a sudden...I don't know why. Oh Molly! Do you think I'll ever remember who I am?'

'Of course you will. It will all come back. You'll soon see.'

'That's what Doctor Rathlin said, almost the same words.'

'There you are then...AND Rhoda Lambay, I wouldn't be half surprised if you're not some fine lady, by all accounts.'

Rhoda laughed and for the first time she felt some of the despair lifting.

'If you turn out to be some rich lady can I be your maid?'

Molly gave a curtsey. 'What do you say M'Lady?'

'I would say you are mad Molly, really.... MAD!'

Suddenly, the stink of sweat came to her, the weeping mothers, the children clinging to their mother's skirts like frozen limpets. Rhoda caught sight of the small boy with the wide blue eyes staring at her again. God knows how he was feeling. Then a surge of sickness rose up in her as she was escorted to see the ship's surgeon...Doctor Mackay.

Rhoda looked down at the desk. Doctor Mackay was busy writing details in the open book before him. He hardly glanced at her. She could see the date, 11th November 1850 and the name of the ship 'Sea Duchess.' She could read what he had written, even though it looked upside down to her.

MOLLY WILLIAMS: Dairy Maid
Ship: Sea Duchess
Age: 19 years
Hair: Dark Brown
Eyes: Brown/Black
Nose: Medium
Height: 5 foot 5inches
Slight scar on left cheek.
Mole on right lower jaw.

Doctor Mackay looked up at her, with a fleeting smile.

'Your name is Rhoda Lambay is it not?'

'It's not my real name. You see I had an accident and ......'

Doctor Mackay looked impatient. He sighed and wrote down Rhoda Lambay, with a steady hand.

'What's your profession?' he asked.

'Err... umm...I don't know,' Rhoda began to answer, but Doctor Mackay was drumming his long fingers on the desk, impatiently, so she decided to carry on.

'I am a good seamstress...and I know all the scriptures.'

'Well that's something I suppose.' he said as he continued to write down the details and look up now and again to study her.

'I didn't steal the petticoat, honestly I didn't. I don't know who put it in my valise at Doctor Rathlin's house.'

Doctor Mackay looked up from his writing when she mentioned Doctor Rathlin.

'Doctor Owen Rathlin?'

'Yes, he lives in Lambay Street. That's how I got my name you see. He gave it to me after my accident. He christened me...well sort of...' Rhoda told him briefly about the accident with the hansom cab.

'I see, so you stayed there to recover after your accident?'

Rhoda nodded her head and stared down. Doctor Mackay looked serious.

Doctor Mackay muttered something. Rhoda watched him as he wrote down her details.

RHODA LAMBAY   Real name not known.
Ship: 'Sea Duchess'
Age: not known 17 or 18 years
Hair: Red, gold
Eyes: Green
Nose: Medium
Height: 5 foot 5 inches
Dimple on right cheek

When he had finished writing he put down his pen and studied her closely.

'Well Rhoda Lambay. You have been found guilty and sentenced. There is nothing I can do about that, I'm afraid. I think I can recall an Owen Rathlin. We studied medicine years ago,'

Doctor Mackay stopped and stood up. 'You seem to be a sensible girl. I suggest you write him a letter, telling of your plight, but there is nothing I can do now.' Rhoda told him that she had already done that.

'Then all you can do is wait. In the meantime if you work hard you could one day get a 'ticket of leave' or a free pardon.' He pushed a lock of sandy coloured hair out of his eyes.

'It means with a good report you could leave Van Dieman's Land before the end of your sentence.'

Rhoda became excited at what he said.

'Before seven years...When? One year...Or two?'

'Like I said it depends on how you conduct yourself. On a good report you get a ticket of leave or a free pardon, but it may take a few years.'

Doctor Mackay stood up and rubbed his chin.

'I need someone to help me in the ship's dispensary. Do you have any experience of nursing?'

Before she knew what she was saying she had said yes 'and my friend Molly Williams will help you all we can. You can depend upon us to work hard.'

She left the dispensary with renewed hope in her heart. She had at last met someone who knew of Doctor Rathlin. She felt sure that Mrs Evans would get the letter to him somehow. She would have to be patient and wait for any news. Everything seemed to be happening to raise her hopes. She suddenly swayed, felt the wooden floor lurch beneath her unsteady feet. Then she realised what was happening. The Sea Duchess was moving...They were leaving land...They had cast off...

It would be seven long years before she was free. Maybe sooner, if she could get a 'ticket of leave' and a good report.

But something deep down in her heart and soul told her, although she tried not to have such morbid thoughts, that everything was not right. There was something deep, rooted and dormant in her mind. It was red. The red blood she kept seeing on her hands. It was there again in her mind. Try as she may she couldn't fathom it out.

Someone was approaching her, along the gangway. It was a woman, tall and thin. Her head of hair resembled a bird's nest. It shook as she walked, her thin hands grasping the handrail in her effort to steady herself. Then as she got nearer to her Rhoda noticed her eyes. They were almost hypnotic in their stare, like a hooded cobra Rhoda had once seen in a picture. In her sudden fear she turned and grabbed the handrail, turning her face away from the sinister stare. The serpent stopped and clawed at Rhoda with her free hand then started to sing in a deep voice.

> *There is a dreadful hell*
> *And everlasting pains*
> *There sinners must with devils dwell*
> *In darkness, fire and chains.*

When she had finished her song she released Rhoda's arm. She continued her walk along the gangway, laughing quietly then the laughter became louder. Rhoda looked behind her. She had vanished in the gloom of the lamp.

For some unknown reason something told her, but she couldn't say what it was, that she would never again see the shores of England. Her life was to change - an adventure! BUT... to what end?

VIII

It was when they had sailed past 'The Lizard' and encountered heavy seas that a new fear entered into Rhoda, something she had never experienced before. It felt like fear and excitement mixed with a death-like draught, slow and deliberate in its advancing mass. It started inside her head, then like a fine net dragged the powerful potion down through her quivering body. The sheer potency of it terrified her. But it didn't linger there. It was dragged down further to the unfathomable depths of her inner soul. She stood rigid and held on to the table. Molly came over to her, wiping her wet hand on her apron.

'Do you feel faint?' she asked.

Rhoda sat down on one of the stools. She felt drained of blood. When she had sipped some cool water she felt a little better.

'No this was a different feeling....I've never felt before.'

Molly looked concerned and put her arm around her.

'It might be the motion of the ship. Try to take more rest.'

'It's better to work. I must be occupied Molly.'

'We've volunteered to do so many things. I hardly know where we are.' Molly wiped her red face. The ship seemed to surge forward with more powerful movements.

'I heard the mate say we had passed 'The Lizard'. Rhoda stood up.

'I'm so tired. When we get our small cabin Doctor Mackay promised us it will be better conditions for us Moll.'

Sleep seemed to be impossible. The nights were like Bedlam with the screams and cries of women. Hatches were battened down for the night. Rhoda thought she was in a tomb but glad they were separated into groups from the hardened core. Their door was held with three padlocks which gave them some security but there were times when the noise was unbearable. The nights seemed long, endless. Sometimes she slept the sleep of exhaustion, but there were countless nights when sleep eluded her. Every thought filled her mind with turmoil, thoughts that advanced in legions, thoughts that invaded her, thoughts that captured her sanity for a righteous ransom.

Sometimes there were dreams, where Isabella Rathlin was beckoning her over a sea of white fluttering petticoats. And then the dreams of Doctor Owen Rathlin, bending over her with anxious brown eyes. As she reached up to touch his lean angular face, it vanished. It had frozen into the coldness of the morning light, leaving her empty, so alone.

Her life became a form of routine. She had volunteered to read the scriptures and look after the prayer books, Bibles and catechisms. She loved reading to the children.

It was when she was reading to the children one morning she met the Reverend Arthur Slyne and his wife Gladys Slyne.

'You read the scriptures well, my dear,' said Arthur Slyne.

He seemed to appear from nowhere. Rhoda was startled. She instantly disliked him. It wasn't just his appearance. He was short, almost bald, with no appearance of a neck. His face had a waxen pallor. His breathing seemed laboured but it was his eyes that Rhoda dreaded looking at. Huge dead fish eyes of a watery grey blue. Never had she seen such eyes. He rested a podgy, childlike hand on her shoulder.

'That's it my dear. Make useful labours to attain your salvation.'

Rhoda squirmed as he squeezed her shoulder. The children started to sit up straighter on their benches, with arms folded staring with intent. Mrs Gladys Slyne beamed at Rhoda. Small black eyes that looked like hard aniseed balls stared down at her through thin rimmed spectacles. A bird's nest of grey wiry hair shook and almost toppled over her thin pointed face. Her thin, hard lips looked slightly blue.

'I'm pleased you are well versed in the scriptures, my dear. Even though you are a convict, if you continue to do God's work you will have a good report from us when we reach Van Dieman's Land.'

Rhoda smiled and thanked her. Gladys Slyne bent down closer to her. The hard aniseed ball eyes changed colour to a purple black.

'But we must have total obedience from you.'

She hissed the words at her. She reminded Rhoda of a giant serpent. Her thin pointed fingers with long hard nails threatened to tear into Rhoda's arm. She suddenly felt very vulnerable and afraid of Reverend Arthur Slyne and more so of his peculiar wife, Gladys Slyne.

Rhoda hated them both. There was something evil about them. Gladys Slyne looked deranged but Rhoda knew she had to obey them if she wanted a good report. She was too afraid of them not to abide by their will. It was going to be a long voyage. She thought there would be a feeling of more freedom on the 'Sea Duchess.' The work for Doctor Mackay was hard, but he rewarded them with thanks and small portions of extra food - bread and scraps of chicken. Apples and a secret glass of port wine. The more they worked the kinder he became to them. They were bound to get a good report from him, if they kept up their 'diligence.'

Rhoda was happier with the work she was doing. She even undertook to keep the ship's library in order. More work made the time go faster. The only shackles that hindered her were...the Slynes.

It was when they were allowed up on deck one morning and standing together, taking in deep breaths of fresh sea air, that Molly told her she was beginning to get some colour in her cheeks. Rhoda felt a tug on her sleeve. She looked down. It was the small boy with the wide blue eyes. Rhoda had seen him in the group of children, in scripture readings, but he had always appeared shy and reticent to speak to her.

'Hello. What's your name?' she asked him smiling.

'Tom,' the boy answered quietly.

Rhoda noticed a bruise on the young boy's face. She touched it gently.

'What happened to you then?'

'Nuffin'...he didn't do it honest. He said it was nuffin'.'

'Who said? What Tom?' She crouched down low to look into his eyes. He obviously wanted to tell her something but he was afraid.

'You can tell me Tom...it will be our secret, just you and me I promise.'

'What's your name Miss?'

'It's Rhoda Lambay...Now tell me about this.'

'It must be kept a secret Rhoda.. I mean Miss Lambay.'

Rhoda nodded. 'Our secret...just you and me...promise.'

'Say God's Honour,' said Tom licking his forefinger and making the sign of the cross on his sallow, thin throat etched with grime.

'God's Honour,' said Rhoda as she did the same.

Tom pointed down the deck towards a small group of people.

'Him! It was HIM! Called me a wicked child. I didn't remember my words. Look, there he is, it's him!'

Rhoda looked towards where Tom was pointing.

'It was him. He hit me.'

The Reverend Slyne left the group to go below deck.

'It was him, he hit me.'

Rhoda was incensed at what Tom had told her. She took him to the dispensary and bathed the bruise with cold water. Tom appeared more afraid now that he had told her his secret. It was only when she had reassured him, and made another promise not to tell anyone, that he gave her a smile.

'You're my friend Rho....sorry Miss Lambay.'

'And you're mine Tom.' She ruffled his fair hair.

Later there was no time to tell Molly. They were busy storing their bags of belongings into the small cabin Doctor Mackay got for them.

There were only fifty women convicts on board the ship and ten children. Their cabin was small, just enough room for her and Molly. They stowed their things under their bunks and put on clean white aprons.

Their day was spent helping Doctor Mackay in the dispensary, sorting some clean linen and helping with minor injuries. There were always some accidents on board ship, heads bumped against low timbers, falls from the rigging. Doctor Mackay inspected the convicts daily. Molly or Rhoda would assist him. There were several children with bruises and cuts on their faces. They were silent about them. Rhoda was suspicious. Something would have to be done about it. She waited until they were eating their tea, bread and butter and tea they had made in their own kettle. Rhoda told Molly about Tom, and other children with injuries.

'You can do nothing about it Rhoda.'

'But he shouldn't be able to get away with it,' Rhoda protested.

'If you tell anyone, you'll be breaking your promise to Tom.'

'Yes I know that could mean more trouble for him. But there must be a way to keep an eye on him and the rest of the children.' Rhoda was getting angry.

'Why don't you ask Reverend 'SLIME' if you can do more with the children. Teach them to read. That way you will be with them more.'

Rhoda laughed at the word 'slime', but as Molly had said she would have to be very careful not to get on the wrong side of both the Slynes. It could put her in jeopardy, especially as Doctor Mackay would have to make a report on her. She couldn't afford to take any chances. She would have to be cunning and observant. She could act her way into the role of a deeply religious person. A smiling veneer, but underneath a simmering anger at the cruel, supposedly Christian, teaching of convict children.

Rhoda was convinced that Gladys Slyne was unstable. She could see it in her eyes. The way she clenched her hands in frustration. One time Rhoda had caught her rocking to and fro on a wooden chair, a faraway look in her eyes. Humming some made up hymn. But what was disturbing to Rhoda was that she was singing praises to 'Rhoda' but the name of her friend 'Molly' was uttered with blasphemous speech. Rhoda had left Gladys Slyne, slipping away silently. She had never mentioned it to Molly but in that moment Rhoda knew she would have to be on her guard against Gladys Slyne. She chose to play a 'cat and mouse' game watching her silently, waiting until the time was right.

There had to be some way to expose their wickedness to the children. Rhoda knew the helpless position she was in. She was just a convict. Far better to wait and bide her time. And play Gladys Slyne at her own game.

IX

Mrs Rebecca Evans made her way along Lambay Street. Finding the area where Doctor Owen Rathlin lived had proved difficult. It had taken her many weeks but she had promised Rhoda Lambay she would deliver the letter to Doctor Rathlin. Now she was about to fulfil her Christian duty and deliver the important letter. The huge black door swung open to reveal a short plump, jolly looking woman with freckled arms wearing a snow white apron.

'Good Morning. Is Doctor Owen Rathlin at home?'

'I'm sorry mam but Doctor Rathlin is not available.' Martha studied the rosy cheeked elderly lady.

'Oh dear....Is he expected soon do you think?' Mrs Evans gripped the letter tightly in her black gloved hand.

'No I'm afraid not. He won't be back for several months.'

'Oh no! Oh dear...months you say?'

Martha opened the door wider.

'I'm sorry but he's gone away to Italy with his wife. I'm looking after the house until they return.'

Mrs Evans held on the white pillar to support herself.

'Oh dear, oh dear. I really don't know what to do now. I promised Rhoda I would find him.'

Martha picked up on the name quickly.

'RHODA did you say? Would that be Rhoda Lambay by any chance?'

'Yes it is.'

Mrs Evans looked relieved.

'Do you know her?'

'Why yes of course I do. But wait, come in. I'll make you a nice hot cup of tea. I'm sure you could do with one. You look frozen.'

Mrs Evans was ushered into the wide hallway. Her trained eyes took in the large vestibule and the stained glass windows on the inner double doors. The ornamental ceiling looked clean. She glanced down at the patterned floor tiles. Yes, everything looked as if it had had a good cleaning. The potted plants in gleaming jardinières almost stood to attention as she passed through the long hallway. She caught a glimpse of herself in the gilded mirror and patted her hair, quickly trying to straighten her bonnet. This lady had been very kind inviting her into the house.

Martha paused at the parlour door. From the look on Martha's face, she wasn't quite sure whether or not to ask the visitor into the parlour. Mrs

Evans sensed her hesitation.

'It would be warmer in the kitchen, I'm sure. That's if you don't mind.' Mrs Evans said with a smile.

Martha agreed with her. Then on her way to the kitchen Mrs Evans stopped.

'Oh dear...dearie me. Whatever must you think? I haven't told you my name.' She held out her hand. 'I'm Mrs Rebecca Evans.'

'And you must think me most uncivilised. I'm Martha Thomas, the housekeeper to Doctor and Mrs Rathlin.'

Mrs Evans told her briefly that she visited ladies who had fallen on unfortunate circumstances in prison.

'PRISON!' Martha echoed the word. 'Don't tell me the poor lamb is in a prison.'

Martha held open the kitchen door. The smell of freshly baked scones wafted in the warm air and hung there. Martha made sure Mrs Evans was seated comfortably at the well-scrubbed table. After she had made the tea and left it to brew, Martha set about splitting warm fruit scones, spreading them with rich yellow butter, then placing them carefully on two large, blue flowered tea plates.

Taking off her worn leather gloves Mrs Evans told Martha all she knew about Rhoda Lambay and her stay in prison.

'But I can't believe this has happened!' Martha exploded. 'She was such a nice young lady. Well mannered. I'm sure she would never have stolen anything, never mind a white petticoat belonging to Mrs Rathlin.'

'Were you here when Rhoda was arrested then?' Mrs Evans asked between slow sips of her scalding strong tea.

'No... it was my day off. I was quite surprised to find she had gone when I returned here.'

Martha handed Mrs Evans the plate of buttered scones. She took one and bit into it, wiping some of the runny butter from the side of her mouth.

'These are quite delicious,' Mrs Evans said.

'She had left a letter on the dressing table in her room, thanking Doctor and Mrs Rathlin for letting her stay,' Martha said importantly. She took a sip of her tea then placed her cup firmly on the saucer.

'But to find out now that she's in prison...well I...'

'I'm afraid she's not in prison any longer.'

'You mean she's out...free?' Martha's eyes lit up.

Mrs Evans put her hand on Martha's arm. 'No my dear...She's on her way to Van Dieman's Land. She's been sentenced to transportation for seven years.

Martha looked stunned at the news. She clutched the edge of the table.

'Oh dear God no....oh the poor lamb!' Martha wiped away a tear with the clean tea towel next to her. 'What on earth can we do?'

'I have a letter from her to Doctor Rathlin.' Mrs Evans held out the letter. 'I was hoping to give it to him.' Martha took the letter.

'I'm sure Rhoda wouldn't mind your reading it in the circumstances.' Martha opened the letter with a kitchen knife. She read it then shook her head. 'Oh dear! She must be terrified. She doesn't know her real name, because of the accident, you see.' Martha bit her lip. 'Oh dear! What a terrible position for her to be in.'

'Yes I know. She told me. Do you think we could get this letter to him somehow?' Mrs Evans stood up. 'I'm afraid I don't know quite what to do about it now. I can't very well take it back, can I?'

Martha picked up the letter. 'I could try and post it to Florence, in the hope that he may get it. But by the time the letter reaches there he will have moved on. They are going on a voyage you see.'

Mrs Evans was not to be defeated. A staunch member of the Ladies Committee, dedicated like her former predecessor Mrs Elizabeth Fry, no situation was impossible for her.

'Why not keep the letter here safely until Doctor Rathlin returns from his travels?'

She placed her empty cup and saucer on the tea plate. 'There isn't much else we can do at this time is there?'

'We could try and find out who she really is, I suppose,' Martha said.

'I'm afraid I won't be able to help you there. I have so much work visiting the ladies in prison. But if I hear of any news, I will inform you of course.'

'Yes of course. You're right. I will keep the letter safe. Meanwhile I'll try and make some investigations about her real identity and find out what happened before her accident.'

Mrs Evans stood up and pulled on her well worn leather gloves.

'I'll write and tell her that I've left the letter with you shall I?'

'You've been so kind already in bringing it here. But no doubt you writing to her will give the poor dear some hope.'

'I will be sure to tell her. And thank you for the tea and scones.'

Mrs Evans shook Martha by the hand. They walked together towards the front door.

'How I wish I had been here that morning when the petticoat was found in Rhoda's valise,' Martha sighed and wiped away a tear again with the corner of her white apron. 'How on earth did the petticoat get there? I would dearly love to know.'

'Well I don't suppose we'll ever know that mystery.'

Mrs Evans straightened her bonnet and stepped out into the street.

'Well goodbye, Martha. I'm so glad we met.'

'Goodbye Mrs Evans. You are such a good Christian woman.

And tell her Martha sends her love. I'll find out things, never fear. I'll have more free time now they are away. I'll find out who she really is.'

Mrs Evans gave a final wave and she was gone, walking briskly back along Lambay Street.

'Yes I'll find out Rhoda's real identity. I'm determined I will.'

Martha was still talking to the figure that had long disappeared from her view. 'Poor lamb, never fear, there must be someone who knows you. And I'll find them soon enough.'

X

Molly's suggestion of 'doing more with the children' so that she could keep an eye on Tom proved difficult. She approached the Reverend Slyne one morning after prayers.

'I would like to volunteer to help the children with their reading and writing,' Rhoda said, quietly closing the prayer book.

'That's very kind of you Miss Lambay but you mustn't tire yourself too much with the good work,' he rasped.

'It's no trouble at all Reverend Slyne. There are only ten children. I am sure it would benefit them to be able to read and write.' Rhoda tried to choose her words with care.

'Able to read the scriptures you mean?' He looked sternly at the children. Rhoda knew she had to agree with him. There would be another time to approach him about other lessons for the children.

'Well...err...yes of course...the scriptures.'

Rhoda watched him rub his hands together. Then he seemed to hesitate.

'I want them to be able to recite from memory some of the tracts.' Rhoda nodded her head remembering Tom's bruise on his head.

'I'm sure they will all do their best if we can recite them altogether.'

She smiled at him. His glassy fish eyes held a glimmer.

'And it will give Mrs Slyne a rest. I've heard her sea sickness is very severe.'

'Yes very severe, Miss Lambay. I try to do everything for her but I succumb to it myself...err... pardon me but I must take my leave of you.'

The Reverend Arthur Slyne left her side quite speedily, a large handkerchief pressed to his mouth.

Rhoda watched the children's faces. Some of the older ones started to smile, obviously glad, as she was, that the Reverend Slyne and his wife were both indisposed with sickness, hopefully for a long time.

The days were passing swiftly for Rhoda. She heard from Doctor Mackay the 'Sea Duchess' was making good progress. The prevailing winds swept the ship on through heavy seas. She loved the ship. It was as if it were a part of her. The sense of freedom it gave her, on deck and below. Never had she been so busy, teaching the children, cleaning and helping Doctor Mackay in the dispensary whenever she had the time. Lizzie, the young convict girl, helped Molly those times when Rhoda was with the children and helping in the library. Rhoda was surprised that she and Molly were able to carry out their duties without falling sick. They both hoped for a good report at the end of the voyage.

She dismissed the children. Watching them file out, the girls in their brown serge and worsted stockings, the boys in their Kersey jackets, waistcoats and trousers. Never had they been given such clothing in their young lives.

'It's dinner time Miss Lambay.' Tom was last to leave.

'I know...go on... off you go to your mother.' Rhoda smiled back.

Tom waved and ran off. Rhoda walked along the gangway. She stopped and tried to steady herself against the swell of the ship. It lurched suddenly. A flash of memory engulfed her. She was inside a large barn looking into a box with three small kittens mewling inside. She was afraid, not because of the kittens, but there was something else in the barn with her. 'NO.....No....I won't remember,' she whispered hoarsely. She turned around, held her head in her hands and tried to block out the images. They faded. But she knew they would return with more terror.

It was later when they had finished tea. She decided to go ahead and check some items in the dispensary for Doctor Mackay.

'I'll catch up with you later,' said Molly. 'Just a few more stitches....I'll soon get this done.'

Molly had proved to be a fine seamstress, like herself. Between them they had managed to do some repairs to clothing. Molly was sewing a tear in the Captain's shirt.

'I'll make a start before the thunderstorm hits us.' Rhoda said. She was amazed at how much work the ship's doctor was expected to do. As well as making sure of the rations for convicts and crew and his daily rounds of the ship, his priority was to work as speedily as possible on a patient.

'Everything must always be at the ready,' he told them in his instructions. 'This way it will help to eliminate infection.' Infection was a silent killer. Rhoda, Molly and Lizzie worked hard to keep the dispensary as clean as possible.

Rhoda checked the items in the cupboards, listening to the distant rumble of thunder. They had already made up beds. She put the spare pillow cases and sheets ready to hand in the cupboard. Kettles, mugs, and other items had to be made secure in heavy seas. She could feel the swell under her feet lifting her up. Then just as she was about to put a glass tumbler secure in the cupboard...it happened...she dropped the glass. It smashed into jagged pieces. She stooped to pick them up. A shard of glass seared through her flesh. She watched the blood run down her hand. Red berries...popping... bursting... Holly berry red.....She stared unable to comprehend what was happening to her but watched the berries of blood dripping...Then gently, drop by drop trickles of memory, like water slowly sliding down a frozen window pane. They formed pendants of the lightest crystal and...crystallised, hardened together into her memory.

'Oh God what's happening to me? What madness is it?'

The blood from her hand was real. She could smell it, she could taste it. Her hand was starting to throb with real pain, it was hurting her. This was real. But there was more. The teasing trickles became more sinister, searing into her mind. They wouldn't go away.

'NO...NO...I won't remember...I can't remember. Don't make me remember!' Rhoda cried and rocked to and fro. 'Please dear God take my memories away.'

XI

And then like giant breakers, the waves pushed forward, like a high tide. She held her breath and waited for the highest wave of all to flood her memory, like a foaming cataract. She was afraid. She didn't want to remember. But the memories in that very moment surfaced like a drowning swimmer...surfaced from their cryptic past......to crystallize.

Thunder rumbled closer. Rhoda was unaware of it. She wasn't on the 'Sea Duchess' she was far away.......

It was a watery sunny day as she left the house. She was so happy. After picking up a few odd things packed hastily in her valise, she had made her way across the yard. She stopped suddenly. She knew who it was and grew afraid. Her first thought was to ignore it and run away. But he appeared in the doorway of the barn. Ezra Blackwell.

'Come and see the new kittens, Alyce, before you go.'

She walked towards the barn. At least she wouldn't have to suffer at the hands of her brutal stepfather any longer. She had taken the post of Governess to a family with two children. She was to meet them at Waterloo, then via the boat train to France. She couldn't wait to meet Jack Stone with his horse and trap to take her to get the London coach.

'Come on Alyce...be quick… in here look!

Ezra Blackwell stood and beckoned to her. She should have known then she was acting foolishly. But still, one look at the kittens and she would be gone. She looked down, into the box and gently picked one up. She held it close to her cheek. Then she heard his harsh laughter.

'Soft and innocent like you Alyce Wilson.'

She dropped the kitten into the box, then turned quickly to run, but he was between her and the barn door, barring her way to freedom. He struck out and caught her on the cheek. She turned, not quickly enough, and he struck her again. She screamed, but as she screamed she knew there was no one to hear her cries. He caught at her arms pinning them to her side, fiercely.

'You insolent, blasphemous brat, there's no one to help you now. Start praying Alyce,' he raved. 'Pray for your salvation, harlot.'

He held out his arms and in that moment she ran, but not towards the open door. She ran towards the loft. Realising her mistake she climbed the rickety ladder. Halfway up she stared down at him. There was no way she could escape his terrible wrath...He was going to violate her, then kill her. He leered up at her and swiftly grabbed a hold on her ankle with a bear like hand. How could she ever escape his overwhelming strength?

'Pray for your soul.....Alyce,' he snarled and started to climb up after her. She looked around in desperation, for something, anything to help her.

'OH God...help me!' she called out. 'Help me, for God's sake.'

And then she saw it, almost half hidden in the hay...a pitchfork. She snatched it up and held it with the prongs facing down towards him.

'LEAVE ME ALONE,' she screamed in terror. She watched mesmerized. Slowly, deliberately, savouring her fear, he climbed the ladder, licking his lips. Two more rungs. He was almost there, eyes glittering. With her fear giving her strength she lunged towards him with the pitchfork. His eyes widened in disbelief as the prongs, finding their mark, plunged into his chest. He fell back. Alyce hesitated. She waited anxious long moments. Was he playing one last deadly game with her? She waited.... Would he rise up to attack her again? She waited. Then aware that Jack was waiting for her in the lane she clambered down the ladder. She looked at him, blood seeping from the wounds in the chest. The pitchfork rigid in his chest.....He was dead....... She had killed him. MURDERED him. 'Murdered.' She said the words softly.

She had to get away quickly. Jack was taking her to meet the 'fast four' to take her to London. No one would find him. Her mother was visiting with her Aunt in Dorchester...no one need ever know that she had killed him. She could make it look like robbery. Rhoda rifled through his pockets and found the five gold sovereigns in his jacket pocket. She quickly shoved them in her valise. This money would pay for the brutality she had suffered through the years. She covered his face with hay, closed the barn door, picked up her valise and ran swiftly to Jack Stone, her heart elated like a bare fisted fighter's win.

'What kept you Miss Alyce ?' Jack looked at her chalk white face, but said no more. He grinned down at her. He was slow in the head, couldn't remember much. But Jack was a good friend, in his childish way.

'We'll have to get a move on Jack, as quick as you can now.'

She was on the coach to London, thinking and wondering if she would ever get to meet her new employers at Waterloo. Her trunk had been sent on in advance. She had been making her way to the station when the accident with Doctor Rathlin's hansom cab happened.

A crash of thunder startled her. She looked down at her hand. Blood had dripped down onto her stiff white apron, in crazy patterns. Dear God in heaven what on earth, what on earth had she done?

She sat on the side of the made up bed, wishing that her memories would leave her, go away. But they would never leave her now. She was a murderer.

Rhoda stood up. She had to find Molly. She had to tell her. What would Molly think when she told her? Rhoda was near the door when she came in. Thunder and lightning seemed to rent the air apart. Rain fell like a deluge. Molly took one look at her face and made her lie down on the bed.

'What is it? More memories?' She tied a piece of fresh white linen around Rhoda's hand and pressed it tightly. 'This will stop the bleeding.'

'Promise you'll stay with me Molly...please don't go.'

'I'm here. I won't go away. Is it the thunderstorm it will...'

'No... no...there's so much blood Molly.'

Molly looked down at the bound hand. 'It's not a bad wound. It will stop bleeding soon.'

'NO Molly...not my blood...My Stepfather's blood.'

Molly looked anxious. She fetched a small glass of port wine for Rhoda. She sat up and gulped down a few mouthfuls. Some of it trickled onto her hand and she stared at it. She sat up on the edge of the bed.

'Take your time now. Tell me what's frightened you?'

'Oh Molly you're such a good, dear friend...and now I'm going to need your friendship more than ever.'

'Why you're more than a friend to me. You're like a sister.'

'I've done a terrible thing Molly. I've done a MURDER!'

Molly stared at her in disbelief.

'Whatever are you saying? You've been dreaming...'

Rhoda waited for the applause of thunder to wane. She wanted to shout out the words for Molly to hear but they struck the back of her throat in pain and made only a rasping sound.

The rain battled with the hiss of the sea. The coiling wind snaked its way around the ship like an unseen enemy. It seemed to Rhoda that the whole of nature was against her and that she would drown right here at this moment, in a boiling sea, for her terrible sin. She felt Molly shake her gently. 'What is it... tell me?' She put her arms around Rhoda to comfort her.

Rhoda heard only the lull in the storm, there was only restlessness as the ship parried and schemed its way against the waves. And thunder, like a cowering coward slunk away, to fight another day.

Molly held her against her shoulder. 'Then don't tell me... hush now.'

Rhoda pulled away from her. She didn't want to hush, not now, not when everything was so clear in her mind. She told Molly everything that she remembered.

'Molly, I murdered Ezra Blackwell, my stepfather. What can I do?'

She stared at Molly's face, expecting to see a look of horror at what she had told her. But Molly showed no such fear.

'DO?' she retorted. 'You do nothing. There's nothing you can do.'

They both looked towards the open door. Someone had closed it making a loud click. Someone had overheard what she had said about MURDER.

Molly darted across the room, flung the door wide open and looked along the dimly lit gangway.

'Who was it Molly?' Rhoda whispered.

'I couldn't see. Whoever it was disappeared quickly.'

'Someone must have overheard......What shall I do?'

When they were safely back in their cabin they spoke in whispers.

'Whoever it was couldn't have overheard you, what with the noise from the storm. Your stepfather deserved what he got.'

Rhoda started to cry. It seemed better to cleanse herself with tears, briny tears that trickled into her mouth. She caught them with her tongue and licked them on her lips, like a healing balm, to soften the words she had to tell Molly. But then only in the softest whisper.

'He always used to beat me, for no reason. My mother ignored it. She told me I had to mend my ways.' The words tumbled out easier now. 'He would rave at me, calling me 'wicked', 'insolent', 'blasphemous.''

'The wicked bastard. He deserved to die.' Molly muttered.

Rhoda wiped her wet face, pressing damp knuckles into her cheeks.

'Worst of all was learning The Catechism Molly.'

'Don't tell me if it hurts you.'

'The hurts been done now. Telling you is harder. He used to try and drown me, holding my head under water. To cleanse my soul he held me naked under cold water, a baptism, for my wickedness, he said it was.'

'Can you remember your name?'

'Yes it's Alyce Wilson. It sounds very strange, like another person.'

'Then you must forget you were ever Alyce Wilson. You are Rhoda Lambay now. And Rhoda Lambay it must always be. You can never go back to being Alyce do you understand?' Molly looked at her sternly.

'But I'm a murderer Molly. How can I ever forget that?'

'You had every right to defend yourself. He was going to kill you.'

'Who would ever believe the word of a convict?'

'You've been given a new name. You must keep it. Blot out the memory of Alyce forever.' She took hold of Rhoda's hand. 'No one knows who you are or where you are. It must remain a secret between the two of us.'

'But someone must have overheard me in the dispensary. Someone already knows about it and they might have reported what I said.'

'We can't be sure of that. We must wait and see what happens. Whoever it was might not disclose it. You would have heard something by now I'm sure.' Molly settled down on her bunk then sat up. 'Anyhow the noise from the storm would have stopped anyone from hearing properly.'

It was later when she tried to sleep on her bunk she realised Molly was right. She had to forget Alyce Wilson ever existed. Parts of her memory were still clouded over. She couldn't remember anything about her father or her mother. As to anyone knowing where she was, or who she was, it gave her a smug feeling that she had got away with the murder of her stepfather. Who would ever look for her on a convict ship bound for Van Dieman's Land? She couldn't be further away from being found out if she tried.

Then almost at the same time a worrying thought about the letter to Owen Rathlin unnerved her. The letter she had written when she was at Millbank, the letter asking him for help. She had implored Mrs Evans to find him. What if Mrs Evans managed to find Doctor Rathlin's address? She prayed with all her heart the letter would never be delivered to him. For him to find out that she had been convicted of stealing was bad enough. But if he found out she was a murderer. There would be no help for her. He must never find out what had happened to her...never.

The name Rhoda Lambay had been given to her by him. It now seemed to be like a rebirth. She had been allowed to be born again. Unknowingly he had given her a new identity. A christening of her new name...Rhoda Lambay....The way he had said it. His last words to her, remembered for ever.

'Let me know your real name...in the meantime...Be good Rhoda Lambay.'

He would never know her real name. Now.... Not ever.

Yet she would never forget his name. Now.... Not ever.

A sudden movement outside their door made her sit up in fear. Someone was outside. She could hear their heavy breathing. A rasping noise. Footsteps pacing up and down. It could be one of the guards coming for her. She was terrified that whoever had heard her confession had sent the guards. Rhoda strained to hear more. The footsteps stopped. The rasping noise became familiar. Where had she heard a sound like this before? ......

'Molly,' she whispered hoarsely.' Are you awake?'

Molly was asleep. The rasping sound stopped. Whoever it was had gone away. Somewhere in the deep recess of her memory she had heard that same sound before. The rasping, grating sound like someone taking their last breath....A death like rattle from deep down in the throat. Rhoda stared wide eyed at the door. Still waiting. Till at last sleep rescued her.

XII

With each day came a renewed fear for Rhoda. As she went about her work on board ship she feared that the convicts and crew she knew looked at her. Could they see into her mind? Did they know her terrible secret? She tried to avert her gaze if someone stared too hard at her. Surely it must be written all over her face. How could they not suspect she was a murderer? The feeling that everyone knew would not leave her. The fear that she had left the door open to her secret soul came more often. She had tried to sit down and steady herself. By taking deep breaths she had managed to keep the secret door ajar. She made herself work harder than ever in the hope that sheer exhaustion would drive away the terrible dreams at night.

Taking some deep breaths on deck one morning, she was alone during the exercise time, Rhoda was beginning to think she was safe. That no-one had overheard her confession to murder on the night of the storm. Then someone put an arm around her shoulders. She rested her head against the shoulder thinking it was Molly. The hard grip on her hurt and took her by surprise. Gladys Slyne peered down at her through her thin spectacles. Rhoda moved away from her. Her death- like closeness made her recoil in terror at the suddenness of it all.

'I hope I didn't startle you my dear but I could see you were not feeling well.' Mrs Slyne continued to hold on to Rhoda's arm. She was surprised at the sheer strength of the woman. That she was concerned over her well being was equally surprising.

'Yes...err...thank you Mrs Slyne. Thank you for your help.'

'That's alright my dear...Why not call me Gladys?...It sounds more informal than Mrs Slyne doesn't it?'

Rhoda was perplexed at this show of friendliness by Gladys Slyne.

'And you Mrs Sly.......I mean Gladys, are you feeling stronger now?'
Gladys Slyne ignored the question.

'And YOUR name. What is YOUR... first... real name my dear?'

Rhoda blanched at the words 'first real name'. This was a strange question to be asking her. Didn't Gladys Slyne already know her name as Rhoda Lambay. What did Gladys know? Was she testing her to fall into a trap? Was this part of the 'cat and mouse' game she was playing? Rhoda decided to play the game with her.

'My christian name do you mean?'

'Well of course I mean your christian name. You haven't got another one have you?' Gladys gave a harsh laugh.

'No.. No...Of course not. It's Rhoda...Rhoda Lambay.'

'What a lovely name. RHODA is a biblical name. Did you know?'

'No I didn't know.'

'Yes it is. I'm surprised that you don't know. I would have thought your parents would have told you when you were christened.'

Rhoda knew her face would give her away. She had to brazen it out. She tossed her red gold hair in defiance.

'No. I can never remember my parents...telling me.'

'I'm surprised you do not know.' Gladys stared at her. 'It's from Acts Chapter 12 Verse 13.' The grip tightened, like a coil. 'Look it up and read the verse...I advise you study it sometime.'

'I will and thank you again.'

The grip on her arm relaxed. Rhoda made her way below deck for lessons with the children. She couldn't wait to get away from Gladys.

Later, when she told Molly about Gladys Slyne, they both laughed.

'I think she is a very peculiar woman.' said Molly sipping her tea. 'When I meet her she gives me such angry looks. Once she even pushed me out of her way, causing me to fall.'

'Well next time I meet her for goodness sake come and rescue me, if only from her grip of iron, the bitch.' Rhoda rubbed her aching arm. They laughed again. Rhoda was beginning, but only just beginning, to lose some of her fear and concentrate on every day things, to try to forget her past.

It was when they were at Santa Cruz taking on fresh water, fruit and vegetables that the weather became hot and sultry. Rhoda heard some quick words from the ship's carpenter that they were taking on board English missionaries bound for Cape Town.

Rhoda and Molly were allowed to sit on deck sewing. Rhoda was mending a tear in Gladys Slyne's dress. She was sure Gladys had deliberately cut the dress with a pair of scissors. It was a strange thing to do. She was saying this to Molly when she heard someone call her name.

'Hello ALYCE! Hello!'

Rhoda and Molly looked up astonished to see a young woman of about their own age hurrying towards them. A white gloved hand waved wildly at them. Rhoda squinted her eyes in the strong sunlight, trembling at the thought of someone calling her name. She was aware of Molly hitting her hand quickly as a warning but Rhoda was prepared although her heart seemed to leap up into her throat hurting her with its rapid beat.

A young woman stood before her breathing heavily.

'IT IS YOU!..It's Alyce Wilson...isn't it?'

The straw bonnet hid her eyes in the strong sunlight. Rhoda stared at the long fair ringlets, the sprigged muslin dress with pin tucks down the front. It had been so long since Rhoda had seen such pretty clothes she was taken aback at the appearance of the girl. But now she had time to recover from her shock, she was more astonished that she had called her Alyce Wilson. She didn't know what to say to the girl, who had suddenly stopped smiling and was staring down at the convict's dress. If it hadn't been for Molly jabbing her sewing needle into her arm, she would have given the game away.

'Ouch! ...you've made a mistake Miss...I don't know you...'

But before Rhoda could finish the girl interrupted her.

'But you must remember me. I'm Ruth. We were all there when they found your father. We were horrified...Oh dear! Surely you remember Alyce?' Ruth's eyes filled with tears. 'We were such good friends you and I.'

Rhoda clenched her hands. It was too much for her to bear. Suddenly the safe world she had spun around herself threatened to be split wide open. The protective cover of her cocoon was slowly, hideously, unwrapping its fragile covering. She felt her face blanch with fear, felt the rush of it sweep down inside her. She was going to faint.

Already Gladys Slyne was curious, her darting glances missed nothing as she made her way across the deck towards them, a frown on her face.

'I don't know you at all. I don't know of any Alyce Wilson. Look I'm just a CONVICT on this ship.......Just go away.'

'Go away,' Molly snarled. 'You're not supposed to talk to the likes of us convicts. We are thieves and prostitutes and....'

The blonde haired girl stepped back as if she had been struck. She looked down at Rhoda still not convinced. 'I'm sorry but you look so much like Alyce.' She turned away to join her male companion.

Rhoda and Molly gave each other wily looks. They could hear her talking to Gladys Slyne about the ship taking them to Cape Town. The young man kept looking across at Rhoda and Molly, smiling. Rhoda tried to avoid him, muttering to Molly with her head bent over her work.

'Molly what does she mean, she was horrified about when they found my father?... I wish I could talk to her. There's so much she must know about my past life.'

'Don't be such a fool.' Molly hissed the words. 'You can't afford to take any such risk.' She stabbed the needle into the sewing angrily.

'You'd be a fool to jeopardise your life, especially now.'

Rhoda's head ached. It had been a shock to hear someone who must have known her and her father. Now she would never know any more. Molly tried to take Rhoda's mind off the missionary girl.

'Rhoda do you know the good looking young man with her?'

'No Molly. I must get away from here. I must get down below.'

Rhoda stood up, her head aching. She wasn't interested in Molly talking about the young man. Molly was trying to make light hearted conversation to take her mind off what had happened. Everything started spinning around her. Her face was burning.

'Not as handsome as Owen Rathlin though,' Molly teased, unaware that Rhoda was shocked at the recent news.

At mention of his name, Rhoda felt the soft flutter of the unknown butterfly again. She could feel the soft, feathery wings flicking against her strong heartbeat. The whirl of emotions was too much for her.

'There I knew it.' said Molly proudly. 'You love Owen Rathlin.'

Rhoda's face flushed at the sound of his name. She looked up. The young man had misinterpreted her look as one of interest in himself. He waved. Rhoda became flustered. The shock had suddenly become too much for her. As she came around, she was aware of the young man with blonde hair leaning over her. Gladys Slyne pushed Molly aside and thrust a damp cloth at Rhoda.

'Get below, where you belong, Rhoda Lambay. You are not allowed to talk with the passengers. Remember you're a convict.'

'It's my fault entirely Mrs Slyne. It was I who approached these women. I didn't realise they were convicts. They were so occupied with their sewing I wanted to see their work.' For one moment Rhoda thought the young woman was going to say more. She appeared concerned about what had happened.

'I'm so sorry, I broke the rules too,' said the young man. 'I caught you as you fell down. I didn't realise I made women faint,' he laughed.

'Thank you...but it was the heat,' Rhoda murmured.

Molly helped Rhoda stumble down below deck.

'It was the HEAT of shock that made you faint Rhoda.'

'Oh God! I thought I was going to be found out then. I really did. To be confronted by someone who knew me Molly. Thank God you were with me.' Rhoda splashed her face with cold water.

'You've got to try and be a better actress than that, Rhoda Lambay. You must be prepared for anything to happen to you. Brazen it out, when things are against you. Stand up for yourself.'

'Thank you Molly for being by my side. I'm going to try and remember what happened to my father. I can't seem to remember him at all.

'What could she mean by 'they were horrified when they found your father'?' Rhoda wiped her face with some more cold water. 'Found him where? And who on earth are they?' She sat down and let her hand ripple the cold water. 'I wish I could remember what happened to him.'

'It may be that YOU don't want to remember.'

'Why do you say that?'

Molly folded up her sewing. 'Because you've erased the memory from your mind, for some reason or other.'

Rhoda examined the neat darn she had mended in Gladys Slyne's dress.

'Do you mean I might have been there when they found my father and I was so horrified by it...' Rhoda stopped and put her hands each side of her face..... 'That I can't remember it?' she whispered hoarsely.

'It might be, I don't know, I'm merely suggesting it.'

Rhoda looked at Molly, deep into her eyes.

'Then why did I remember so clearly killing my stepfather? I remembered every sordid detail. Why didn't I erase that from my memory? That was horrific enough surely, Molly?'

Molly sighed. 'I can't answer that. One day your memory will come back and you will remember it all. It will become clear as crystal.'

Rhoda murmured the words softly 'Clear as crystal, when will that be I wonder...and will those memories hold more terror for me?'

XIII

A few days into the voyage the 'Sea Duchess' was becalmed. There was no wind for days. It was as if the ship had become embedded forever amongst the slight ripples of waves. The weather grew unbearably hot. Rhoda and Molly made the most of their time allowed on deck to get some cool air. Doctor Mackay made a request that all convicts were to spend as much time as was allowed on deck. The captain was a compassionate man and preferred to see his human cargo afforded such privileges.

Rhoda shaded her eyes and gazed out over the horizon. Something stirred in her memory. The swell of the emerald waves became a mesh of grassy fields. The crests of the waves white daisies. There were milk maids, cowslips, buttercups, a field full of flowers. And she was gathering them up, making fresh posies for her mother.

Her mother, with green eyes like her own. Sandy coloured hair that had once been red gold, like her own. Her mother was holding a man's hand. But it was not her father. It was Ezra Blackwell. His face became vivid again, the black eyes, harsh laugh and stink of ale that always surrounded him. It seemed to seep out of his very pores. His leering sneer made her stomach twist and knot and heave when his arms, hard, roughened like tree branches, held her. And she, screaming louder, as he pushed her ever higher, and faster and higher on the tree swing as she clung on in terror of falling. Her mother, laughing at her fear, provoked him to insane laughter.

Then more terrors in the night as he prowled like a predator outside her bedroom door. She became a trapped, wounded animal and had used all her cunning to scream for her father, that she was having a bad dream. Screaming for her mother made the blood thirsty, hungry hunter slip away into the night.

The mesh of green was changing. The emerald waves becoming a fine mesh of molten gold. Rhoda gasped at the beauty of it all. All her bad memories of the past dissolved under the surface. It was only the sight of the gold sheets of water that burnished in their stillness, rubbed hope into her heart. One day she would remember her father. She was puzzled as to why she had called out for her father when he wasn't there. Why hadn't she called out for her mother?

It was when Rhoda and Molly were alone in the darkness of the night that they talked. Molly told her stories about her twin brother Hawtin.

'He had his mind set on becoming an actor,' Molly said.

She propped herself up on her bunk, eating half an apple that had been given to her by Doctor Mackay.

'An ACTOR? Why I would have thought he would have been a farmer or worked on the land with your father. Why an actor?' Rhoda finished munching her piece of apple and decided to eat the stalk as well.

'He was always larking about, pretending to be an actor,' Molly laughed. 'One night he wrapped the sheet around himself and gave us a speech like this.' Molly slipped from the bunk and stood up in her drawers and camisole reciting, 'Friends, Romans, countrymen lend me your ears... Then he pretended to collect ears from us and stick them on the side of his head.'

Rhoda giggled. 'He sounds like an amusing brother. I wonder if I might have a brother or a sister. Well I've got you for a sister now Moll.'

'You have. We were always laughing at his antics.'

Rhoda became serious. 'I must say the name Hawtin Williams has a certain ring about it. It sounds like an actor's name.'

'That's why I must get a ticket of leave, then I can go home and find him. He wanted so much to be an actor.' Molly sniffed.

'Perhaps he is by now. He may be famous for all you know.'

Rhoda jumped from her bunk 'My Lords, Ladies and Gentlemen, may I present to you...Sir Hawtin Williams, the greatest actor of our time.'

'It would be wonderful if I could just find him, see him again, that's all. I must get back home. How I miss my family.'

'I can't ever go back...ever.' Rhoda whispered. 'Not that I want to.'

'What about Owen Rathlin?'

'Owen Rathlin is married with a wife.' Somehow when she said his name something happened. She couldn't explain what it was. It was as if his name was meant to be her secret. Hers alone. 'He is and always will be a very good friend...nothing more.'

Rhoda wanted to talk more about Owen. She kept saying his name to herself as she closed her eyes. Praying she would dream of him. There were times when she linked her name to his. Rhoda and Owen Rathlin.

During the long nights, when the blackness like a giant inkwell tried to blot out her memory of him, she strived to defeat the hostile army of fears. Rhoda knew that even if the force of the fiercest thunderstorm might send her and the ship to the bottom of the ocean. Knowing that Owen Rathlin had shown her warmth and kindness in the brief time they had together, it was as if they had known each other always.....

She didn't see much of the two missionaries, but she wished there could be some way of talking to Ruth. Gladys Slyne always seemed to be watching her closely. She was afraid Gladys would find out her real name. She had to be very careful not to give the game away with anything that would make Gladys suspicious.

She loved teaching the convicts' children. They liked her and called her 'Miss Rhoda' now. She was pleased with their progress in singing hymns and Religious Instruction. The Reverend Slyne did not want her giving them other lessons. 'To make them aware of what God had done for them, they would have to learn their Catechisms by heart.'

The children's once pale faces now had a healthy glow due mainly to the fresh air and a good balanced diet of fresh fruit and vegetables. Doctor Mackay made sure everyone on board ate as well as possible. There were sherbet drinks of limes and lemons to avoid any scurvy. The Captain's aim was for everyone to arrive alive in Van Dieman's Land. It was of no use carrying sick or dead convicts to work in a new land.

The Reverend Slyne walked around the children as they recited their words, prodding some who were not concentrating.

'Look to the front and LISTEN,' he hissed.

When they had finished their reciting Rhoda smiled and thanked them.

'I'm sure the Reverend Slyne is pleased with you all.'

Rhoda looked at him. He looked far from pleased.

'I think they all need more instruction Miss Lambay.'

Arms behind his stooped back he glowered at the children. His dead fish eyes rolled from one child to another until they fixed on Tom. Tom shifted uncomfortably in his seat. Rhoda sensed what was going to happen. He was going to single Tom out.

'Tom!' she called out quickly. 'Come here beside me.'

Tom walked slowly towards her, head down, expecting the worst.

'Now,' she continued brightly. 'Let's show Reverend Slyne how we remember our words.' She prodded Tom. 'Go on start. Do no sinful action...' Tom held his head up high. She held on to his shoulder. Rhoda knew he was doing it for her not the Reverend Slyne. He stammered at first, then recovered.

> *'Do no sinful action,*
> *Speak no angry word*
> *Ye belong to..... Je...sus*
> *Children of the Lord.'*

'Well done Tom you remembered your words.' Rhoda patted Tom on the back. She looked at Reverend Slyne for some approval but he just muttered 'Hmmmph' and glared at the children with hate in his eyes. After a chorus of 'All things bright and beautiful' the Reverend Slyne made a hasty retreat, a large handkerchief held to his mouth. The Reverend Slyne's sea sickness didn't seem to improve. A small voice piped up. It was six year old Letty bubbly and chatty.

'He's a wicked ole bastard,' Letty laughed out loud.

'You mustn't say such things Letty. It's wrong. You must never say it again.' Rhoda looked aghast at Letty.

'Well my Mum says he is, so there!' She started to cry.

'Right, come along now, we'll say the Lord's Prayer and go to have some dinner. Put your hands together.'

Letty stopped crying at the mention of dinner. Rhoda smiled to herself. She watched the small screwed up faces, with eyes half shut, hands clenched tight in front of them. 'Out of the mouth of babes,' she thought.

Suddenly there was much excitement coming from voices up above. Molly came running in to her.

'Quick come on...your name is being called!'

Rhoda wondered what on earth was happening.

'What do you mean, my name is being called? What's happening ?'

'A passing ship has mail on board for the 'Sea Duchess' that's what! It's a good thing we've been stuck here for ages. The mail's caught up with us.' Molly was breathless with excitement.

'Wait a moment,' Rhoda hesitated.

'Oh come on Rhoda. There's a letter for you.' Molly grabbed her hand, almost pulling Rhoda off her feet.

'But who can the letter be from?' Rhoda was afraid. Her heart plummeted...... like a dead gannet.

XIV

The whole ship had gone quiet with the arrival of the mail. Rhoda stared intently at the thick brown envelope in her hand.

'I'm afraid to open it Molly,' Rhoda's hands were trembling.

'Here give it to me. It won't bite you.'

Molly opened the letter and handed it to Rhoda.

'Go on. You read it to me. Please.'

'I...can't read much at all,' Molly said. Her face reddened.

'I'm sorry. I didn't realise.' Rhoda took the letter. 'Then I'll read it to you.'

> *Rowton House*
> *Steepfield Street*
> *Euston*
> *London*
> *December 30th 1850*
> *Dear Miss Lambay,*
>
> *I'm sorry to be the bearer of unpleasant news. But all my efforts to find Doctor Owen Rathlin and give him your letter were in vain. When I eventually found his house in Lambay Street I was informed that he was travelling in Florence with his wife ....*

Rhoda breathed a sigh of relief at this good news. She didn't want Owen Rathlin to find out where she was, or what crime she had committed, not now. Whatever would he think of her as a murderer? She looked up at Molly and smiled briefly.

'Thank God Molly...thank God!'

'Is that all? There must be some more to the letter.'

'Yes there is a second page.'

Rhoda held the letter in a trembling hand and read the second page.

However, I was fortunate to talk with Martha, the housekeeper. What a kind soul she is. I'm certain she can be trusted. She quickly recognised your handwriting on the envelope. We talked about your predicament. Dear Martha was most concerned. She promised to keep the letter safe until Doctor Rathlin returns home. I divulged the contents of your letter to her. Martha is determined to do all she can to find out your real identity, rest assured. Martha has considerable time in which to indulge her search, with Doctor and Mrs Rathlin away from home. Have faith. Pray to the Good Lord. Rest assured you can put your trust in Martha. She sends her love to you.

May God bless you and keep you safe.
Rebecca Evans.

Rhoda's eyes brimmed with tears. Dear Martha. She was going to try and find out who she really was, not knowing she was a murderer. If Martha found out what would she do? Would she inform the proper authorities? They would catch up with her. Her fate would then be at the end of a rope, hanged for murder. She told Molly her thoughts.

'What's going to happen to me now?'

'Happen? Nothing. It will be no easy task for this Martha to find out about you. She doesn't even know your real name.'

'I don't know.'

Rhoda bit her lip so hard she could taste the blood in her mouth. She spat it out. It was easy to say do nothing but when she really thought about it, Molly was right. Molly was always right about everything. She couldn't do anything about it. Only Molly knew her real name...except someone might have overheard her confession on the night of the storm. She shrugged it off. She wasn't going to worry about it.

'You're a dear friend to me Molly. I don't know what I would ever do without you. I can't see Martha ever finding out my real name or where I lived. It would be an impossible feat.'

Later when they had finished their chores they sewed together. Molly looked up from her sewing. Their quilts were nearly finished.

'You've got to be strong in this life Rhoda, if you want to survive. Look after number one, my Dad used to say. And this is what you must do.' Molly grew serious. 'Don't be afraid of anyone – ever!'

Rhoda snipped off some loose threads on her quilt.

'But you've always looked after me. You've never put yourself first. You're a true Christian Molly, much better than me.'

Molly flushed. Her rough hands smoothed the patterns on her quilt.

'Well I've always loved you like a sister Rhoda. As for being a Christian...well...I'm not afraid to say I believe in God...Do you?'

Rhoda flinched at the direct question. She had never heard Molly talk like this before. And the question, well, it was something she had never been asked.

'Oh I don't know. I try to teach the children about the scriptures and things. But, well, they are afraid. I can't stop their fears but I try to help them.' She stopped and became angry. 'Well how can God let this happen? We are branded as CONVICTS. I didn't steal any petticoat. And, well, you only took a cheese because you were hungry. And look at Arthur Slime. The way he treats the children isn't Christian!' She stopped and pursed her lips.

'No Molly, I don't think there is a God who listens to us at all. He would try and stop all this.'

Molly put down her quilt.

'You can't say that. I keep praying that I'll get a ticket of leave. I'll go back to England, meet some nice young man and get married and find my twin brother Hawtin.'

'Molly,' Rhoda whispered. 'Many times I've thought of ending my life. You know…I mean after what I've done.'

Molly threw down her quilt. She grew angry. She took hold of Rhoda and shook her.

'That's a wicked thing to say. Life is sacred. You must never think such a thing - ever. Always remember, your life is sacred!'

'I can't help it. Sometimes when things get really bad I just don't want to live anymore.'

Molly stood up. She looked serious… She put her hands on her friend's shoulders and looked deeply into her eyes.

'Things will get much worse than this Rhoda, you'll see. Then just when you can't take anymore, everything will be alright. Now promise me this. No matter how bad things get, you will never, ever do such a dreadful thing like take your own life.'

Molly held up her right hand, and with a solemn face said, 'SWEAR!' Rhoda had never heard Molly speak in such a way before. She tried to make light of the situation.

'Alright I swear.'

Rhoda held up her right hand 'Lord strike me dead if I do.' Rhoda realised what she had just said and grinned. Molly smiled sardonically.

'Come on Rhoda. Let's finish these quilts. We're nearly in Rio.'

Molly stuck her sewing needle in Rhoda's hand playfully.

'Ouch… that hurt!'

'It was meant to…Death by needle stabbing!'

They both laughed out loud as they continued sewing. When they had finished Molly held up her quilt.

'There we are Madame. What do you think? One guinea to you

Madame.'

Rhoda joined in the fun. She pretended to be haughty.

'One guinea. What will you do with it girl?' Molly thought for a moment.

'Why. Invest it Madame. Make more quilts for more guineas.'

'Very wise my girl, very wise.'

It was later when they were together in their cramped cabin submerged in the inkwell of blackness that the legion of fears came. Stealthily at first, one by one they crept upon her, taking her by surprise. Surrounded, overwhelmed by them, she gave herself up to the unrelenting foe. She was haunted about what she had said to Molly. The commandment she had broken. The tenth commandment – 'Thou shalt not kill.' She had killed. Murdered her stepfather. How could God ever forgive her? Would he understand how it happened? The pitchfork was in her hand before she realised. Something made her pick it up. Then she remembered the words she had said before she thought she was going to be killed. 'God help me!' Could it be that God had helped her in that terrifying moment…helped her see the instrument to deliver her from evil?

She tried to be silent. The wind had strengthened. The 'Sea Duchess' creaked and groaned softly as it rode the rising waves. She sobbed. The tears trickled down into her mouth. Molly heard her sobs.

'God will help you if you want him too,' Molly whispered.

'WHAT? What did I say?' Rhoda pretended she had been asleep.

'You said 'God help Me' and 'Thou shalt not kill'.

'I never meant it Molly. God never listens. He never hears.'

'I listened. I heard you Rhoda. If I heard you then God listens too.'

'I think God only hears what he wants to hear. He wouldn't want to hear me, a murderer.'

'God knows you were only protecting yourself, your own life. Kill or be killed Rhoda? The decision was yours. What else could you have done to protect yourself against that evil man?'

'But I needn't have killed him Molly.'

'Then you wouldn't be here then, would you. YOU would be dead!'

XV

The next morning just as Rhoda and Molly were putting on their clean white aprons to help Doctor Mackay in the Dispensary, there was an impatient knock on the cabin door. Rhoda was surprised upon opening it to see Gladys Slyne standing there, in what appeared to be a dishevelled state in her nightgown.

'Is there anything wrong Mrs Slyne?' Rhoda asked. She was roughly pushed aside as Gladys thrust her way into the cabin. It was barely large enough for two people but with Gladys there it had become a tight squeeze.

'I want that letter Rhoda Lambay. Do you hear me. I want that letter now. Gladys could hardly control her anger.

'What letter do you mean? I can assure you I have no letter of yours Mrs Slyne, you are mistaken.'

'Not my letter you little fool. YOUR LETTER – I WANT THE LETTER YOU RECEIVED YESTERDAY!' Gladys shouted the words. Spittle ran down the side of her mouth. Her eyes blazed with madness. Rhoda and Molly cast each other worried glances. They had to calm Gladys down. One of the guards might hear. It was Molly who spoke.

'The letter belongs to Rhoda not you Gladys Slyne. It is not your property. It was addressed to Rhoda.' As Molly was speaking she squeezed herself past Rhoda and Gladys through the open doorway.

'You insolent brat! This is not your business! Hold your tongue!' She whirled on Rhoda. 'Now give me the letter Miss Lambay!' Her tone became a quiet menace. 'I advise you to or you will be very sorry!'

Rhoda was shaken. She stooped to find the letter but it had gone from where she had put it, carefully folded.

'It's not here.Look it's gone!'

Gladys became more agitated.

'It can't be gone...where is it?' she grabbed at Rhoda's wrist causing her to cry out in pain. Molly sprang to her defence. 'Leave her alone you BITCH! She hasn't got it........ I have.' Molly waved the letter. 'This isn't yours Gladys Slyne...You will never get it.' Molly darted away along the short gangway and up the stairs to the deck.

Gladys and Rhoda ran after her. Gladys stumbled on the stairs, over her long nightgown. Rhoda caught up with Molly on the deck.

'What can we do? She'll always try to find it. We must get rid of it Molly.'

Gladys appeared and walked towards them with slow determination.

Molly held the letter over the side of the ship.

'Do you want to keep it Rhoda?' she shouted.

'No let the wind take it. It's of no use. Throw it away!'

Gladys swept forward, pushing Rhoda down on the deck in her haste. Molly held the letter up for one fleeting moment, just as Gladys was about to snatch it from her grasp. Then it was gone. It fluttered in the wind then a strong gust caught it and swept it away. Gladys struck out at Molly and caught her a stinging blow to the side of her face. Molly reeled back almost falling over the side of the ship.

'You will be very sorry you did that you slut. You will have to pay for that. Pay for your sins.' Gladys looked up into the sky in disbelief. She turned towards Rhoda.

'You will be very sorry you didn't let me have the letter, Miss Lambay. Rest assured you will rue the day.'

Gladys turned away and stumbled from the deck to the stairway and disappeared from view. Rhoda and Molly clung on to each other breathless from the attack on them.

'Why did she want the letter from you?' Molly said.

'I'm glad you threw it away Molly. It was no use keeping it. The woman is mad. Perhaps now she knows it's gone she won't bother us again.'

Molly looked serious. 'We'll have to watch out for her Rhoda. She is an evil woman. She had no right to demand your letter. We should tell Doctor Mackay about her.'

'No we can't do that. There might be questions and trouble for us. Remember we're only convicts. We have no rights.'

Molly looked up and around the deck to make sure the letter had gone.

'I suppose you're right. We must keep quiet about it.'

'Thank you for protecting me Molly. I don't know what I would do without you – ever.' Rhoda slipped her arm through Molly's and together they left the deck.

'Then you can make us some hot tea Rhoda.'

That night there was a terrifying storm. The ship trembled with fear. Rhoda could hear the creak and groan of the strong timbers. The heavy bulkheads wrestled with the sudden forces of the storm. Frothing seawater swirled into the hatches, sweeping everything with it. Rhoda and Molly grabbed a hold of anything that floated around them.

'We're going to drown here!' Rhoda cried.

The wind howled in the rigging. There were screams of terror from the women convicts down in the hold of the ship.

The 'Sea Duchess's' bulwarks creaked, threatening to turn the ship over. With every sickening roll of the ship they thought they would be flung into the seething ocean to be lost souls forever. Molly managed to open their cabin door when the swell of the sea water subsided. Then it quickly rushed in again. They stood together in the freezing water. The gangway had shipped a great deal of water.

'It's up to my waist. Can you swim Molly?'

Molly shook her head. The lanterns had become drenched with seawater, leaving them in choking, soot like blackness.

'Oh God! Where are you Molly?' Rhoda stretched out her arms to try and find her. When she caught hold of her they clung together like limpets swaying, sometimes falling against the wall. Rhoda managed to grab hold of the handrail and pulled Molly towards it. They both clung to it. Rhoda coughed and spluttered as the swell rushed in between decks. They could see a light coming towards them. As it got nearer they could see it was Ethan Davies carrying a lantern. He held it aloft until it shone into their white faces. The shipmate waded towards them.

'What are you doing out here? GET BACK TO YOUR CABIN! Here, take this lantern and keep it well out of the water...The storm will abate soon.'

'Are we all going to drown? We're terrified. What can we do?'

'Just keep calm and stay in your cabin. Go on now.'

They took the hurricane lamp from him with the flame protected from the wind and thanked him for the light then sat close together on their wet bunks. The burning lantern became their warmth and hope.

The ship was driven relentlessly forward, waves lashed by a howling wind. The rasping wind seemed to screech salt. They could taste it on their stinging lips.

'We're going to drown Molly. I know we are. I am being paid out for my terrible sins,' Rhoda screamed above the noise of the storm.

'Ethan says the storm will abate soon. We have to hold on!'

They shivered in their wet clothing, but the light and warmth from the lamp became their lifeline. They clung on to it together, willing it not to go out. Rhoda was half asleep, her hand clinging on the lamp aching with tiredness. Molly had fallen asleep in an upright rigid position. Rhoda watched as the water gradually receded. The wind still howled but had lost some of its fierceness. Ethan had been right. The storm had abated.

As Molly slept she watched as the swirling sea water was swept away by an unseen force.

Rhoda loved the sea, she loved being on the 'Sea Duchess' but never had she felt so close to death as when the violent storm hit them. She marvelled at the strength of the ship, to stand up to the fierce battering of the sea and wind. Never wavering, the ship had taken all the beatings, all the abuse of the pounding waves and had saved them. A silent tear slid down her cheek in gratitude. She wiped her hand across the tear and licked the salt. She felt some of the ship's strength in that quiet moment – the taste of salt made her belong and in some way she was secure, lulled in the cradle of the 'Duchess'.

Rhoda and Molly were clearing up the damage from the storm. They had cleaned their cabin, the hatches were open and every trace of the damage from the night storm was fast disappearing. The sky was blue and there was a strong wind to take them forward. Rhoda was tidying the ship's dispensary when the door opened quietly. Ruth, the missionary girl, stood in the doorway. She entered the room quickly looking over her shoulder then closed the door.

'You mustn't talk to me Miss. Go away please or I'll be in trouble.' Rhoda was afraid that Gladys would appear at any moment.

'I will only be a few minutes, Alyce. It is Alyce isn't it? You really are Alyce Wilson of Bellington Hall, Frogmorton.'

Rhoda bit her lip. She couldn't admit to being Alyce Wilson. Molly had warned her against anyone knowing her real name. Ruth stepped forward and hugged her.

'It's alright...I'll call you Rhoda. I know you are afraid of Gladys Slyne – so am I really. If she appears here you can pretend you are giving me some treatment.' She sat down on the chair and made herself comfortable. Rhoda knew she was determined to stay there. 'Now tell me quickly how you became a convict. I don't believe for one moment you did any wrong to warrant being here.'

Rhoda filled a dish with some cold water and wrung out a cloth. It was better to play at the game of Ruth being in the dispensary for treatment.

'Had a bit of a fall, have you Miss. I'll clean it up for you,' Rhoda said quite loudly for fear someone might be listening outside the door. She couldn't trust anyone overhearing this conversation. Ruth gave her quick wink. 'Good thinking,' she said. 'Now tell me while I groan a bit, as if in pain,' Ruth whispered. 'But hurry I'll soon be missed.'

Rhoda decided to trust her. After all she had to know about what had happened to her father. Ruth would be able to piece some of her life together. The missionaries would be only going as far as Cape Town and she would never meet them again. She told Ruth about her accident and loss of memory and the supposed theft of the white petticoat. She didn't tell her about killing her stepfather Ezra Blackwell and in the next instance she was glad she didn't.

'You poor soul, losing your memory like that, but I'm sure it will all come back, given time.'

Rhoda rolled up her sleeves. Ruth continued to wince as if in pain as she spoke quietly in answer to Rhoda's urgent questioning. The most urgent one was what had happened to Rhoda's father.

'Rhoda I'm sorry to tell you your father, Daniel Wilson is dead.'

Rhoda gasped in shock. Ruth went to comfort her. 'No, stop! Please go on. I must know everything. I can't remember it at all.'

'Your father was found strangled on his estate, Bellington Hall, Thruxington, Frogmore. We were there near the river when they found him. Do you remember it? It was the 3rd September 1836.'

Rhoda shook her head.

'Well you must have only been about four years of age at the time. The year was 1836. I can remember it more perhaps because I'm four years older than you Alyce...sorry - Rhoda. I was eight at the time it happened. I was staying with you at the Hall.'

Rhoda sponged her own face with the wrung out cloth.

'My God! Ruth! Is it any wonder that I can't remember my father at all? I hardly knew him but I have some very bad memories of my stepfather.' She couldn't say his name to her, her face might have given her away. She might have looked like a murderer.

'You mean that terrible man Ezra Blackwell? A drunkard, a blasphemer. Your mother married him two years after your father's death. We stayed away from making any contact after that. I'm sorry, perhaps I should have written to you.' Ruth caught hold of her hand. There were tears in her eyes. 'We should have kept in touch by letter.'

'Don't blame yourself Ruth. I wish I knew who killed my father. Did they ever find out who was responsible?'

'There was always a considerable amount of strangers around, gypsies and the like. Your father might have seen one. The constable thought it might have been a poacher and your father caught him in the act.'

'Thank you for coming to me and telling me this Ruth. I wish we could talk some more. There is so much I want to know but...'

They heard someone turning the handle on the door. Someone was coming in. Rhoda immediately started to sponge Ruth's face, as she started her groaning act. She had to make it look like she was getting some help. Doctor Mackay came into the room, his unlit pipe in his mouth.

'Ah we have a patient I see. What can we do for you young lady?'

'Nothing at all thank you Doctor Mackay...Rhoda has been very kind and helpful. I just felt a bit faint that's all.'

'Perhaps you should rest Miss Ruth. We can't have you getting ill can we? I suggest you rest in your cabin. If you continue to feel faint come back and see me.'

Ruth stood up. 'Can Rhoda escort me back to my cabin please Doctor?'

'Well, be quick Rhoda. I have to do my visits around the ship.' Doctor Mackay waved them away impatiently.

Rhoda put her arm around Ruth's waist and made to escort her. On their way back to Ruth's cabin they met Gladys Slyne. She barred their way. Rhoda strangely enough didn't feel threatened by her presence, even though she loomed over them, her eyes darting back and forth to each of them.

'What's happened? Are you not feeling well Ruth? You should have come to me for help, not a CONVICT.'

Ruth was prepared for her. 'I'm sorry but I went to the dispensary. I've just seen Doctor Mackay. He suggested that I rest.'

'Yes that's very wise.' She turned to Rhoda. 'Go away Miss Lambay. I'll attend to Ruth now...Go on girl, get away with you.'

Rhoda knew it was hopeless. She had to obey Gladys. There was nothing else she could do. She gave Ruth a fleeting look and a smile.

'Thank you Rhoda,' Ruth whispered.

Gladys whirled in anger on Rhoda. 'How does she know your name?'

Rhoda was at a loss for words. How could she explain it to her? But Ruth was quicker. She sensed quickly how the game was played.

'I heard Doctor Mackay call her Rhoda. That is your name isn't it... young woman?' she said with a mock of sternness in her tone. Rhoda gave her a quick smile. Gladys would never know about their hasty conversation. This time Gladys was not a part of the secret game. Rhoda tossed her head in defiance.

'Yes it is Rhoda Lambay – RUTH,' she almost chortled.

Rhoda caught a glimpse of a red faced Gladys as she made her way back to the dispensary. She was sorry that she and Ruth didn't have the opportunity to carry on their conversation. Yet she had learned some more about her past life, be it just a small piece, tinged with so much sadness. She would tell Molly all about it and go over and over it again in her mind. She had to remember her home address and the date her father died. There was another thing she had meant to ask Ruth - the date of her birth. She decided to make her birthday the 3rd September 1832. The day her father died. It would be a tribute to them both.

XVI

Since the day Rhoda had received the letter from Rebecca Evans she had tried to put it out of her mind. It was in the safest place now, carried on the wind to God knows where. She had become stronger since her secret conversation with Ruth. Each day made Rhoda feel more secure and safe. At least Ruth was someone from her past, someone who had known her. But Alyce Wilson was no longer. What mattered now was to try and be strong.

They had sold their quilts in Rio de Janeiro, for a guinea each. They had crossed over the Equator. The children never stopped talking about the dolphins and the flying fish. Tom had kept looking for the equatorial line then came to the conclusion that the line must lie on the bottom of the Atlantic. They were well on their way to Cape Town when Molly came rushing up to her one morning. Rhoda caught hold of her.

'What's happened? What have you done?'

Molly was holding her arm, her face contorted with pain.

'I've scalded my arm!' she cried.

Rhoda caught hold of her and plunged Molly's forearm into a bucket of cold water. Molly winced at the shock of it but it helped with the pain.

'Oooooh that's better! It's stopped hurting so much.'

'Keep it there for a while. How on earth did you do that?'

Rhoda held Molly's arm in the water.

'Gladys Slyne scalded me with her cup of tea,' Molly sniffed.

'WHAT! An accident was it? The stupid woman.'

'Not really. She tipped it over me.' Molly bit her lip in pain.

Rhoda was aghast. 'What are you saying?'

'She tipped it over me deliberately!'

Rhoda tore a strip off the hem of her white petticoat. She was angry. She spoke quietly. 'Why would she do such a terrible thing?'

'She's mad that's why…She laughed at me.' Molly took her arm out of the cold water. It was red and sore. Rhoda bound a strip of white cotton petticoat around her forearm and tied it securely.

'This is what Gladys Slyne meant about I'd have to pay for my sins – when I threw your letter away Rhoda.'

'Doctor Mackay will look at it for you later,' Rhoda said. 'Come on let's go up on deck. Some fresh air will do you good.'

They wandered around the deck. The cooling breeze caught the white sails. They flapped and slapped against the wind like fresh washing out on a line to dry. Rhoda looked up. The sails looked like large white cotton petticoats stark white against the blue sky. She watched Molly walk towards the port side of the ship. Suddenly a cry went up.

'WHALE...on the starboard side!'

There was so much excitement for the ones on deck at the sight of seeing a real whale. Rhoda, caught up in the stampede, was overwhelmed at the size of the creature and its graceful movements. She looked around to see where Molly was. She wanted to share this moment with her. The children pushed their way forward to get a better view. They had never even seen a picture of a whale before. Now seeing a live one at such close quarters drew gasps of wonder and admiration.

'Cor luv us all. Look at the blinkin' size of it!' Lizzie shouted. 'They wouldn't 'ave one of them at Billingsgate!' Everyone laughed. She pointed her long thin arm towards the fast moving whale. Rhoda gazed at the colours of the sea. She had always imagined the water to be green or grey but the sea was always changing its colour. It was like a master of disguise, capable of wearing so many colours, forever changing, light green, turquoise, dark green, pale blue, mixing the colours on some giant palette. Then with sudden sweeps of the master's brush it changed again, soft violet, indigo, port wine and even shimmering silver and molten gold.

As she watched the froth of waves and listened to the excited voices of children, people pressed together in moments of wonder, a sweeping surge of happiness drifted through her body. It was as if her life had been planned to arrive at this moment. Never had she felt such freedom. It was as if the sight of the magnificent whale, mastering the vastness of the sea, was showing her a rare glimpse of nature. The supple movements of the glistening black creature that kept abreast of the ship somehow made her feel secure. She clasped her arms tightly around her chest. Her hair streamed out in the breeze. Thoughts of Owen Rathlin standing by her side. She imagined him watching the sight of the whale in wonder.

She looked down to see Tom at her side. She laughed at the joy that shone from him.

'LOOK!' he yelled at her. 'He must be as big as the ship!'

Rhoda nodded and moved away from Tom. She knew what was to follow, questions about the whale. Questions she couldn't answer. She left him chatting to one of the crew and went to look for Molly. It was nearly time for dinner. Molly must have gone below to bathe her arm again or gone to see Doctor Mackay about the scald. Rhoda went first to the dispensary. Doctor Mackay was there attending to young Ethan

Davies. He had slipped on his way down from the rigging.

'Ah Rhoda!' Doctor Mackay called out on seeing her. 'I need your help here – quickly.'

Rhoda forgot about looking for Molly and assisted Doctor Mackay with a splint and bandages for the young man's leg.

'You're lucky it's not broken Ethan. You must have twisted it when you slid part of the way down.' Doctor Mackay worked quickly.

'Now lad you can get up on the deck and get some air but try and rest it as much as you can. Go on lad. Get some dinner inside you.' They watched Ethan hobble out of the dispensary.

'Has Molly been to see you Doctor Mackay? She has a bad scald on her arm?'

No, he hadn't seen her but insisted she came to see him about the scald.

Rhoda cleared up and went to the cabin to look for her. She really must see Doctor Mackay about the bad scald on her arm. The bucket of water was still there. Rhoda washed her hands and face then went to find her to get dinner.

When Molly didn't even appear for dinner Rhoda became concerned. It wasn't like Molly to miss it. She was always hungry. She checked the library, stores, kitchen, then back to their cabin. On the way back to the dispensary she saw Doctor Mackay.

'I'm worried. I can't find Molly anywhere. Have you seen her?'

He looked at Rhoda's troubled face.

'Where did you see her last?' he enquired.

'On deck when we were looking at the whale.'

'Did you leave the deck together?'

'Well no...I mean Molly wasn't standing by me. The last I saw of her was when she went to the port side of the ship.'

'The port side...So she didn't see the whale?'

'I don't know.' Rhoda became agitated. 'Doctor Mackay, what's happened to Molly? It's not like her to go missing.'

Doctor Mackay looked serious. He took charge of the search for Molly. Rhoda grew afraid with each passing minute. Where was she? Everyone was aware that Molly was missing. She had to be somewhere on board ship. What if she was trapped somewhere? A thorough search of the 'Sea Duchess' revealed no sign of Molly. They even checked the bilges.

Doctor Mackay called Rhoda to the dispensary and sat her down. He looked serious. He tapped his empty pipe.

'It has been known for convicts to jump overboard ship.' He paused and looked uncomfortable. 'Do you think your friend could have jumped?' She told Doctor Mackay the about the talk they had together. Molly had said what a wicked thing it was to end your life. He listened patiently, holding an unlit pipe in his mouth.

'I see.' He stroked his chin thoughtfully. 'Look it might well have been an accident...she could have fallen overboard. Perhaps she leaned over too far looking for sight of the whale.' He said the words gently. 'It does happen all too often I'm afraid.'

'But she must be on board Doctor. She must be somewhere on the ship. Please look again, I implore you.'

'I'm afraid she is nowhere on the ship - it's been thoroughly searched. I'm afraid to say your friend Molly is lost at sea.'

'What about searching the ocean for her?' Even as Rhoda asked she knew it was hopeless. He shook his head.

'There's no hope of finding her now. I'm sorry. The wind is for us. The ship is moving too fast .We can't put about, not now.'

Rhoda sat still. She was numbed by what Doctor Mackay was saying. He was wrong. Molly would be found, she just knew she would.

'Why don't you let Lizzie stay with you in your cabin tonight – it will be company for you. She will be able to help you?'

Rhoda knew he meant to be kind to her. Through the long voyage he had shown such kindness to her and Molly. He said they reminded him of his own two daughters.

'Yes, thank you. I don't want to be by myself. I couldn't bear it.'

Rhoda felt very afraid. There was something very wrong but she couldn't disclose her fears to him, not yet. She had to find Molly first.

That night Rhoda could not sleep. There was so much going on in her mind. How would she ever sleep again? Molly could not be gone. She would never take her own life. She just wouldn't. Rhoda stared at the cabin door expecting it any moment to swing open and Molly would appear. Tomorrow when up on deck, she would search for Molly herself. She had to be somewhere, which was obvious, but never in the ocean as Doctor Mackay had suggested. She thought about it being an accident. An accident that she had fallen overboard?

She sat bolt upright in her bunk. That word ACCIDENT. That very morning Molly said about her scalded arm. That hadn't been an accident at all. Gladys Slyne tipping scalding tea over her had been deliberate.

Molly wasn't one to tell lies. If it had been done deliberately then why? Gladys had said Molly had to 'pay for her sins.' Gladys would never have pushed Molly over the deck of the ship, would she? She was reminded how Molly had very nearly toppled overboard when Gladys had tried to snatch at the letter. Gladys was livid with rage. What reason did that bitch Gladys Slyne have for hurting Molly?

Then another thought...drop...by drop...drenched her thoughts with such a force that it threatened to drown her sanity. What if Molly had not met with an accident at all? What if Molly had been pushed over the side of the ship? What if...Gladys...?

She stopped herself. Her thoughts were running away with her. She was not thinking logically. There could be a number of reasons. Tomorrow will be different. They would find Molly. She knew she would be the one to find her. She would search all over the deck for her. Rhoda said a small prayer for Molly. She didn't cry, there was no need too. Molly would turn up tomorrow.

She looked at Lizzie sleeping. Her slender arms clutched her blanket. Lizzie was so thin. Rhoda wondered where she got her strength from. Poor Lizzie was such a comfort to her. If she would keep her promise to work hard for her and Doctor Mackay, he would repay her with kindness. Rhoda liked her but she couldn't replace Molly. No one would ever could.

She stared at the narrow wooden door of their cabin. Now she felt more afraid than ever. There it was again, the rasping sound, like a laboured breathing. She was afraid to go to sleep. She called quietly to Lizzie. Lizzie stirred softly. She caught Rhoda looking at her.

'What is it Miss Rhoda? Are you afraid?'

'Yes. I can hear someone outside the door Lizzie. Can you hear it?'

Lizzie stretched and yawned.

'It's the noise of the ship Miss, they always creak and groan. Try and get some sleep. You'll feel better if you sleep Miss Rhoda.'

'Thank you for being with me Lizzie. I miss Molly so much.'

'I'm sorry about what happened to Molly. I truly am sorry Miss Rhoda. I'll work hard for you. I really will, you'll see if I don't.'

'I know you will. Go to sleep Lizzie. I'll find Molly tomorrow.' Rhoda sniffed. This is one of Molly's tricks. She's playing a game with me.'

Rhoda whispered into the darkness. 'I'll find you Moll... just you wait...I'll find out where you're hiding.'

XVII

Rhoda couldn't wait for the night to end. The dread of being without her dearest friend was impossible to think about. Doctor Mackay was wrong. Molly was somewhere on the ship. She would have left a message for her if she had taken her own life. But Molly would not have done even that. She had even said life was sacred.

When they were allowed up on deck Rhoda ran quickly to the spot where she had last seen Molly. She half expected to see her friend standing there laughing at her as if it were some game she was playing with her. She wandered along the port side of the ship keeping her eyes down looking for something, anything that would give her a clue about Molly's disappearance. And then, out of the corner of her eye she saw something...something white. It twisted and turned as if to free itself. Something was flapping in the wind like a trapped, fragile white moth. Rhoda stared at it as if it were a living thing. Even as she reached out for it she knew. It was the white strip of petticoat she had bound around Molly's scalded arm. Tears stung her eyes in the breeze, as she clutched the white strip close to her chest. This was all she would ever find of Molly.

Gazing down into the unfathomable depths of the ocean, she cried tears of anger. Some of them fell on the crumpled piece of petticoat. Then someone had taken hold of her hand. Rhoda gasped thinking it might be her friend but it was the young missionary woman, Ruth.

'I'm sorry about your friend,' she said. 'I'll pray for you.'

'Keep your prayers for yourself. I don't need them.'

Rhoda unleashed her anger upon Ruth. She had to blame someone. The young missionary woman was visibly shaken. She stepped away from her as if she had been struck, white faced, her lip trembling.

'I only meant to give you words of comfort and assist you in your time of need.....'

Rhoda's eyes blazed 'Who assisted Molly? What comfort does she have now? She's dead isn't she, lost forever in the sea? Someone murdered her.'

At the word 'murder' Ruth's face blanched with fear.

'You mustn't say such wicked things.'

Rhoda shouted the words, 'Whoever killed Molly was wicked! Evil! Caught up with the devil! But I'll find out who it was! I'll make them pay for it. Molly didn't take her own life. I just know it!'

Her words were caught up and carried on the wind far out beyond the listening waves but they reached someone else's ears first. Gladys Slyne was on the deck moving towards them. Rhoda felt the lump in her throat grow harder threatening to choke her. She felt like a useless pawn in the deadly game. She just wasn't strong enough to compete against her.

Rhoda felt an enormous rush of hatred as Gladys drew closer. The urge to lash out at her, tear into her, became a primitive force deep within her. Never had she been consumed with such a gnawing vengeance. If only she had given Gladys the letter Molly would still be alive. She had to suffer the simpering Gladys Slyne. Her close contact made her retch as her clawed hand gripped her arm like an eagle's talons.

'I couldn't help hearing what you were saying Rhoda Lambay. Just be grateful for God's gifts my dear. Taking one's own life is wicked and sinful. It's against God's law.'

'MURDER is against God's Law! Molly didn't take her own life. I know she didn't. She always said life is sacred.'

'And so it is my dear...life IS sacred. You would do well to remember that.' Gladys Slyne's voice shook with emotion. Her bird's nest head quivered. 'Are you saying then that your friend...was PUSHED overboard?'

Rhoda was taken aback at the question. Her cheeks flamed with anger.

'YES! I think Molly was pushed over the side of the ship.'

'In that case, this is serious. There is a murderer on board this ship.'

She gripped Rhoda's arm tighter and looked directly into her eyes.

'I WONDER WHO SHE IS.' Her tone held menace.

The Reverend Arthur Slyne came bustling forward. His dead fish eyes glanced from Rhoda to the sea, unaware of the barbed conversation.

'We must all pray for the soul of your friend.' He clasped his podgy hands together. Rhoda nodded her head in agreement, suddenly aware that the mask should not slip, play the part, participate in the game, stay on good terms with the Slyne's no matter how revolted she was by them, which meant striving to survive and find out how Molly disappeared from the ship. A mortal dread shook her. Now she would have to play their game and it was going to be a more sinister one. She would have to try and act her part to perfection, show them no fear, for Molly's sake. Arthur Slyne's hand slid across her shoulders with a limp thud.

'We must look after Rhoda now, mustn't we Gladys?'

'Yes, you need to have friends like us Rhoda,' she wheedled. 'Good Christian friends. You must hold close to your faith. Yes indeed. Have faith in the Good Lord, Rhoda. Keep your faith.'

Rhoda nodded in agreement. 'Yes, I will keep my faith, even in adversity. You evil bitch,' Rhoda whispered. But Gladys never heard her.

It was only when the Slynes had left her and gone below deck that she realised Ruth was standing near and had heard every word that had been said. She looked staggered. 'I can't believe what I just heard. What is this talk of murder? You think Molly was pushed over the side of the ship? It's too evil to contemplate, Rhoda. You must be mad to even think it.'

Rhoda gazed out to the sea. 'Perhaps the voyage has made some of us mad.' Her eyes narrowed. 'But I believe the madness was brought aboard the 'Sea Duchess' when we left England. It's catching - like a disease. I've more than likely caught it. If I have then I must use it to my advantage.'

Ruth looked confused. 'What do you mean? I don't understand you.' Rhoda stared at her and tossed her head defiantly.

'Well I have heard it said that it takes a thief to catch a thief. I wonder if that applies to someone who commits murder' Rhoda stared at the stillness of the sea. 'Do you imagine me to be mad Ruth?' Ruth drew her cloak around her. 'I can't answer. All I can do is wish you well – we will probably never meet again. And no matter what you say, I will always continue to pray for you and your friend Molly.' Rhoda hardly heard her voice. There were too many tumblers of thought cart wheeling across the shaking ground of her mind.

She didn't see Ruth and her brother leave the ship when they reached Cape Town. There was a sombre sadness of finality about their leaving. It was then Rhoda knew...she was utterly alone.

Rhoda was relieved when Cape Town was far behind them. There were times when she became sick and tired of the voyage but Lizzie proved to be a good companion. She had tried hard to be a friend to Rhoda but no one could ever replace Molly. They had taken on board fresh vegetables, bread and meat which gave them more variety to their diet. They were crossing the Indian Ocean, bringing them closer to Van Dieman's Land.

There were more gales and storms and times when the east wind was against them and times when the fog spiralled its way around the 'Sea Duchess'. Rhoda felt the opaque vapour like a layer of membrane on her face. She opened her mouth to inhale the breath of it deep inside her. It was like willing the dampness of the sea to come and heal her. Thoughts of Molly seeped into her mind time and again.

Alone one morning she unfolded the strip of white petticoat she had found on the deck. The shape of a red patterned butterfly emerged caked with dried blood. She hadn't noticed the pattern before. The more she stared at it the more convinced she became. Why hadn't she noticed it until now? Was this message from Molly? Was it Molly's blood? Or THE MURDERER'S?

'There is a murderer on board this ship and I wonder who SHE is?' Gladys Slyne's words sprang into her mind. Why ever didn't she think of it before. It was staring her in the face. Gladys Slyne had killed Molly. NO...WAIT...Her thoughts were running away with her again. Someone on the night of the storm had overheard her confession that she had murdered her stepfather - Ezra Blackwell...My God! Gladys knew she was a murderer. Did Gladys think that Rhoda had murdered Molly, her dearest friend? If you commit one murder, why not two? Whatever was she to do?

'DO....YOU DO NOTHING'...They were Molly's words. She could do nothing but wait. She recalled Molly saying that Gladys Slyne must be mad. It seemed so long ago now. If Molly had been scalded deliberately, then why? If Molly had been murdered by Gladys, then why? The bandage had come off Molly's arm in a struggle. She was hardly likely to take it off. It was wrenched from her arm by someone with a strong grip. That only left Gladys Slyne. Then she was right. GLADYS MUST HAVE KILLED MOLLY. It didn't make any sense to her. WHY would Gladys kill Molly? What was the motive for it? Did Molly have to pay the price with her life? Now Gladys would have to be paid back, when the time was right. It all seemed like delusions.

'I'm sorry about what happened to Molly.'

Rhoda was startled. She had been deep in her thoughts. It was the young man, Ethan Davies, who had fallen from the rigging on the day when they were all watching the whale. Fog swirled around his head like a halo.

'Thank you,' Rhoda smiled at him. She didn't really want to talk about Molly. 'How's your leg? Is it getting any better?'

He tapped his leg with a stick. 'It gets better every day, thanks to Doctor Mackay and your helping me.'

Rhoda said she was pleased about his progress and made to move away.

'Wait a moment. I saw your friend that day when everyone was looking at the whale.'

Rhoda stopped and turned to him.

'You saw Molly! Where was she?'

'On the deck. Port side, like she was talking to someone.'

'Did you see who it was that she was talking to?'

'No. I was up in the rigging. When I next looked down there was no one on the port side.' He looked awkward. 'Umm, I didn't see her jump over the side. Doctor Mackay asked me that.'

'I don't believe my friend jumped.'

'If your friend didn't jump over then she must have been pushed or she fell over the side.'

Rhoda shook her head in disbelief.

'Although the waves weren't that high for her to have been swept over, I'm sure.'

Ethan moved away and leaned over the side watching the spray hit the sides of the ship. He leaned over further, waving his arms at her.

'See look at me,' he called to her to watch. 'I'm leaning over but the swell is not enough to tip me over. The swell of the water that day wasn't as heavy as it is today.'

Rhoda was glad when Ethan stopped leaning over the side.

'Thank you for telling me what you saw that day.'

She went to go below when Gladys Slyne came into view on deck. Ethan called out loudly to Rhoda.

'WHEN I REMEMBER WHO I SAW FROM UP IN THE RIGGING, I'LL TELL YOU MISS LAMBAY.'

Just as Rhoda had her foot on the stair to go below, Gladys caught her by the arm. She was smiling down at her. She had been listening again.

'Rhoda, we want you to come and work for us in Van Dieman's Land.'

Gladys stood erect like a swaying serpent towering over her, ready to strike. Her beady eyes glittered. Rhoda composed herself quickly.

'I would like that very much Mrs Slyne...err... I mean Gladys.'

'Good, then you don't have to work in Cascades factory. You will be able to teach the children their religious tracts and do household duties.'

Rhoda's heart thudded. At least she would be with the children.

'What about Lizzie, Mrs Slyne. Poor Lizzie has received very little in the way of religious instruction – I'm afraid she is quite ignorant about such things. I'm sure her mind would be greatly improved in such matters if some place could be found for her in a good Christian household.'

Rhoda was amazed at her own rhetoric. If only Gladys could see into her mind at that moment. Even Molly would have applauded her act.

'Well we can't let Lizzie flounder. I'm sure she would appreciate our kindness to her. She would have to be obedient to us, the same as you

Miss Lambay. We can't ignore the pleas of the simple girl.'

'Thank you Mrs Slyne. I know Lizzie will be overjoyed at the prospect. I will make sure she knows her place.'

Gladys's eyes narrowed. Was there just a hint of disbelief in them?

'AND you Miss Lambay. Make sure you know YOUR place.'

And she knew even then that once they were in Van Dieman's Land she would be in their clutches for a very long time. Rhoda almost bobbed a curtsey. 'Yes I think I know where my place is Mrs Slyne, in servitude and obedience. You will have to excuse me. Doctor Mackay is waiting for some help in the dispensary.' She left Gladys staring after her. She made her way down below anxious to get away from her.

Rhoda set about her work with a renewed interest. Her mind seemed to be bubbling with some unexplained excitement and partly fear. She was pleased that she had had the courage to ask about Lizzie. That she had been sufficiently audacious to ask set her giggling to herself. Molly would have approved of her performance. She was beginning to learn how to handle Gladys Slyne. She was excited that Ethan Davies might remember who Molly was talking with. Could that someone have been Gladys? Ethan might have the only clue to Molly's disappearance off the 'Sea Duchess.' She would try and see him again as soon as she could.

Then, washing away the imprints of exhilaration were tempting trickles of fear. Fear like footprints trod in wet sand. Clear, alone, stretching along an alien shoreline. The footprints were hers. She had made them. There were no footprints of Molly's alongside hers. There never would be. She had to wait alone for the incoming tide of patience and cunning to wash them away. As the cold water trickled through her fingers, she watched in horror as the water turned from a pale pink to blood red. She pushed the bowl away from her. In her haste she spattered her clean apron. Blood stains slowly spread over the fresh white laundered apron. Rhoda sank slowly to the floor, at the same time trying to untie the knot at her back. Sobbing, she tried to rid herself of the bloody mess.

It was Doctor Mackay who found her and came to her rescue. 'You're getting yourself into a proper tangle aren't you?' he laughed as he helped her up. He deftly untied the knot. Rhoda looked down at her apron. There were no signs of any blood stains there or in the water.

XVIII

The next morning Rhoda heard the terrible news that Ethan was missing from aboard the 'Sea Duchess'. Rhoda was stunned. It was terrible news. Rhoda told Doctor Mackay she had left him on the starboard side of the ship. She couldn't imagine Ethan, a well trained sailor, leaning over the side of the ship and falling into the sea. What did Doctor Mackay think about it?

'It's very sad. A tragic accident,' Doctor Mackay said thoughtfully. Poor young Ethan Davies. He was a good ship-mate.'

'Yes he was.' Rhoda was shocked. She folded a clean pillowcase. Her hands were trembling. She was thinking about Molly's death.

'It seems strange don't you think. Two people falling overboard the ship?' Doubts came crowding into her mind, jostling her to find out the truth. 'Molly was assumed to have jumped overboard and Ethan met with a tragic accident.' She was afraid to put down the pillowcase. Doctor Mackay looked at her and frowned.

'Why is it strange? People are always having accidents, being swept overboard, falls, even deaths. It's a common occurrence on board any ship, believe me. I've seen it all.'

Rhoda didn't want to get into deep conversation about the death of Ethan. It resembled the loss of Molly too much. She was suspicious and at the same time very much afraid of what could happen to herself. She would have to stay more vigilant now. They were nearing the end of their voyage.

Doctor Mackay stopped her as she was about to leave the Dispensary. He dropped two guineas into her hand.

'The guinea from your quilt,' he said. 'And Molly's guinea.' Before she could say anything he added. 'I'm sure Molly would have wanted you to have it. She worked hard for it. You're going to work for the Slynes aren't you?'

Rhoda nodded her head. She was close to tears.

'Well that's better than working at the Cascades factory.'

'I've heard that it's terrible place.....' Rhoda's voice faltered.

'Terrible is too soft a word for it. It's a HELL HOLE I can tell you. Harsh punishments are given out. The women are divided into three classes, sewing, coarse dresses or doing heavy laundry work. Some good seamstresses are picked for fine sewing. You will be better off with the Slynes. They are a good Christian couple. Work hard - you'll soon get a ticket of leave Rhoda. I've given you a good report for the work you've done for me. I can only wish you well and hope that one day your memory will fully return to you.' Doctor Mackay stopped and tapped his empty pipe.

'Thank you Doctor Mackay and yes I did hear all about Cascades. I am lucky me and Lizzie are going to work for the Slynes.'

'Well what you heard is true. You're very lucky the Reverend Slyne and his wife have chosen you. Very lucky indeed!'

Rhoda shook his hand. 'Thank you for your kindness to me and Molly.'

'Do you want any letters to go back with the ship? Is there someone you might like to contact back in England?'

Rhoda was just about to say no one then changed her mind.

'I was wondering about Molly. I never thought to ask her address back in England. She wanted to contact her brother, Hawtin Williams, but I'm afraid she never knew where to find him. He wanted to be an actor Molly said.'

Why she was telling Doctor Mackay this she didn't know. It was just that he had been so kind to her. She wanted to throw her arms around his neck, to thank him. He was like the father she never knew, or could remember.

'Well if I ever see or hear about an actor by the name of Hawtin Williams I will tell him about you and your friendship with Molly. Hawtin Williams eh? Sounds impressive I must say. An actor's name if ever I heard one. I'll look out for the name for you.' Rhoda couldn't contain herself any longer. She threw her arms around his neck and kissed him on the cheek. This was a final goodbye to her old way of life. A new uncertain one was beginning. There was a glimpse of a tear in his eyes as they said their goodbyes.

'Goodbye Rhoda Lambay...and....be good.' The same words that Owen Rathlin had said to her, so long ago.

It was later when she had dried her tears and said a sad farewell to the cabin that had been her and Molly's little home for such a long voyage. She told Lizzie about working for the Slynes. Gladys was prepared to accept her into their Christian household. She told her what Doctor Mackay had said, about Cascades being a 'Hell Hole', yet there was another Hell Hole they were going to. This one had the all the facade of a Christian household. If only Doctor Mackay had known the truth about Molly and Ethan. When they left the ship Rhoda knew she would have to remain forever diligent if she wanted to stay alive and play the deadly game...to win.

Rhoda's first sight of Van Dieman's Land almost took her breath away. The triangular shape rising out of the sea looked like a huge emerald in the distance. How she wished Molly was with her to share this moment, the end of a long voyage.

'Cor blimey, I never thought it would look so green. Did you Miss Rhoda?' Lizzie stood alongside Rhoda staring into the distance.

'No I never dreamt it would look like this.'

'Blimey it looks like Paradise don' it Miss?'

'It isn't Paradise Lizzie. But it looks beautiful from here.'

Lizzie turned to look at Rhoda. She took hold of her hand.

'Bless you for getting me work with the Reverend Slyne and his wife.'

There were tears in Lizzie's eyes. Rhoda had come to rely on Lizzie more each day to overcome her grief at the loss of Molly although she would never forget her loving friendship. Lizzie had proved her worth, helping her with the dispensary and the children. Gladys had noticed her diligence, that's why she agreed to let them work together.

'Remember what I told you Lizzie. You MUST obey the Slynes. You don't want to be sent to Cascades do you?'

'Oh my gawd no! I'd die, I know I would. I'll scrub, clean everything proper...' Lizzie started to raise her voice. 'Sshhh It's alright Lizzie, just do as Mrs Slyne tells you. And listen to what I tell you.' She put her arm around Lizzie's thin shoulders. Together they watched Van Dieman's Land rise towards them, looking like a jagged emerald diadem resting on a cushion of shimmering sapphire sea.

As they sailed nearer to the shore Rhoda gazed in terror at the gigantic jagged cliffs that seemed to tower over the ship. They stood like a clutch of sharp pointed knives guarding the entrance to the emerald island, one on each side. She strained her neck back until it hurt trying to see the tips of chiselled rock.

'Look Miss Rhoda. It doesn't look like paradise no more. These must be the gates to Hell.' Lizzie held on to Rhoda clutching her tightly as the foam and the waves hissed their disapproval. There were moans of despair from the women. Shouts of rage and sobs which were lost in the rage of the fierce ocean. Rhoda looked through the gateway tearing her eyes away from the cold facade. She stared out at the enticing green of the emerald and knew then in that moment that behind the facade was a hardness to this alien land. They would be leaving the womb of the 'Sea

Duchess' to be left naked, like new born infants, to make a new life, a new beginning.

PART TWO
1851
VAN DIEMAN'S LAND

XIX

Rhoda wiped the damp morning mist from her face and looked down over Cockle Creek towards Recherche Bay. The sight and smell of the sea made her feel somehow closer to Molly. Sometimes she hated the sea for taking Molly from her. She missed being on board the 'Sea Duchess', the kind Doctor Mackay and the strict routine of the ship.

Even when they worked hard there had been a sense of freedom on board. The ship had become the mother she couldn't remember. The wooden strength of her timbers had held her fast through all the storms. She had curled up in the womb of the ship on her wooden bunk to be rocked securely. She had cried to her, laughed with her, talked to the 'Duchess' of her little threads of hope and made a promise that one day all would be well.

This alien land, wild mountains, rivers, lakes - the rushing lushness of it all had overpowered her thoughts - had held her hostage with the sight of vast green forests. She had to grapple with sinister sounds, smells that seized her senses and mocked her memories. The powder white sands that lined the bay gave her a false sense of freedom. Would she ever become as free as she had felt on the ship. She had no choice but to obey the Slynes or things could be much worse for her and Lizzie.

Shading her eyes Rhoda looked up to the top of the hill at a high wide tower. She could just about make out heavy ornamental gates that led to the carriageway and on to a mansion with a wide veranda, the home of Lady Elizabeth. She wished she could work for her. She was known for kindness to her convict employees, vastly different from the coldness of the Slynes.

Rhoda was tired of her chores. Even with Lizzie helping there was so much work for them. It was only when she was alone, like now, in the small schoolroom adjoining the Slynes cottage, that she could taste a few potent sips of freedom. In the short time since they had found their 'land legs' they had received very little rest. The Reverend Slyne and Gladys were busily engaged with the Church work and their local parishioners.

Rhoda waited in the doorway as the guard who escorted the convicts' children came into view. She was happy that the children were doing so well. The long voyage had taken its toll on some of them. Fever and disease had taken some of the younger ones to a watery grave. But now, after three months in Van Dieman's Land, they looked healthier and stronger with some colour in their thin cheeks. Rhoda was angry that they had to be taught separately from the 'settlers' children. The haughty settlers made it clear to Rhoda that they didn't want their children mixing with the 'convicts' brats'.

The children filed in quietly. Standing very still, waiting for the Reverend Slyne to enter the room, muffled coughs and sniffs were contained quickly in clenched fists. Letty, the smallest, had a fit of coughing just as the Reverend Slyne made his appearance. He stopped and peered at them as if they were all plague ridden. His glassy, dead fish eyes rolled over each one of them. The children shuddered at his cold gaze.

'Stop that coughing girl,' he hissed, giving Letty a clout on the side of her head. Letty wailed with fright. Rhoda gritted her teeth. It was hard to stand by and do nothing. 'STOP THAT NOISE CHILD!' he shouted as he gave Letty another clout. Letty stopped coughing and wailing, stood upright and sniffed back her tears before he could deliver another blow.

'The children are getting unruly, Miss Lambay,' he announced, his podgy hands clasped together. 'You must all be grateful for God's gifts.' He snarled the words, puffed out his chest then with hands on his widened hips barked out an order.

'Each child will come and tell me - God's gifts. Then you will be allowed to sit down.' One hour later the exhausted children sat down.

'Sit up straight now...backs straight.' He tapped each child with his cane. The children strived to sit up straighter. Rhoda could hear their sharp intakes of breath in their efforts.

Arthur Slyne's voice droned on and on. Even Rhoda had to fight to keep her eyes open. When he left with threats of 'Bad Reports' on the children, they all relaxed and puffed out their cheeks.

'Why is 'e so 'orrible?' Letty piped up.

Rhoda remembered the last time when Letty had piped up on board the ship. She had to chastise her. One day the Slynes might overhear her words.

'Letty. I won't tell you again. You must not say such wicked things about the Reverend Slyne.'

'It ain't wicked. My mam says he's a wicked, evil old basta....'

Rhoda stopped her before she could finish. Some of the children started to snigger. Rhoda knew that she had to be firm with them or things could get out of hand, heaping more trouble on them all.

'STOP IT AT ONCE!' she shouted. 'Next time you say such a thing I will have to report you to Reverend Slyne.'

Upset they all looked at one another. They knew only too well what the word 'reports' meant. There could be 'good ones' or 'bad ones'.

'You won't get a ticket of leave. You or your Mam,' Tom said smugly, 'if you don't get a good report. That's true isn't it Miss Lambay?'

Letty shouted at Tom, 'I want a ticket...I want a ticket!' She trembled and started to cry. They all started talking at once, arguing and sniffling. Gladys Slyne appeared in the doorway.

'Tickets of leave?...What's this unearthly noise all about?'

Rhoda had to think quickly. She looked sternly at the children. Instantly the children stopped. They had come to know the stern look that Rhoda gave them. It was a warning for complete silence.

'I was just telling the children Mrs Slyne that they must strive to get good reports or they won't get a ticket of leave...that's all.'

Rhoda was surprised at herself, how quickly she could imitate Gladys Slyne. She folded her hands in front of her and nodded her head. Gladys Slyne wavered in front of the children. Her sharp eyes seeking out the inattentive ones. They stared at her hypnotised.

'That's very true,' she rasped. 'You should all seek to gain a good report.' She turned on Rhoda and gripped her arm fiercely. 'Even you Rhoda Lambay...remember, I have to give you a report... but you will not renounce the Devil and all his works, will you?'

Her eyes blazed with madness of fire. She came closer and whispered quietly so that only Rhoda could hear.

'You are an evil murderer...YOU will burn in HELL!'

Rhoda felt the blood leave her face. A cold, death like cape had been flung over her, without any warning. The secret door that had guarded her inner soul had now been thrown wide open. What unnerved Rhoda was that she had not been prepared for the swiftness of the crucifying blow and Gladys Slyne barred the threshold. She felt faintness come upon her. Then an uncontrollable rage blazed through her, like wild cataracts of untamed ocean spray.

'And if I burn in hell YOU MURDERER, you Gladys Slyne, will burn with me!' The grip on Rhoda's arm slackened. Rhoda hadn't bothered to whisper her words to Gladys, she had said them loudly, like reciting some religious tract. The children looked bewildered. They sat still - watching the scene being played out before them.

The bird's nest hair quivered violently. The children had heard what had been said. Rhoda composed herself and dismissed the children for their rest-time with Lizzie in the back yard then she made her way quickly to her room. She had never meant it to come out in this way. Gladys had taken her by surprise in the deadly game. Now it was out. It was Gladys who had overheard her confession to Molly of the murder of her stepfather, Ezra Blackwell. In her mind she had always known this. She knew it had to be Gladys Slyne. But Rhoda had been unprepared for the way Gladys had thrust the deadly words at her. Rhoda sat down, but hadn't she fired back at Gladys? Hadn't she called Gladys a murderer? The bitch had been taken aback by the force of her words Rhoda thought smugly. Well that will teach her.

Rhoda flung herself down and started to weep soft tears then racking sobs controlled her. She wept for herself, for Molly, for Ethan. It was only when her face became blotched and blazoned with stinging brine she stopped weeping. Hate and anger gripped her. Would she ever be able to wrench herself free from Gladys Slyne? She would have to try and find freedom another way.

Rhoda dried her eyes. Someone was tapping on her door. It was Gladys. She came quickly into the room, looking anxious and flustered.

'Rhoda my dear. Come and sit here beside me. Do you feel a little better now?' Rhoda bit hard on her bottom lip. She trembled as she watched Gladys open the big, black bible on her lap. Rhoda knew the deadly cat and mouse game was going to resume. She would have to be on her guard once again. This time she was more prepared.

'Now then... Acts Chapter twelve, Verse thirteen. Listen Rhoda, I will read it out to you...' As Peter knocked at the door of the gate, a damsel came to hearken, named...RHODA.' Gladys paused and smiled. 'You see, I told you your name was a biblical one. You didn't know that?'

Rhoda smiled faintly, playing the game. 'I didn't know 'Rhoda' was a biblical name. No, I was never told that.' Rhoda shook her head.

'Oh yes. But there's more. Rhoda didn't open the door to Peter. Did you know why?' Rhoda shook her head and frowned at Gladys. She had to play along with her. She didn't know where this was leading.

'Why didn't she open the door to Peter Mrs Slyne?'

Gladys clenched her hands under her chin. 'Because they thought her MAD...They all called Rhoda...MAD!'

'Why did they call her mad Gladys?'

'They didn't believe her when she told them Peter was at the door. You see everyone knew Peter was in prison.' Gladys leaned closer to Rhoda. She could smell her acid breath. Gladys folded her arms, her head shook.

'That is why they won't believe you Rhoda Lambay. No one will believe the word of a CONVICT girl.'

'Was Rhoda a convict Mrs Slyne?' Rhoda smiled sweetly.

'No she was not. They thought she was mad.' Gladys looked down at the black bible again. 'You see, it's all written here clearly. They won't believe you Rhoda, my dear. You are MAD you see. Surely you must know that. You do understand that dear Rhoda don't you? Look it says so here. Look.' Gladys gave her a twisted smile. Rhoda took the heavy bible with trembling hands and read the verses. There had to be something more about Rhoda. She found what she wanted. Gladys had read out only part of the story.

'But there's more to the story. It says here, and I will read it to you Mrs Slyne.' She sat up straight. Rhoda looked at her and began to read in a patronising tone. 'But she constantly told them Peter was at the door. Then when they saw him...they believed her.' Rhoda showed her the verses. 'See it says here. Do look Gladys. They believed Rhoda. She wasn't mad after all.'

Gladys took the bible from her and patted her wiry hair.

'Be grateful for God's gifts Rhoda Lambay. Learning enables the mind. BUT...IT COULD LEAD TO YOUR OWN DESTRUCTION.'

Gladys lifted the heavy bible and hurled it at Rhoda's head. She reeled back against the tapestry cushion as she tried to ward off the heavy blow. She heard Gladys leave the room slamming the door behind her.

She sat up and wiped her hand across her wet forehead. It was wet with fresh blood. She rested there for a while unable to move. Then she picked up the fallen bible and noticed the red streaks that slid across the black leather. She wiped them with her hands and stared down at the streaks. Holly berry red blood. She wiped her forehead again, continually looking down at her hands. The blood didn't vanish. It stayed there. She smelled the freshness of it, wiped it across her face and looked into the mirror. She smiled at her image, a bloody victor of the game. Gladys had drawn blood – the game was getting more dangerous.

Very slowly Rhoda had the feeling she was winning. She had struck out again at Gladys. The blows that Gladys dealt her no longer mattered.

It was the final blow that counted. The deadly blow. Rhoda clenched her hands and her nails dug into her fists. And when it came she would be ready for it.

XX

Rhoda's head continued to hurt her for days after. Lizzie looked concerned about her wound. She stopped dusting.

'What really happened to you Miss Rhoda?'

'I walked into the door. It was a silly thing to do.'

Rhoda looked at the copybooks for handwriting on the table. Lady Elizabeth had managed to get them for the children, from goodness knows where. She had also brought slates, chalks and three counting frames. Rhoda had kept them well hidden, waiting until the time was right, until the Slynes were in a good mood. They would have to remain hidden somewhere. Rhoda placed her hands quickly on top of the pile of copy books.

'What are you hiding there Miss Lambay? I demand to know.'

Rhoda spun around at the tone of voice. She knew it was Gladys Slyne. But instead of Gladys, Lizzie stood there. Her thin hands clasped in front of her, her head quivering and her wide eyes staring at her. Rhoda pressed her hands on her chest.

'Oh Lizzie you gave me such a fright. You sounded just like Gladys.' They both laughed. 'You'd make a good actress that's for sure.' Lizzie continued to walk around like Gladys, her head quivering, her eyes darting around the room. Every now and again she would stop, fold her arms and give Rhoda a haughty look.

'Why are you staring at me like that girl?' Lizzie whispered with a rasping voice, 'Stop it at once, do you hear?'

Rhoda looked away from Lizzie towards the open door.

'Good morning Reverend Slyne,' Rhoda said.

Lizzie stumbled as she turned around quickly, almost losing her balance. Rhoda laughed and rushed to catch her.

'Let that be a lesson to you, wretched child,' Rhoda said with mock severity. She shook Lizzie and tried to take her duster. They didn't hear the Reverend Slyne creep into the room.

'What's this about a lesson Miss Lambay? What lesson?'

Rhoda gulped for air. 'Good morning Reverend Slyne.'

He waved his hand. 'Yes, yes, what's this about a lesson?'

Rhoda knew she had to think quickly. Lizzie kept opening and closing her mouth like a fish gasping for air.

'Well, you see Reverend Slyne, I was just telling Lizzie about...er... um...learning a lesson...of...um...the Catechism.'

'The children must learn their Catechism Miss Lambay.'

Rhoda straightened her dress and apron, quickly patting her upswept hair. Thank goodness the Reverend Slyne hadn't appeared sooner.

'They must learn it by heart...Why are they so slow?'

'We are learning it. Every day we recite part of it together...'

'It's no good part of it Miss Lambay. They MUST know all of it. How many times do I have to tell you? I will test them myself.'

Rhoda shivered at the prospect of it. She knew what that meant. She whispered to Lizzie to stay and make a pretence of dusting the heavy oak benches.

Gladys Slyne came into the room. 'Are you being industrious Lizzie?'

Her bird's nest head nodded in approval. Lizzie stumbled and dropped her duster in fright. Rhoda swiftly picked up the duster and covered the copy books with it. They would have to be hidden later. Rhoda had a thought. If Lizzie were allowed to stay with the class of children, the Reverend Slyne might not be so harsh on the children. It would also give Lizzie the chance of a rest sitting with them.

'Mrs Slyne, Lizzie has asked to be allowed to attend the class to learn the Catechism. Would you kindly allow her to?'

Lizzie looked as white as her clean apron. She glared at Rhoda. Mrs Slyne looked pleased. The Reverend Slyne looked aghast at the shaking Lizzie.

'You mean you've never learned the Catechism girl?' he snorted.

'Err no sir...I... Reverend ... sir. I never did...but ...umm ... I would love to learn it sir...really I would.' Lizzie's eyes filled with tears. Rhoda smiled to herself. Lizzie was learning fast how to handle the Slynes. This could mean a rest for Lizzie sitting with the children. Rhoda gave Lizzie a wink.

'But of course you must learn it Lizzie. You can start now when the children arrive.' Gladys grasped her shoulder. 'You can work later.'

Gladys escorted Lizzie to the front bench. The children trooped in and sat quietly, backs straight, arms folded. Lizzie looked petrified at Rhoda.

'You boy....What is your name?' Reverend Slyne commanded.

'Thomas Robertson sir,' Tom answered proudly.

'Now then...Who gave you this name?'

'My mother and father sir...'

The Reverend Slyne's face grew white with rage. His glassy fish eyes enlarged as if they would pop out of their sockets. He swung his podgy fist into the boy's head. Lizzie gasped.

'Recite the Catechism with them Miss Lambay. All day long. It's obvious the boy is stupid. He should have a good beating.' He caught Lizzie looking at him, terrified of what was happening. He turned away sharply.

There was nothing to be done but practise. All day long they practised. The children became bored with words that had little meaning for them.

'One more time children before we finish,' Rhoda smiled at them.

'Question : What is your name?'

'Answer: N or M'

'Question : Who gave you this name?'

Tom looked very grave faced as he answered with the others.

'Answer : My Godfathers and Godmothers in my Baptism...'

'Question: What did your Godfathers and Godmothers then do for you?'

Letty started to cry. 'I don't want gold feathers on a gold mother. I want my own mother.' Poor Letty wanted her mother to stay the same. Rhoda was distraught but she had to drum the words into them for their own sakes. It was too much for the children to understand.

'Now children, answer all together now.' Rhoda repeated the question. The children recited it like parrots. Some merely mouthed something. They could not remember such strange words and meanings. The children were becoming very tired...

'Answer : They did promise and vow three things in my name. First that I should renounce the devil and all his works, the pomp and vanity of this wicked world and all the sinful lusts of the flesh.'

Tom became serious.

'Where does the Devil have his works Miss Lambay? Does he work for the Reverend Slyne?'

Rhoda ignored his question then Tom asked another one.

'What are the sinful lusts of the flesh Miss Rhoda?' Rhoda took no notice but something from her past reared its horned head.

'Secondly, that I should believe all the Articles of Christian Faith. And thirdly, that I should keep God's holy will and commandments and walk in the same all the days of my life.'

'Does the Devil WORK in Van Dieman's Land?' asked one boy with a face full of freckles. 'AND how can we all walk the same way?'

'Why is God's WILL FULL OF HOLES?' Tom asked. 'What's a will?'

Not to be put off by his other unanswered questions, Rhoda wiped her hand across her forehead. 'You will understand these things when you are older. Now we have done enough for today.' Rhoda was exhausted when the children finally went back down the hill with the guard.

She laughed with Lizzie about the children's questions. How could small children be expected to understand? Yet there was something uneasy in her childish laughter. When she was alone a copious although only brief memory of learning her own Catechism came to her suddenly, when she had been laughing with Lizzie. Now, nightshade memories simmered in the poison cauldron. Simmered, bubbled gently to the surface...

She remembered Ezra Blackwell sitting her on his knee, the slow squeeze of his hard, cruel hands on her bare flesh. He held her tightly. One night she could feel the strength of him there in the bed beside her. She could smell his fetid breath, could see the evil glints in his eyes. She had spluttered out the half remembered words. Strived and willed herself to remember them in sheer terror of what he might do next, but he would only sneer at her and grip her tighter to him.

'What is your name evil one?'

Before she could whisper 'Alyce Wilson' he stopped her, his hand over her mouth. 'NO...you're name is Evil One... Now say it.'

She had repeated it, her voice inflamed with a primeval passion.

'Now...Who gave you this name? Answer me evil bitch.'

'You did... YOU gave me this name... You... YOU.!'

'No,' he whispered in her ear. 'God gave you this name. And one day I will have to get rid of you and your evil. Your beauty brings evil to anyone who touches you...evil whore.'

When he had left the room, she sprang from her bed. She tried to loosen the heavy bolt that had been crudely stuck and daubed with paint. She had strained at it for hours, picking and scraping the paint away. All through the gawping, gloating night, in fear he would return, Rhoda had prayed to God to help her release the bolt. She heard Ezra's quiet footfalls padding towards her door... She freed it...forced it safely home. She listened. She, the quarry, sensed his festering breath behind the locked door and listened as the stealthy hunter turned to seek out other prey.

She remembered black nights, when she heard him prowl outside her locked and bolted door. It was then she used cunning, the animal instinct of self-preservation. Rhoda screeched out that she was having a bad dream. Her nightmare screams sent him scurrying like vengeful vermin. It was only when the healing light of the moon stopped the pummelling that pounded her heart beats into raw shreds of innocence that she dared to close her eyes. Then sounds would make her watch and wait, expecting the darkness to leap at her. Leap at her like some wild, undiscovered animal that could hold her down and wait until her shuddering frame was still and then devour her. She watched the shocked face of the moon as it peered down at her like some prying neighbour bathing herself in her pale, blue cold light until in shame, the moon withdrew her light and pulled a thin veil of curtained clouds slowly across her ancient hardened face......

Rhoda wrapped herself in a cocoon of soft eiderdown, tucking in the edges around her slender body, almost suffocating herself in its warmth. Shrouded in shameful loneliness she cried herself to sleep.

XXI

Martha was very determined to find out Rhoda Lambay's real identity. Since her meeting with Mrs Rebecca Evans of the Ladies Committee all she could think about was trying to help poor Rhoda. She made many journeys between the Old White Horse Cellar in Piccadilly and the George and Bear in Holborn. It wasn't as if she liked drinking but she knew so many of the coach drivers that frequented the public houses. Her father had once been a coach driver, so she was well known about the premises and she did fancy a port and lemon on several occasions. She had even arranged for bill posters to be displayed in each establishment with a full description of Rhoda. She had the feeling that Rhoda was not a Londoner and had come to the city via a coach.

Martha had proved to be relentless in her quest. She had always fancied herself to be a bit of a sleuth. Besides, she had taken quite a liking to Rhoda. She battled her way through the crowd in the George and Bear. The coach drivers asked her about the progress she was making in her search. The stormy weather was making things more difficult for her to get around London. She decided that tonight she would concentrate her efforts around Holborn. It was near to Lambay Street. Some form of feminine intuition steered Martha in this direction.

The public bar was stifling. Smoke stung her eyes as she struggled past a tall, thick set gentleman. He stopped to look at the placard. Martha watched him. Her sharp eyes took in his appearance. He was about six feet tall with a black cape slung over his shoulders and was dressed in an evening suit with a silk top hat. He carried a silver topped Malacca cane. Martha wondered if he was about to visit the opera house. At first he looked shocked, almost taken aback at what he was reading. Then he stared again at the description, muttering to himself.

'Surely it can't be her...but then again it must be...'

Martha overheard his muttering and decided to approach him. There was nothing to lose in talking to the elderly gentleman.

'Excuse me for being so forward sir, but would you by any chance know something about this poor young girl?'

The gentleman turned towards her. Martha caught a glint in his eyes. Believing it to be a tear, she steered him towards a quieter corner of the bar. He stroked his grey beard and wiped at his tear-filled eyes.

'I can see you're upset sir. Do you recognise the description?'

'Indeed I do madam.' He looked serious. 'Tell me, do you know her?'

Martha watched his thick black brows draw together in a frown. His dark eyes looked fiercely at Martha.

'I do know her sir, but only as Rhoda Lambay. She stayed with us a short while.'

'A short while...why ?' He looked astonished.

'Well, in fact it was only one night sir. The next morning she had gone.'

Martha was intrigued by the grey-haired gentleman. He was handsome looking. He sipped his ale. Martha took sips of her port and lemon. He leaned closer towards her, whispering as if it were a secret between them.

'Did this girl say her name was Rhoda Lambay?'

'Why no! She didn't know her name poor lamb.' Martha told him about the accident and her loss of memory.

'Lost her memory now has she?' He smoothed his chin. 'She's gone, disappeared again...Well now.'

Martha took a deep breath and a large gulp of her drink. It was obvious this man knew of Rhoda. Why had he said 'disappeared again'? Why had Rhoda disappeared in the first place? And from where? She had to find out.

'Well she hasn't exactly disappeared sir.' Martha had trouble finding the right words to say. She didn't want to upset this gentleman but then if he knew Rhoda then she had to tell him more about her. 'She's been transported to Van Dieman's Land.' Martha told him gently for fear of shocking the gentleman, all about the arrest and transportation as a convict for seven years.

He looked at Martha with a mouth wide open. 'Transported? A CONVICT?' He raised his voice. People stared at the mention of the word convict.

'I'm sorry to distress you sir, but please can you tell me her real name. I must write her a letter. I promised I would try and find out who she was. Do you know anything of her sir?'

He coughed violently and clutched his chest.

'Why I believe her name is...Alyce Wilson.'

'Oh praise be to God! At last...after so long! Such good news sir.'

Martha remembered something else, just to make sure she had found the real Alyce Wilson.

'One more thing sir. Alyce had marks on her face and body as if she had been in some sort of accident or other.'

'Did she? I'm sorry I don't know anything about any marks.'

Martha hesitated about giving the gentleman her own name. She continued.

'Yes she had quite a few. We were concerned. Yes, and in her valise were five gold sovereigns, a silver hairbrush and…'

'Tell me do you still have the items?' He leaned forward.

Martha considered this to be very strange. He was putting the items in importance before Alyce. He hadn't even introduced himself to her. Martha decided not to give her name to the gentleman but pushed the conversation further. She took another sip of port and lemon.

'Perhaps you would like to write to her sir. Are you a relative?'

'No…She won't remember me. Not if she's lost her memory.'

He stood up and shook her hand. He wasn't going to give her his name. There had to be a way to find it out. She picked up his smooth silk top hat, tipping it slightly towards her to see the satin inside. She waited as he pulled on his white kid gloves. Martha noticed the cut of his clothes which were well made. He made it obvious the conversation had ended. He thanked her.

'Well, good day to you Madame.'

He quickly strode away after raising his hat to her. Martha had wanted to ask him more but it was too late now. He dissolved into the steaming crowd like a draught of doom. Martha pulled on her warm gloves and downed the last dregs of her port and lemon. She was pleased with herself. No doubt about it she would make an excellent detective. She had been able to catch a glimpse of the name inside the top hat. Embroidered with gold thread were the name of the hat maker 'Poteroes' and the address of the gentleman - Bellington Hall at Threxington. She knew Poteroes well. They were near Holborn, quite close in fact. Martha grew excited. What's more she knew the very man who would help her. Josiah Skillard. He worked there as a clerk. He could get the name of this gentleman for her. Then she could investigate further. It seemed to be a very strange affair to Martha.

It wasn't easy to get the information that she wanted. For one thing Josiah was extremely loathe to disclose names of customers. He had to spend more time than he could afford to search back several years until he got the correct address and match with the name of the gentleman. Martha thanked him with a ginger cake she had made and assured Josiah that her intentions of finding out the gentleman's name 'was to aid a poor young girl to regain her memory.' Josiah wrote down the name and address - Sir Daniel Wilson of   Bellington Hall, Frogmore, Threxington.

'Sir Daniel Wilson. Well I never and he didn't so much as introduce himself. Wait until Rhoda hears about this,' she laughed.

Martha was anxious to get started in her search. She had found out the name and address of the gentleman. Now all she had to do was call at the house and make sure all her information was accurate. After all she had to write this in a letter to Alyce ... no it must be Rhoda Lambay. It would be too confusing to address the letter to Alyce Wilson. After all she might have to be addressed as a Lady or something more formal.

Josiah, in his initial search, could find no evidence of Bellington Hall in the recent account books. Martha had to wait for several weeks before Josiah could give her the vital information. Besides, the weather was bad, with more snow on the way. It was early March when she decided to make her journey to Threxington. Martha was going to make the most out of her journey. She would call and visit her sister on the way back home from Threxington. All she had to do now was take a coach to make the journey and then stay with her sister Jess for a night and catch the coach back to London the next day. Martha became more excited at the prospect of an adventure. Although there was something she didn't quite fathom out about it all she had to go on with it now for the sake of poor dear Rhoda. Martha was going to find out all she could to help Rhoda remember her past life. She would write it all down for her in the letter. After all it might help the poor lamb to remember her real identity...Martha was sure Rhoda would be overjoyed with the news.

XXII

Martha wrapped up warmly against the sudden blasts of a dry March day and settled herself into the corner seat of the coach that was to take her to Threxington. She instructed the coach driver, Bill Perkins that she wanted to be dropped at Frogmore. It was a good four hours later when the coach pulled in at Frogmore and stopped for rest at the 'White Lion.'

Martha felt all the aches and pains of the cramped journey as fatigue began to take effect on her. She pushed the bar door open ahead of the other travellers and ordered a port and lemon. She knew their dalliance about making their decisions on what to eat and drink would tax her patience. She couldn't wait to see Bellington Hall.

She sipped her drink and made conversation with a plump, dark haired girl who was drying and polishing glassware.

'Excuse me, but can you tell me where I could find Bellington Hall?'

The girl looked at Martha and continued polishing the tankard with care. She frowned when Martha said Bellington Hall.

'It's down past Apple Tree farm madam, on the left, then you go along Yew Tree Lane. It's down that way. You can't miss it.'

Martha quite enjoyed being called madam. No doubt it was because she had asked about Bellington Hall. They probably thought she was someone of importance.

'Thank you my dear, you've been very helpful.'

She made her way down past Apple Tree farm, then down Yew Tree Lane. She was getting quite tired walking and wished she had asked the girl how far it was to Bellington Hall. Just then she heard the sound of a horse and cart coming up behind her. The vehicle stopped alongside her.

'You going far? You can have a ride in the cart if you want,' the young man with the untidy hair shouted down to her.

'I'm looking for Bellington Hall...do you know it?' Martha asked as she climbed aboard with some hesitation.

'Course I do. I lives over in Apple Tree farm.' He pointed back the way she had come. 'No one there now though, they've all gone away... yes, gone away they have, a long time.'

They arrived at the gateway to a long drive. The Hall looked quite large through the oak trees. Ivy clawed at the walls, but it was clear to see the hall was shut up. All the windows were shuttered. It was obvious there was nobody at home. Her journey had been wasted. She had come all this way hoping to find out something to help Alyce Wilson remember something about her past life.

'Oh dear I was hoping to talk to someone who might have known Alyce Wilson,' Martha said. 'Do you mind taking me back up Yew Tree Lane to the crossroads?'

'Miss Alyce? I took her to catch the coach - long time now.'

The young man looked lost in thought. It was obvious to Martha that the poor lad had difficulty with his thoughts. 'I'm Jack Miss. It was me that took Miss Alyce to catch the coach. In a terrible hurry she was.'

Martha pulled her warm scarf around her and climbed back into the bumpy cart. Jack hadn't said yes about taking her back up the lane but she assumed he would. He turned the cart around. Martha was intrigued now. Here was someone who had known Alyce and had taken her to catch the London coach.

'Did you know where Alyce was going Jack?'

'To catch the coach, I told you...She's gone now...away.'

'Is Alyce's mother alive Jack?'

'No, she's gone now...away, she has...in the river...drowned.'

'Drowned! Oh the poor woman! What about her husband Jack?'

'The Master...he's gone now away he has.'

Jack put his fore finger in front of his mouth 'Shhh! It's a secret. Jack mustn't tell no one. You must never tell anyone. I made a promise I did.' Jack shook his head. Martha was more intrigued than ever that Jack would never tell her his secret. It was annoying her, as to what it could be.

Martha was feeling very cold and desperate for a cup of hot tea. Jack dropped her back into the village outside a small cottage. He jumped down, knocked at the door and waited. An elderly lady with snow white hair answered. Martha couldn't hear what was being said but the next thing she was being escorted into a small parlour with a crackling fire. Jack's horse and cart cantered away before she could thank him. She watched him through the small window tearing down the road.

'Sit down my dear and make yourself comfortable. I'll make you some nice hot tea,' the woman said. Martha thanked her and introduced herself as Mrs Reed. When they were seated comfortably with their hot tea and buttered muffins Mrs Reed spoke. 'Jack says you're looking for Miss Alyce?'

Martha looked at the old lady with the knitted shawl pinned with a peacock brooch fastened tightly around her shoulders.

'Well I'm not so much as looking for her. I know where she is...'

'Oh thank God you've found her, Martha. I've got something for dear

Alyce. She must have this before we do anything else. Before he died my husband insisted I was to give it to her when she was older. I don't know why but she was too young at the time. Then somehow I forgot all about it through the years. Then she went away to her new post as a Governess in France. Well you know how it is…let me see now.'

Martha was about to tell her what had happened to Alyce then thought twice about it. To tell the old lady she had been transported to Van Dieman's Land might have shocked her into fainting. Whatever Mrs Reed was going to give her, she could send it on to Alyce Wilson.

Mrs Reed searched through the heavy oak drawer and pulled out an old notebook. 'This is it…well not all of it, just this page 54. This is what you must give to her.' She handed the page of a well worn notebook to Martha. 'You will give it to her won't you…please?' Martha took it. It was written in pencil though some of the writing appeared to be fading. It looked like a report of some kind. Martha looked hastily at the clock. She would have to leave to catch the coach to stay with her sister for the night.

'You can rest assured I will see that Rh…' Martha checked herself just in time 'I will see that Alyce gets this. I promise you.'

'Thank you Martha. You see my husband was the constable that was assaulted in the course of his duty.' She pointed to the note page. 'Alyce will remember my husband Alfred, she'll know about it. The rest is secret.' Mrs Reed looked extremely vague. Martha was not going to hear the rest of the story...the secret.

Mrs Reed stood up. 'Perhaps you might like to call on me again and tell me about dear Alyce. I suppose she has quite settled into being a governess – an important family so I hear. Has she settled down, do you know Martha?'

Martha didn't want to say anymore about Alyce Wilson. Certainly not to leave this old lady with the news that Alyce was not Alyce any longer but Rhoda Lambay convicted of stealing a white petticoat and being transported to Van Dieman's Land for seven years. The dear old lady might drop down dead in front of her at the terrible news and that would never do. Martha smiled warmly at Mrs Reed promising her she would call again when time permitted her.

'Thank you Mrs Reed for your warm hospitality...and...YES...I believe Alyce might have settled down in her new position. She is a resilient young lady, able to overcome any difficulties I'm sure. I will see to it that she gets this note as soon as possible.'

Mrs Reed waved her off from the doorway.

'Oh Martha, please be sure to give her my love and my prayers are with her, please tell her,' Mrs Reed called out.

'I will,' Martha answered. 'Love and prayers will comfort Alyce.'

It was only when Martha was seated in the coach it became clear that trying to find out about Alyce Wilson had become a greater mystery. And even more puzzling when Martha read what was on the note paper. 'This is going to be a pretty kettle of fish to sort out my dear Rhoda. I only hope it will help you to remember your past when you get this.'

XXIII

Rhoda woke up early one morning. She listened to the battering of rain on the window pane. But she could hear another sound. She strained to hear it above the squall. It sounded like a wounded animal. She slipped quickly from her bed, hurried to the window and looked far over Cockle Creek. The sound was coming from inside the house. Lizzie's bed was empty. She had to rise earlier than Rhoda. She stood behind the bedroom door and listened. There it was again. This time it was a whimpering sound. She opened the door carefully, wary of what might be lurking in the passage way. Lizzie almost fell through the doorway into her arms.

'Lock the door Rhoda...she's after me!'

Rhoda shot the small iron bolt into place. Lizzie fell onto the bed. Rhoda looked at her arm. She knew instinctively what had happened. Lizzie had been severely burned....

'OH MY GOD...Not again! Did Gladys do this to you?'

Lizzie could hardly speak. 'No...I walked into a door like you did.'

Rhoda bit her lip in anger. 'I know what happened Lizzie.'

She opened the window, filling a large china bowl with cold rain water. Lizzie protested but once her arm was in the cold water, she felt some relief.

'Oh that's better...Oh, the relief from the pain.'

After a while she told Rhoda what had happened. It was identical to what had happened to Molly on the 'Sea Duchess'. This was too serious to ignore. She had to tell Lizzie that the same thing had happened to Molly.

'But why did she pour it over my arm? It wasn't an accident Rhoda.'

Lizzie whimpered with the pain. 'I didn't do anything, honestly I didn't. I was just making her tea, like I do every morning.' Tears trickled down her face and ran down her arm into the cold water.

'It was done deliberately. Why did she do it? Why? Why?'

Rhoda put her arm around her for comfort.

After she had bound Lizzie's arm with soft white linen and given her cool drinks of rain water, Lizzie became calmer. She rested on Rhoda's bed propped up with two pillows and her arm resting in the bowl of water. With frightened eyes she kept looking towards the locked door.

'Try and rest Lizzie. You're safe with me here now.'

Lizzie's eyes darted towards the window then at the door again. Rhoda sat beside her, soothing her with the cold water and stroking her long brown hair.

'Now listen to me Lizzie.' Rhoda's voice was serious. 'I've got to get you away from here...I...'

'No...No Rhoda - What do you mean.....away from here?'

'You must listen to me Lizzie...This is serious. There's danger for you if you stay here with Gladys Slyne.' Rhoda took hold of her hand. 'Real danger I mean.'

'I don't care - I'm not going away from here.' Lizzie pulled her hand away from Rhoda. 'The guards and them terrible dogs of theirs will be after me. You don't know what you're saying. I don't care how much she hurts me. I'll stay here with you... please Rhoda.'

Rhoda had tried not to tell Lizzie too much about Molly and the scalding but she had to tell her now for her own safety. She told her everything. It was the only way to convince Lizzie of the real danger she was in. She was convinced Gladys Slyne had murdered Molly and Ethan. Lizzie stared at her, mouth wide open in disbelief at her words.

'Molly AND Ethan? Oh my God!...Oh my God!' Her voice started to rise in disbelief. Rhoda had to silence her.

'This is why you must get away from her, for your own safety.'

Lizzie sat up quickly. Her arm dangled out of the bowl. She winced with pain. 'You mean she might try to MURDER me?'

'Not TRY Lizzie. She WILL murder you.'

Rhoda didn't give her a chance to say any more. 'I don't know when it will be. It might even be tonight.' Lizzie put her arm back into the cold water. 'What can I do Rhoda? Whatever can I do? I'm so afraid.'

'Shh...Hush! Now listen. I have a plan. Only for a short time but you must trust me. And don't ask questions. Do you understand me?'

Lizzie nodded and took long gulps of water.

'Gladys Slyne is a dangerous mad woman. She is about to kill you. I don't know why she killed Molly and Ethan yet, but I have to try and trap her into making a confession. I have to do this. For both Molly's sake and Ethan's. Do you understand Lizzie?' Lizzie nodded her head slowly.

'What about the danger you'll be in Rhoda? We could get help. Tell the Governor about what happened aboard the 'Sea Duchess.' We can do that Rhoda couldn't we?'

Rhoda shook her head and sighed. 'And who's going to believe two young convict girls Lizzie? Gladys Slyne is supposed to be a good Christian woman, the wife of a Reverend. Now, who do you think they will believe?'

Rhoda picked up a pencil from her washstand and a piece of paper.

'I'm going to write a quick note to Lady Elizabeth. She is very kind and a proper lady. I know she will understand. It won't be long Lizzie I promise you. You will be safe with her.'

Lizzie gazed at Rhoda as she wrote the letter. When she had finished she put it in an envelope, addressed it and hid it deep inside her apron pocket.

'You must take this letter tonight to Lady Elizabeth. She's very kind to convicts. She will keep you there safely. I promise nothing will happen to you.' Lizzie made to interrupt her... 'No I...'

'I wrote that you are a good worker, but you have been badly treated. I haven't mentioned anything else Lizzie. You must leave tonight. She has other convict women who work for her, don't worry.'

'But what about you? Why don't you come with me?'

'There's something I must do first. I told you I must get a confession from Gladys Slyne. It will all come right in the end, you'll see.'

Lizzie didn't feel happy about the guards and the savage dogs, but Rhoda promised her to wait and see what the plan was. She told Lizzie to try and get on with her work as best she could and not to arouse suspicion.

'Try and keep out of her way. Dust the schoolroom when I'm in there. Better still, sit and read the bible with the children.'

'But I can't read Miss Rhoda,'

'No one knows that. Now do as I say. Go and try to act as if nothing has happened. I know you can do that Lizzie. Remember, you're a good actress.' She gave Lizzie a hug and a smile. 'Go on now.'

When Lizzie had left her, Rhoda clenched her fists to stop her hands from shaking. First the scalding of her victim...then the murder. But when? She was determined Gladys Slyne would never win this part of the game but she needed to act quickly. She had to be on the alert if she was to help Lizzie this time. If she had only known about the scalding before maybe she could have saved Molly's life. This wasn't the time for reflecting now. It was the time for speedy action.

That night the heavy rain ceased. There was a slight drizzle. Rhoda stood at the window in the darkness of their room looking down the hill. Lizzie was ready to leave, the letter clutched tight in her hand, a dark grey cloak muffled around her. Her face was white as chalk.

'What if something goes wrong? Oh Rhoda I'm scared.'

'It won't go wrong...Look here he comes now.'

Rhoda opened the window quietly and called softly. 'Albert...Albert!' Albert turned, trying to make out who it was in the darkness.

'Albert, over here...it's Rhoda.' She waved her hand to him. She had seen Albert many times passing the Slyne's cottage on his way to and from the tavern at the bottom of the hill. She had met him at times on her way to market for the Slynes. He made his way swiftly across the garden. Rhoda could smell the ale fumes on his breath. 'Albert please help us.'

'You can get into serious trouble for this young lady.'

'Albert, you were a convict once. Will you take this poor girl with you to Lady Elizabeth's house? Please. She is in danger from Mrs Slyne. She works hard. I've given her a letter to explain it all.' Rhoda was out of breath trying to explain it to Albert before the guards were due to make their rounds across the hill. Albert went to move away from them. He looked anxiously around him in the black night for any sign of a light carried by the guards. Rhoda was sure she could hear a dog barking some way off.

'It's more than I dare do Miss Rhoda. This could be serious.'

'Is there anything more serious than being murdered Albert?'

'What!' he almost shouted. He looked over his shoulder quickly. 'You mean she's being murdered?'Albert pointed to the frightened Lizzie. It was difficult to give any details and explain everything, there just wasn't the time. Rhoda could hear the dogs barking nearer. They would soon be up the hill.

Albert shook his head and turned to move away. Rhoda thought of a quicker, faster way to convince him, something that Albert understood.

'Wait, I have something for you if you'll take her with you.'

Rhoda slipped Molly's guinea into Albert's rough hand. He stared at it in wonder. 'Take it. Go on...TAKE IT...please!' Rhoda became agitated. 'We haven't got much time left before the guards and dogs are here.'

'My God you must be serious. A whole guinea. Is it real?'

'It's real alright. The same as the situation Lizzie's in. Come on Lizzie, get out of the window. For God's sake be quick now.'

Albert pocketed the guinea. He pulled Lizzie out of the window and she started to cry. 'Stop it at once Lizzie, you'll be safe now. Go on.'

Rhoda stood at the window for a long time until they disappeared into the cloak of night. Lizzie would be safe once she got to Lady Elizabeth's house. A tear ran slowly down her cheek. If only Molly knew how her guinea had helped to save the life of Lizzie. In her heart she knew everything would be alright for Lizzie. She watched as a light from a lamp came up over the hill – the guards with their snarling dogs. Rhoda prayed that Albert and Lizzie got away in time. She waited, hardly daring to breathe. The minutes ticked away. Only then did she know they got away safely.

But now what about herself? How did she fair in the deadly game? She smiled to herself. Well she had won this part. But what about the predicament she was in? To face Gladys Slyne in the morning would be demanding on her inner strength. Gladys would want to know what had happened to Lizzie.

She thought about it until the small hours of the morning. She would have to be a good actress to play the part. Rhoda had a feeling it would work. If it didn't, she would have to face the wrath of Gladys Slyne... alone...There was no one to help her now.

When she met Gladys the next morning Gladys didn't look well.

'Where's that brat of a Lizzie?' she shouted.

'I haven't seen her this morning Mrs Slyne. Did she bring you your tea?' Rhoda smiled sweetly and tried to act innocent.

'TEA?...No she did not bring me my tea. Where is she?'

'Lizzie had a bad scald on her arm yesterday Mrs Slyne. So I said to her she must be more careful handling scalding hot tea. I mean she's so stupid. She could scald someone with it. Couldn't she Mrs Slyne?' Gladys stared at Rhoda through her thin spectacles.

'Scalded herself then did she?'

'Yes.' Rhoda started to wash the floor. 'Yes the stupid wretch of a girl scalded herself, so she said. I'm glad she's gone.'

'GONE...Lizzie's gone?' Gladys clenched her bony hands. Rhoda stretched herself up and rubbed her back.

'Oh yes, she's gone alright. She's gone in the head as well if you ask me Mrs Slyne.'

'Gone? But she can't have just gone.'

Rhoda puffed and blew. 'Oh yes. She said she wanted to get away. Of course I didn't know anything until I saw her empty bed this morning.'

'I gave her a good Christian home. I'll find her and when I do she'll be sorry.' Gladys paced up and down shaking her wiry head.

'She was lazy and couldn't cook. Lizzie wouldn't learn her Catechism no matter how hard I tried to help her.' Rhoda stopped washing the floor, wrung out her cloth and looked at Gladys. 'Worst of all she didn't believe in God.' Rhoda stood up with her hands on her hips.

'I believe she may have gone to Lady Elizabeth's house to work. Let her have her I say. Lizzie was useless.'

Gladys's face became red with anger. She seemed lost for words.

Rhoda took advantage of the situation.

'It's a shame Mrs Slyne...err ... I mean Gladys. She never appreciated what you or the Reverend did for her.' Rhoda waited for more anger to spill.

'Why would she go to Lady Elizabeth's house?' Gladys fumed.

'I suppose she thought Lady Elizabeth was important. Don't worry yourself Mrs Slyne, Lady Elizabeth will bring her back in no time.'

Gladys flew into a rage. For one moment Rhoda thought that she might have to receive severe blows. Gladys reared up and stared at Rhoda.

'Did you hear anything in the night Miss Lambay?'

'No. Not a thing Mrs Slyne. I slept like the dead. She must have stolen away like a thief in the night.'

'I WILL NOT HAVE HER BACK. I don't want that type of girl in my house.' Gladys sniffed. 'This is a good Christian Establishment.'

Gladys marched out of the room, almost slipping on the wet floor. Rhoda felt very relieved and pleased with herself. Gladys had believed every word she said. She had brazened it out against her alone. Yet still she had to be more aware, more watchful and more alert than ever before. There was no one to turn to now for any help, just herself, alone. AND at any given time Gladys could retaliate. She had to be observant, sly as a fox to smell out any clue or any suspicious moves made by Gladys. Rhoda started shaking. It was an exciting fear that held her. She had never experienced such a feeling before. Something clawed at her stomach. Was it the searching, probing fingers of madness? Would she become like Gladys to end her days in the relentless game of cat and mouse, or would she ever be able to penetrate the smiling veneer and find the Achilles heel, the fatal flaw in the Christian armour of Gladys Slyne?

XXIV

The days without Lizzie became lonely ones for Rhoda. With forever being on her guard against Gladys and no one of her own age to talk to or confide in Rhoda became filled with despair. She noticed it one morning when her hands began shaking. She started getting fainting sensations similar to when she was on board the 'Sea Duchess.' Sometimes her head would start to ache violently and she felt sickness surging up in her. She began to wonder if Gladys Slyne was trying to poison her. Dreadful thoughts began to take over her mind. Rhoda began drinking copious draughts of water for fear of being poisoned. At night she would wake up startled, listening for Gladys. Was she outside her bedroom door waiting?

She began making plans to get away from the Slynes forever. She was making tea for Gladys in the kitchen one bright and sunny morning when Gladys appeared quietly. Rhoda poured the boiling water off the stove into the teapot. She tried to remain calm and turned to Gladys to wish her good morning.

'I'll pour my own tea,' Gladys announced as she reached across Rhoda and picked up the teapot. Rhoda was taken off her guard for a moment, but it was just long enough for Gladys to pour the scalding tea over Rhoda's arm. Rhoda screamed with pain and leapt back away from Gladys. She ran outside and put her arm in the bucket of cold water. Tears stung her eyes. She was determined that Gladys wouldn't see the pain she had inflicted on her. Gladys was immediately by her side. 'Oh my dear, how careless of you.'

Rhoda decided to play the game. Wincing with the pain, she thought wildly about a quick plan forming in her mind. The scalding had worked for her not against her. She tried not to show Gladys her pain.

'Yes it was very careless of me.' She showed the reddening arm to Gladys. 'It looks bad. Do you think Doctor Jones should have a look at it? It might fester later on.'

Gladys took a hold of her arm and bound a wet cloth around it.

'I don't think so. I want you here today Rhoda. Besides, it doesn't look too badly burned my dear.' Gladys smiled smugly.

Rhoda had to think again of another plan to get away from Gladys. The Reverend Slyne came into the kitchen. He mumbled to himself as he poured his tea, unaware of what had happened.

'Gladys my dear I hope you haven't forgotten that we are to meet the new Reverend James and his wife this morning.'

Gladys's hands twitched nervously. She stared at Rhoda.

'Oh dear! I quite forgot dear. Rhoda has a bad scald on her arm. I think I should stay with her.'

The Reverend Slyne frowned. 'But we can't let them down my dear now can we? They are expecting us. It is important we go.'

Rhoda seized her chance. 'Of course you must go Mrs Slyne. I will take the opportunity to bring fresh supplies from the market and let Doctor Jones have a look at my arm.'

'There we are there then. Two birds killed with one stone as they say,' Reverend Slyne said briskly. 'Come along Gladys.'

Gladys muttered to Rhoda 'NO, Two stones to kill ONE bird Miss Lambay. I've used up one stone already. The next one will be the one that kills the wounded bird,' and left the kitchen.

Rhoda knew the implications behind Gladys's words... MURDER. She had to leave now, this very morning when the Slynes had gone on their visit. This was going to be her only chance to save her own life. First the scalding, then the killing....just like how she had killed Molly. Once again Gladys had made the scald look like an accident. Once again Gladys had murder rooted in her mind. After the Slynes had gone on their visit, Rhoda made quick preparations.

She set off quite calmly, on the pretence that she was going to early morning market like she always did. In her basket were a few items, a bottle of water, some apples, a good size chunk of bread and cheese. And her own guinea. Rhoda gazed down at Cockle Creek and decided to walk in the opposite direction quickly. At the end of the row of cottages was a lane of rough cobbles. She could hear the sounds of farm animals as she hurried over the rough stones. Her boots slid on the wet surface.

The scent of the eucalyptus trees and pine forests filled her senses, overwhelming her with their fragrance. She passed by houses with high walled gardens, set in spacious grounds. English trees, whose names she knew, juniper, oak, ash and chestnut and neatly pruned hawthorn hedges that looked like hedgerows around a farm.

After some time she found the way more difficult, wild flowers and trees of every colour like a thick forest. They tempted her almost calling her to come nearer. She could hide in there quite easily. After she had eaten, she listened to the din of parrots. They darted to and fro like flashing rainbows. Rhoda stood up and walked towards the interior. It looked dark and thick with tangled undergrowth.

She heard what sounded like an eerie growl. Was it a whistle or a bark? She moved closer to the interior of the forest. It looked so cool there. Thinking it might be a dog that was trapped she stepped closer.

'You're not thinking of going that way are you woman?'

Rhoda spun round to see a tall, fair haired man. Tanned by the sun and with twinkling blue eyes that seemed to mock her. He swung off his horse and put his hands on his hips defiantly.

'Well answer me. Are you woman?'

It was his patronising attitude and the way he called her 'woman' that angered Rhoda. For one moment she was lost for words. Rhoda objected to being called 'woman'. Who did he think he was? The impudence of the man! She could do what she wanted.

'If I want to venture into the forest I will. It's no business of yours,' Rhoda answered him tartly.

'You're right of course. It's no business of mine. I just don't want you to get lost in there...that's all.'

He pushed his wide brimmed hat back on his head. He came closer to her. His horse snorted and flared its nostrils. The holes in his trousers needed repairing. His hands were strong, browned to a colour only the sun could give.

'You afraid of horses?' he asked, putting his hat straight.

'No I am not. Is there a pathway through there?' She pointed towards the dense trees. He threw back his head and laughed out loud, then became deadly serious.

'The only path through there is to certain death. No one going into the interior ever comes out alive. You could wander in there for years. No one would ever know. Convicts have tried to run away in there. They've never been seen since. Dead now I reckon.'

Rhoda thought about what he said, especially when he mentioned convicts. She made her way carefully towards him.

'I'm sure I heard a dog growling in there. Do you imagine it might be trapped? Should you take a look and see?'

Again he laughed at her. Rhoda felt her cheeks go all hot.

'It's a dog alright but not the kind you have met.'

Rhoda decided to be brave. 'Well if you're afraid to look then I'll see.'

'Then of course the devils will get you.'

Rhoda laughed. 'DEVILS! What devils?'

'Devils with black coats and sharp teeth like knives. They stink, got a white stripe on their front. You could mistake them for dogs. They're wild and they'd rip you apart in seconds.' He pulled his hands apart with such force Rhoda jumped. 'They attack our sheep so we have to shoot them. They've been known to eat a whole horse.'

Suddenly Rhoda was very tired. She hadn't realised how far she had travelled in her quest for freedom. She was hot, thirsty, dizzy...her head ached and her face was burning. She became aware of cool water being splashed on her face. Strong arms were around her. She sat upright looking around.

'Is it true what you say about the devils?'

He pushed a bottle of water into her sweating hands. 'Yes I'm afraid it is. There are two legged varieties which I think are worse. Now then, you gave me a scare then when you fainted. When did you drink last?'

'I don't remember. Early this morning I think.' Rhoda sipped the cool water he held for her.

'One thing you must always have is plenty of water. You'd die out here without it.'

Rhoda took some more gulps, and wondered why the man was so obsessed with death. As she rested she told him about working for the Slynes and Molly's death. Somehow it was easy to talk to Rosswell Hawkes. She liked him. She liked his gruff manner and she felt safe with him. She felt that he was someone she could talk to, so she confided in him. This was how she had felt with Owen Rathlin so long ago now. Her instincts told her she could trust Rosswell Hawkes.

She trembled as he lifted her up on to the horse. He swung up in the saddle behind her. Never could she remember being so close to a man before. She tried to breathe easily, but she just couldn't. He sensed her nervousness and held her closer.

'Just rest easy now and don't go fainting on me.'

They rode back together, his arms like two strong branches holding twined round her as he gripped the reins. There was a smell of pine on him. And other smells, like bracken burning and log fires. He told her about his sister Maggie, who baked enormous pies, fit enough to make you burst wide open and rich plump berries, golden apples and pears simmering in large copper pots, ready for jam or waiting to be crowned with a thick rich pastry top for belly filling pies. 'I'm starving,' said Rhoda, licking her lips at the thought of food.

Maggie was sixteen but found it hard to learn things except cooking. His mother and father were settlers. They kept rare sheep of good breeding. Rhoda could have listened to him forever. Then she thought of the Slynes.

'Guards and dogs will be out looking for me. What can I do? I'll be sent to Cascades, I know I will. I should never have done this.' She stared ahead expecting at any time for someone to appear. She seemed to know in that moment that her life with the Slyne's would be finished. They would send her to the Cascades factory. What could she say to them? She had no idea how to face them. She told Rosswell her fears as they trotted lazily back to the Slynes.

'Well I have a good plan we can bring into action against these so called Christians, the Slimeys.' Rhoda laughed. It was almost as if they were Molly's words. 'They'll be glad to have you back.' He told her his plan. As they got nearer the cottage they could see Gladys and the Reverend Slyne waiting for her. There were two guards with fierce looking dogs snapping and snarling, straining on their chains.

'Just do as I say....and say NOTHING,' Rosswell whispered.

The dogs were let free. They snarled and barked at them. Rhoda was terrified but kept her eyes closed as Rosswell had told her. Rosswell slipped easily from his horse greeting the guards and their dogs as if they were his friends. As he patted the dogs' heads they licked his hand. Rhoda half squinted her eyes as Rosswell Hawkes carried her easily into the cottage. The children were chattering. The Slynes were fussing. She couldn't resist a smother of laughter in the half conscious state she was supposed to be in. It was only when Rosswell pinched her on the leg that she realised how serious the situation had become.

Everyone listened as Rosswell Hawkes, the arrogant settler and a better actor than herself, told the story of Rhoda being abducted by a mad passionate old settler who carried her off to the dense interior. Gladys brought them hot sweet tea. Rosswell made a face when he sipped it as he continued his story - that it was he who saved her from a fate worse than death. Gladys marvelled at his story but there was more.

'I rode my horse in pursuit until it was exhausted. AND, praise be to God Almighty, I rescued this poor girl.' They were all overwhelmed with his bravery. They started clapping, calling him a hero. But unknown to Rosswell he had made too much of the bravery story.

'Mr. Hawkes, you have shown bravery in adversity. I insist you come to our service of thanks for your safe return.' Gladys announced.

Rosswell look amazed. Rhoda smiled faintly at him as she pretended to come around. 'Oh where am I?' she asked with a hand to her forehead. Gladys fussed around her bringing them more hot strong sweet tea 'for shock.' Rosswell stood up and said he really must leave. He refused another cup of tea, smiling sweetly at Gladys. Rosswell had another plan. He winked at Rhoda.

'My sister Maggie is a good girl, but a bit slow in the head, Mrs Slyne. Could it be arranged that Maggie attend the school to learn her scriptures? I might add that Maggie is an excellent cook and would recompense you by cooking your meals.'

Smiling sweetly Gladys approved, as did the Reverend Slyne.

'But of course Mr. Hawkes, your sister should be encouraged to learn the scriptures. Bring her to us when you're ready.'

Rhoda's heart thumped with excitement. This was another of Rosswell's plans, to be able to see her and talk with her every day when he brought Maggie to the Slynes.

Maggie was shy and withdrawn, but after some coaxing by Rhoda and Rosswell she began to talk with Rhoda. Maggie reminded Rhoda of a younger version of Martha. She seemed capable of taking over the kitchen and the cooking, asking the Slynes for some more kitchen utensils, plates, a rolling pin, bowls for mixing and some sharp knives. Rhoda was astounded but the Slynes were prepared to get the items for Maggie for her famous cooking. Maggie's hazel eyes sparkled as she put on her clean apron. Her long sandy coloured hair was tied back from her face. Rhoda envied her vitality.

She proved to be an outstanding cook. Never had the Slynes eaten so well. Chicken hot pots sweltering with fresh vegetables, fruit filled pies with their juices bubbling through the golden pastry. Even Rhoda's slender figure started to plump out more.

One hot, sultry day Rhoda told Rosswell about killing her step father. She expected him to be shocked as they sat under a pine tree and sipped lemonade. Rhoda had the bible on her lap, to show Gladys she was reading one of the scriptures to Rosswell.

'I don't see what you can do about it now,' he said. 'If you ask me woman, err... Rhoda, he had it coming to him.' Rosswell puffed steadily on his pipe. 'Now Molly and that young Ethan lad, well, that's a mighty mystery. What she did was murder and no mistake. You'll have to trap her like the snake she is but you take care you don't get the fatal bite.'

Rhoda knew what Rosswell said was true. She would have to do it. But how? In the short time she had known Rosswell he had given her back the inner strength she thought she had lost forever. It had been of no useful purpose to run away from the Slynes. She had sought to play the cat and mouse game with Gladys in the hope that one day she would confess. But now she had to force Gladys Slyne away from barring the doorway to her inner soul.

Rosswell had shown her the intangible key. Molly would have done the same if she had lived. All she had to do was reach out and unlock the door.

Maggie was about the same age as her. She was quick to learn her Alphabet. Rhoda had just about managed to teach them all the three R's. The children accepted Rhoda and Maggie like two older sisters. When the Slynes appeared they had all learned to pay attention and listen to the scriptures.

There were days when it all became too much for the Reverend Slyne. He willingly left it all to the 'dutiful Rhoda' to instruct the children. His ministry in the church took all his time. Yet they still had to be aware that Gladys was around. She would appear as if out of the wall, silent and deadly, ready to strike. The children were nervous of her, but even they learned a few tricks on how to look serious and interested in the inevitable boredom of reciting their words.

It was during the children's play time, when Lady Elizabeth made an appearance. She had come to see Rhoda. Gladys eyed her sharply as she bustled in through the door very businesslike in her grey silk gown, her light brown hair threaded with strands of gold. Her warm round face beamed with pleasure when she saw Rhoda.

'My dear...I have some news for you...sit down please.'

Gladys looked amazed at Lady Elizabeth.

'I would like to know the intention of your visit with Miss Lambay. She is MY convict girl after all,' Gladys snapped. Lady Elizabeth sat down and tapped her grey silk fan with her short, well manicured finger nails. She looked annoyed at Gladys.

'And so you shall Mrs Slyne, all in good time. I came here to inform you Miss Lambay is no longer your convict girl as you put it.'

Rhoda gasped and looked at Lady Elizabeth. For one brief moment she thought that Lizzie had told Lady Elizabeth the whole story and that Lady Elizabeth had come to rescue her from Gladys. Rhoda sat perfectly still, hands clasped together. Lady Elizabeth unfolded a letter. Rhoda was frozen in horror. What would the letter contain? What could it possibly be? Who else but Gladys knew about the murder of her stepfather? Who on earth could it be from? Had she been found out? Lady Elizabeth read out the letter. It contained a free pardon... She, Rhoda Lambay, had been pardoned by the Governor of Van Dieman's Land. She was no longer a convict but free to return to England to do whatever she wanted. She was FREE.

'You must be overjoyed my dear,' said Lady Elizabeth taking her hand. Rhoda took the letter from her. She could hardly believe what she was reading. So many thoughts crowded her mind.

'I'm sorry my dear. I didn't know you could read.' Lady Elizabeth looked embarrassed. 'Oh dear you really must forgive me for being so hasty. I am so sorry my dear Rhoda.'

'Don't worry about it Lady Elizabeth. This is the best news ever.'

The letter was a formal one. It stated that Isabella Rathlin had made a death bed confession. That she alone had been guilty of hiding a white petticoat in the valise of one known as Rhoda Lambay...She asked for forgiveness of her crime...' Tears blurred Rhoda's eyes.

'You are a free woman now Rhoda. Do you wish to return to England? You are free to do as you wish my dear.'

Rhoda looked up from the letter. 'Return...NO...oh no...I wish to stay here in Van Dieman's Land.'

'Good for you. We need people like you here. Now then, I have a proposition for you.' Lady Elizabeth stood up and smoothed down her gown. She was taller than Rhoda, with ample proportions. 'I hear that you are a skilled needlewoman.'

'I can do fine sewing Lady Elizabeth.'

'Well done. That's the spirit. Now would you like to sew for me?'

'I would love to. But what about teaching the children? I have chores around the house and....'

'But Rhoda you are a FREE woman now. I can give you a wage.'

A wage...Rhoda had never received any payment from the Slynes. She thought about it. This was a wonderful offer. How could she ever refuse it? And to be offered a wage.....

Lady Elizabeth looked at her with concern. Her pale blue eyes twinkled.

'I can see you are a loyal person, Rhoda. I'm sure Mrs Slyne will share you with me. You can still teach the children.'

Rhoda had forgotten all about Gladys standing there listening to every word. Her face was ashen. Never had she seen such a look of venomous hatred on a face.

XXV

The two stunning blows left Gladys Slyne mortified. That Rhoda had been given a free pardon was a savage blow. And that Lady Elizabeth wanted Rhoda to sew for her, giving her a good wage was the second blow for Gladys. Even when Rhoda assured her that she would still continue to teach the children, there was no mistaking the look of sheer hatred on her face or the menacing tone in her voice. Rhoda sensed Gladys would not capitulate in the deadly game. Gladys drew herself up. She resembled a hooded cobra about to strike. Rhoda took a deep breath. She knew Gladys would dart the deadly venom. Unleash it at last.

'You think you are FREE. But you will never have freedom Rhoda Lambay.'

Gladys stood in front of her as she spoke, her head swaying, eyes like two hard black marbles. But Rhoda was ready for her.

'And your prayers to GOD will never free you of MURDER Gladys Slyne!'

Gladys slumped down onto a chair. Her face was ashen at Rhoda's words. 'Something is very wrong here. I demand to know what it is,' said Lady Elizabeth. She stood up quickly, a puzzled look on her face. She stared at Gladys and Rhoda. Rhoda waited. She took her time. Now it seemed at this very long awaited moment that this was the appointed time for the deadly game to end. She still doubted that she could go through with it. It had come suddenly, unexpectedly, with her new found freedom. It was time to think of number one as Molly had said so long ago. 'Be with me Molly, please be with me.' She whispered the words into her cupped hands. Now she was ready.

'You are right Lady Elizabeth, something is indeed very wrong here.'

Rhoda pulled out something from under her sleeve. 'If you watch you will be the witness, judge and jury to a confession.'

Lady Elizabeth went to say something, but sat down quickly. She gave Rhoda a startled look. 'Is this some form of game you're playing?' Lady Elizabeth asked.

'It is a game Lady Elizabeth. A deadly game has begun.'

Like a magician's sleight of hand, Rhoda produced the strip of white petticoat she had always carried with her, tucked into her sleeve waiting for the right moment. Rhoda held up the white strip of bloodstained cotton. It fluttered in the light breeze from the open window that faced Cockle Bay.

'See a silent witness from beyond the grave Gladys.'

Lady Elizabeth sat watching, entranced by the scene unfolding before her. Rhoda secretly prayed that her strength would not fail her. Not now. Not when this was the right and only time she would have. If she wavered just once Gladys would strike at her and she would be lost forever. Gladys broke the deathly silence.

'WHERE DID YOU GET THAT?' She held out her claw like hand to grasp it. Rhoda held it closer to Gladys, almost in front of her wild eyes. Gladys shut her eyes and screamed 'TAKE IT AWAY FROM ME.'

'Why, it's just a torn strip of white petticoat with someone's dried blood on it.' Rhoda persisted in holding it in the same position. The dark red stain against the white looked like a butterfly pattern.

'LOOK Gladys...Look...a blood red butterfly flown from the grave.'

Rhoda said the words in a slow, serious tone of voice.

Lady Elizabeth intervened. 'What on earth is that?'

'Not on EARTH Lady Elizabeth...but what in Heaven's sake is it?

It was sent to me by my dear friend Molly from Heaven where she is now.' Gladys still kept her eyes closed. Rhoda continued...

'Molly was murdered Lady Elizabeth. Shoved, pushed or thrown from the deck of the 'Sea Duchess' on our voyage to Van Dieman's Land. But you know Molly was pushed. She was murdered, wasn't she Gladys?'

Lady Elizabeth gave a cry, but continued to sit and listen.

'Open your eyes Gladys.' Rhoda raised her voice. 'Look, this came off Molly's arm. You deliberately scalded her arm with your tea that morning. Do you remember Gladys? You threw it over her arm. I tied this strip of petticoat on Molly's arm to stop the pain. I tied it secure. But! YOU...YOU...WRENCHED IT OFF HER IN THE STRUGGLE. You pushed Molly Williams over the side of the Sea Duchess.'

Rhoda's voice was starting to break with emotion.

'No! No!' Gladys screamed into her cupped hands.

Rhoda steadied herself, no longer did her voice quaver with emotion.

'You sent my dear friend Molly to an early grave through your jealous madness. Confess Gladys Slyne, confess to your crime.'

Gladys looked up so suddenly that Rhoda stepped back for a second and almost lost her nerve.

'No...no...no,' whispered Gladys hoarsely. 'I did not pull it off her. It was on her arm when I held her and she did struggle, but I was stronger than her. NO...NO...I didn't take it off her.....I didn't...'

Gladys stopped, realising what she had said. She pressed her hands into her mouth, eyes wide, like glaring black marbles. Rhoda pushed back the hair from her forehead. She dare not stop now.

'CONFESS Gladys! Confess to God. Repent your sin. Confess that you pushed Molly to her death.'

Gladys grabbed Rhoda's arm like the coil of a dying serpent.

'She struggled when I pushed her. You had a biblical name...' Rhoda wiped her face with her apron. 'Rhoda ... you are mad. It's written in the bible.'

'Now Gladys,' Rhoda said firmly but with a quieter voice, 'confess that you killed young Ethan Davies. Confess it now, Gladys. Confess it.'

Gladys smiled at her. 'ETHAN...Is that a biblical name?'

Rhoda folded the strip of white petticoat, pushing it up her sleeve. It had served its purpose, just as Rhoda intended it would. She suspected Molly intended it to happen this way too. But now she had to find out about Ethan. She owed it to him. He died needlessly, as did Molly.

'Gladys, what about Ethan Davies? The boy had fallen from the rigging and hurt his leg. Why did you murder him Gladys?'

Lady Elizabeth kept opening and closing her mouth in an attempt to say something but thought better of it. Gladys folded her arms and rocked to and fro. She held Rhoda's eyes for one hypnotic moment then raised herself up in her chair. Rhoda thought she was about to strike her. With her hand held high Gladys said 'The boy was up in the rigging. He could see me.'

'But Ethan Davies didn't see you push Molly. He only saw someone talking to Molly on the port side of the ship.' Rhoda was emphatic in her choice of words. Gladys Slyne's face twisted into a strange purple shape. Rhoda was vaguely aware the room was filling with people. The Reverend Slyne stood in the doorway. Maggie and the trembling Lizzie were also present by now. Rhoda dare not let her guard drop. Not now. She couldn't let Gladys see how weary she was, in the perseverance of her close questioning. She had to find some inner strength.

'What are you trying to say?' Gladys asked breathlessly.

Rhoda raised her voice again. 'I'M SAYING THAT ETHAN DAVIES DID NOT SEE YOU!'

'But I remember you said to him thank you for telling me what you saw that morning, the morning when everyone was watching the whale...' Gladys paused...'I heard you...I heard...' Gladys stopped.

'Then through your eavesdropping you only heard part of the conversation. You believed Ethan had seen you push Molly over the side of the ship.' Rhoda's eyes narrowed. 'That's why you had to murder him, wasn't it Gladys?' Rhoda heard gasps of horror from the assembled crowd. Rhoda was almost near to collapsing in her efforts. Soon it would be over.

'You are a double murderer Gladys Slyne.'

Gladys sank down to the floor shouting 'Murder, murder, murder, wicked... to kill them both.' She buried her face in her hands. The Reverend Slyne hurried towards her.

It was later when Rosswell Hawkes appeared with a doctor and two guards. Gladys Slyne was taken to The Royal Derwent Lunatic Asylum.

Lizzie and Maggie had sent the children back with the guard. Rhoda couldn't stop shaking until someone pushed a glass of port wine into her hand. Lady Elizabeth came up to her. 'My dear! What you have been through is dreadful. Your poor dear friend and young Ethan Davies both murdered.' Rhoda sipped the wine. 'You are very brave my dear Rhoda. I could not have done what you just did.'

'You were brave Miss Rhoda. I didn't realise what you must have gone through. I'm ashamed to have taken this guinea from you.' Albert held out the guinea. 'You saved young Lizzie's life.' He put the guinea into Rhoda's hand. She shook her head.

'No you earned it Albert. You took a risk for Lizzie.'

'No Miss Rhoda. You took an even greater risk than me. I can't take it Miss, really I couldn't. Use it as an investment, now you're free.'

Rhoda smiled at him. 'Mmm...an investment.' Rhoda thought for a moment.

'For making more guineas, do you mean?' Rhoda had heard those words before. 'Well thank you Albert, I will. I'll do it for Molly and Ethan.'

Lady Elizabeth put an arm around Rhoda's shoulders. 'You did a brave thing for poor young Lizzie. You took a great risk in saving her life. If only she had told me of the terrible danger you were in, I could have helped you my dear. Why ever didn't you let me help you?'

'I had to get Gladys to confess. I had to know who murdered my friend Molly and Ethan. Now they can rest in peace.'

Rosswell Hawkes stood in the doorway. The sun caught his hair in a halo of golden light. Rhoda thought he looked like an angel.

'Well WOMAN, you finally did it. You trapped your serpent.'

Rhoda was happy to see him, even though she was weary.

'Thank you Ross, for being such a good friend to me. You acted swiftly getting help for me. Thank you again.' She held his hand. 'Without you I would never have found the courage. You saved me from running into the wilderness. You saved me from certain death.'

Rosswell's face flushed. 'Can Maggie still stay here with you? She's a good cook. We miss her cooking at home so I'll have to drop in for dinner at times if that's alright.'

'Of course she can stay here. I would be lost without her. Oh I'm so tired I think I'll drop down soon. Can we talk tomorrow Ross?'

When Rosswell had gone she looked around the room. The awful realisation of what she had done dawned upon her. It wasn't like the victory she had imagined it to be. It seemed empty now. Gladys could have reacted swiftly at any time and accused her of killing her step-father. Why hadn't Gladys accused her? Was it because Gladys had never heard her confession on the 'Sea Duchess'? Doubts began casting tiny shadows in her mind, like fragments of grey gauze they wisped away her victorious win of the deadly game.

What had she done? She had acted as judge and jury to prove Gladys Slyne guilty of murder. Not one murder but two. But wasn't she herself guilty of the murder of her stepfather? What would have happened if Gladys had accused her of murder? How would she have reacted then? She had a free pardon over the theft of the petticoat. Yet she had to carry the burden of guilt to her grave. She was just as guilty as Gladys. Suddenly she felt some sympathy for Gladys. The woman was insane but there would be some excuse for insanity. But what about herself? Was she sane?

She went to sit outside in the cool of the evening. She should feel some sort of happiness but all she felt was a lost feeling. There was a new life ahead of her. She could make a new start in her life now she was a free woman. Hadn't Molly told her that her stepfather had deserved his end? She had been justified in killing him or it would have been herself.

She could hear the sounds of Maggie and Lizzie in the kitchen, their laughter and chatter as they made her a special celebration supper. How she wished Molly was here to know about her freedom. They would have laughed and cried together. Dear Molly who had always said things would get worse before they got better. How right her words had been. Then suddenly for some unknown reason she wanted to run and shout it out to someone. She had to tell anyone that she really was free! No longer a convict! She had never dreamed that she would see this day happen.

She walked into the small garden and looked far out from Cockle

Creek, beyond Recherche Bay and out beyond Storm Bay, far out to the eavesdropping waves that seemed to rise up and catch the sunlight. The tops of the waves looked like sparkling white teeth that held bubbling laughter in their ragged jaws. The waves reminded her of Molly. She was far out in the sea beyond the Bay resting now, at peace in the deep, clean, green ocean. Rhoda just had to tell her. She knew Molly would hear her words carried on the breath of the breeze.

'Molly I'm FREE!' she shouted into the waiting mouth of the breeze. 'MOLLY I'M FREE AT LAST! Dear Molly and Ethan, you're both free spirits now,' she whispered.

Then, she felt the softest caress of the breeze, She could have sworn it was almost a touch of warm fingers stroking her cheek. And Rhoda knew it was Molly's answering touch. Rhoda turned away from the sea.

'LIZZIE!...MAGGIE!...Rhoda shouted as she ran into the cottage.

PART THREE
December 1851
VAN DIEMAN'S LAND

XXVI

It was getting near to Christmas when Rhoda suggested to Maggie and Lizzie about making some toys for the convict children. Rhoda was sorting out some of the different pieces of fabric that Lady Elizabeth had given her.

'What about wooden dolls for girls and soldiers for the boys?' Rhoda said holding up some sprigged muslin and cotton. 'We've got enough pieces here to make something for each child.'

'We'll have to get someone to make the dolls for us. I'm no good at carpentry,' said Lizzie making a shawl of light grey gauze and draping it over her shoulders. 'Who can make them for us?'

'I think I know who will make them for us...the Bad Boys,' said Maggie.

'Bad boys? What bad boys? Where are they?' asked Rhoda.

Maggie ran to the window. 'Look, it's starting to snow again. It could be a blizzard. I love the snow Miss Rhoda, I...'

'Yes it looks very pretty Maggie.'

Rhoda turned Maggie around to face her. 'Now Maggie, who are the Bad Boys?'

'Boys that used to be on Point Puer. They make things out of wood, school desks and stuff. They could make dolls couldn't they?'

Rosswell came into the room and stood by the fire. Flakes of snow fluttered from his top coat. 'Rossie you know the boys from Point Puer don't you? Ask them to make dolls for us,' Maggie wheedled. Rhoda took his coat.

'Do you know these boys Ross? Maggie seems to think they carve things out of wood.'

Ross stood with his back to the fire. 'Yes they do. They do carpentry I know. They're boys aged from 9 to 18 years old I believe, why?'

'Would they carve wooden figures for us for the convict children do you think? We were thinking of dolls for the girls and soldiers for the boys,' said Rhoda showing him the materials.

'I could ask about it I suppose,' said Rosswell. 'But don't expect them to make the clothes,' he laughed. 'How many would you want?'

'How about eight? We could paint their faces,' said Rhoda.

When Rosswell had gone they sat and planned what clothes they could make with the materials on the table.

'I could make them some biscuits for Christmas couldn't I Miss Rhoda...that would be nice for the Bad Boys wouldn't it?'

Rhoda went to the window. The snow was getting thicker. Maggie had made lamb stew with vegetables for supper. The appetising aroma made Rhoda feel hungry.

When they had finished supper, leaving a good sized portion for Rosswell, they set about making preparations for figgy pudding for Christmas.

'Let's see what we've got.' Rhoda looked through the items in the cupboard. 'We've got figs from Lady Elizabeth, suet to be grated, sugar, milk and nutmegs.' Rhoda ticked them off her list.

'What about eggs. There's none left' Maggie said.

'Ross is bringing them in the morning...I hope he remembers.'

Rhoda looked out into the night sky with Lizzie.

'It doesn't look so heavy now Miss Rhoda does it? Oh how I remember it back home. We used to have such fun sledging and making snowballs.' Lizzie pressed her nose against the window. 'What about you Miss Rhoda, did you have fun in the snow?'

'I can't really remember. I suppose I must have. I do remember trimming a Christmas tree. It looked so beautiful.'

Maggie started to grate the suet then she stopped and looked at Rhoda.

'Can we have a Christmas tree? It would be nice for the children. I could hang the biscuits on it.'

'That would be nice. Look there's some long bits of ribbon in the scrap bag,' Lizzie said, fishing out the red and blue ribbon. Rhoda looked at Lizzie and Maggie seriously and folded her arms.

'I will have to ask permission first from the Reverend James and his wife.'

'He'll say yes because we have to attend church every Sunday,' said Lizzie folding the ribbons carefully. Maggie plonked the earthen ware pot for the cake and the mould for the pudding onto the well scrubbed kitchen table.

'If they say no, then I'll put salt in their pudding and cake,' she said fiercely. They all laughed at that. 'I'm sure he will agree. He's a gentleman and his wife, although she's prim and proper, is a good Christian woman.'

The next morning when Rhoda looked out of the window it was as if someone had gathered up the white powdered snow and had hidden it away. Sheets of rain fell as she watched the children, shoulders down against the wind, pushing their way up the hill.

'Get the fire blazing Maggie,' she shouted 'There'll be their clothes to dry out.'

Later when they had all dried out, Rhoda asked Tom where all the other children were. Four were missing as there were only eight children in the group. 'What's happened Tom? Where are the others? Tom sniffed and wrapped his rough blanket around his white shoulders. 'They've been taken with a fever Miss Rhoda. They might not even last till Christmas.'

One of them piped up 'It's a shame, a crying shame so my mother said.'

Rhoda was upset. All the treats they were going to give the children and now they were sick. Something had to be done.

'Don't worry, I'll ask the Reverend James if a Doctor could be sent down there. We'll do something to help them.'

When the children had gone Rhoda sought out the Reverend James.

'I'll go down and help. I did some nursing on board the 'Sea Duchess.' Rhoda put on a clean white apron, tying it as she talked. The Reverend James nodded in agreement.

'It appears to be an outbreak of some fever or other. I hope it's not cholera for God's sake.' Rhoda looked at him quickly. 'My little daughter died of cholera back in England. Come on I'll take you down there.' Rhoda said she was sorry about his daughter then wasted no time climbing into the trap and settling herself beside him as it lumbered down the hill.

The children had been put into isolation inside the dirt driven hospital. Rhoda looked around her. There were more children being brought into the wardroom. She could see Letty over in the corner. As she drew nearer she could see a blotchy rash on her thin body. She rushed towards the child, tears starting to fall. Letty had become like one of her own. They had spent so much time together. To see her lying forgotten in a corner of the room was heart rending.

'Letty, look it's me Rhoda. I've come to look after you.'

Letty looked hot and frightened. 'Oh Miss Rhoda, I feel so bad. My head hurts me.' Letty started to cry. Rhoda took hold of her hot little hand.

'The Doctor's coming to make you better Letty, he'll be here soon.' Rhoda made her more comfortable on the palliasse cot.

'I'm not going to last am I Miss. Them 'orrible people said.'

Rhoda wiped her face with a damp cloth wrung out in the little amount of water that was left in the dirty bowl.

'You mustn't listen to them 'orrible people Letty. They don't know what they're saying.'

Rhoda looked around her, feeling helpless in the situation. Children were crying for their mothers. The sounds of vomiting and stench made her angry. There didn't seem to be anyone to take charge or care at what was happening. She tried to find the other children but couldn't see them anywhere. Then through the doorway and as if by magic came...Doctor Mackay.

XXVII

Doctor Mackay took immediate charge of the situation, barking out his orders. The epidemic had taken a hold on the children.

'It's scarlet fever Rhoda and if this young bairn stays here she won't be alive in a few days time. You'll have to get her away from this hell hole of stench and disease.'

The Reverend James came and stood by Rhoda. 'I've been praying for the souls of the departed children. Some have expired already I'm afraid.'

'Be more afraid then Reverend because more of these children will have expired before morning, unless something is done swiftly.'

Doctor Mackay was very brusque in his manner. Rhoda knew the tone was not meant against the Reverend James personally but against the terrible conditions of the sick and dying children.

'We can take some of the children into the new church orphanage until they are well, said the Reverend. I'll make arrangements for them at once. We can take them there in my carriage.'

'They'll have to be kept in isolation, remember that Rev,' Doctor Mackay called out to the retreating Reverend James.

'This place is not fit for animals,' Doctor Mackay said. He examined Letty. Her red throat was sore. 'Shivering, headache and the vivid rash, all the symptoms of scarlet fever.' Doctor Mackay was right in his first diagnosis. Rhoda wanted Letty to come to the house so that she could nurse her.

'No, it's best she stays with some of the other children. You must remember Rhoda that isolation is important at this stage. When the skin peels and if there are no complications later, then we'll see.'

Letty started to cry when Rhoda was about to leave. She placed her woollen shawl on Letty and told her to keep it until she saw her again. She promised Letty that if she was very good, there would be a surprise gift for her for Christmas. Letty's eyes lit up with joy.

'What if I'm on fire by then. I won't get my gift will I?' said Letty, her eyes suddenly filling with tears.

Doctor Mackay cleared his throat. 'Well young lady, we will have to make sure you don't get on fire won't we?' He smiled down at her. Letty started to shiver again and vomited. She fell back on her palliasse closing her eyes with exhaustion.

When all of the children had been removed to the new orphanage

Rhoda felt very weary. The Reverend James had forgotten all about her in his efforts to get the children out of the makeshift hospital. She decided she would have to walk up the long hill to the cottage.

It was a clear starry night. Doctor Mackay was beside her. 'Come on Rhoda, get in, I'll give you a lift home.'

'Did you know I had a free pardon Doctor Mackay?'

'Good for you, young woman. Now you can go home to England.' Doctor Mackay brought the horse and trap to a standstill.

'I'm not going home. I'm staying here. I teach the convicts children. I've grown to love them like my own family. I'll not return again to England.'

Doctor Mackay put his empty pipe into his mouth. 'There was something I had to tell you. Now let me see what it was.' Doctor Mackay rubbed his chin. His eyes twinkled mischievously.

'Ah yes, now I remember. I'm no longer on the convict ships. I last sailed on the 'Lady Mary' from Cape Town, a ship that carries settlers to Van Dieman's Land.' Doctor Mackay stopped and scratched his ear. 'Now what else was it...now I remember! You'll be happy to know that I met a young man by the name of Hawtin Williams. He's an actor fellow, touring with a theatre group or something.'

Rhoda caught her breath at his name and put her hand over her mouth. When she released it she could hardly speak in sentences.

'Hawtin...Hawtin Williams! Oh yes! He must be an actor now... Molly...oh Molly told me so much about him...But where is he?'

'Aboard the next ship to reach here, 'The Lady Anne'. It's long overdue on the journey out from England, what with storms slowing her up.'

Rhoda was breathless. 'Hawtin's coming here to Van Dieman's Land? That's the most wonderful news.' She hugged Doctor Mackay in her happiness then gave him a worried look.

'Does he know about what happened to Molly?'

'Yes he does. I told him about Molly's tragic accident on the 'Sea Duchess'. He seems to have heard about it. You'll have so much to tell him. He's anxious to meet you.'

Rhoda considered telling Doctor Mackay about Gladys Slyne's confession but decided against it. Doctor Mackay was tired and wanted to get back to his quarters. There would be another time. Rhoda climbed down from the cab.

'Thank you for what you did for the children Doctor Mackay. You will call and see us at Christmas time won't you?'

'I'll try Rhoda. I'm kept very busy but I'll try.'

She watched his horse and trap as he drove away down the hill. Rhoda was overjoyed at the news. To be able to see Hawtin Williams, Molly's long lost twin brother at last, was like a miracle. She looked up at the clear night sky and breathed in the cold freshness; after the stench of the hospital it was like isolated pangs of purifying air. There was a tingling sensation deep within her body. It was tantalising. It was more than happiness. What could it be? There must be name for it?

Someone or some powerful force had thrown legions of diamond stars up into the blackness. Was it Molly in her playful mood she laughed, or was it the powerful force she had been denying on her long voyage to this land? Was God the powerful force who had been watching her every move in the 'dangerous game' and was it him who had protected her? Rhoda gazed up at the vast canopy of brilliance. Were they the same stars that had watched her take her last steps from English soil?

She walked towards the cottage door. This was her home now. Maggie, Lizzie and Rosswell were her family and Lady Elizabeth, why, she was like a mother to her. Whatever was left in England of her own family, well, she was glad that she still couldn't remember them. 'It may be that you don't want to remember,' they were Molly's words. Whatever secrets remained in her past life could stay hidden forever.

'You're right Molly, I don't want to get my memory back, not now, not ever,' Rhoda shouted up at the stars. Lizzie appeared in the doorway. 'Whoever are you shouting at Miss Rhoda?' Lizzie looked around to see who was there. 'There's no one to hear you.'

'Yes there is Lizzie. There's always someone who will listen.'

XXVIII

1852

It was late February before some form of normality returned for Rhoda. Letty and the rest of the children had made a good recovery, partly due to good nursing and the assistance of Doctor Mackay. Rhoda wished that Doctor Mackay could have joined them for Christmas but he was already voyaging back to Cape Town aboard the 'Lady Mary'. Rhoda had just finished brushing her hair when she heard a loud knocking at the cottage door. Maggie came into the room wiping her floured hands on her apron.

'Shall I see who it is Miss Rhoda?'

'No Maggie I'll go. You finish off the pastry for the chicken pie.'

Rhoda glanced in the mirror at herself. There was no time to pin up her long flowing hair now. She just hoped it was no one of importance. Rhoda peered out into the weak sunlight. The figure was framed in the doorway with the sunlight almost acting as a halo of light. Rhoda shaded her eyes. 'I'm sorry, I can't see who you are...the sunlight has dazzled me.'

Rhoda was suddenly swept off her feet and deposited in the doorway. The man in the dark cloak swept off his broad brimmed hat with a flourish.

'I'm Hawtin Williams...Molly's brother.'

Rhoda almost fainted with the shock of coming face to face with Molly's twin brother.

'You must be Rhoda with that beautiful red hair...' He stopped as a look of uncertainty clouded his handsome face. 'Oh no! Don't tell me I've made a mistake and you're not Rhoda Lambay...Oh God! I'm sorry I...'

Rhoda finally discovered her voice. 'No, I am Rhoda Lambay, you haven't made any mistake.' They stood looking at each other in an embarrassed silence. Rhoda couldn't hold back her tears any longer. She reached out and threw her arms around his tall, slim frame. She held him as if he were a long lost brother. Then stepping back she pulled him into the warm living room.

After Maggie had taken his cape and hat and he was seated in an old brown leather armchair, Maggie came in with a tray of tea and hot buttered scones. She stood and stared at Hawtin.

'I can smell something good cooking in the kitchen.' Hawtin's eyes twinkled as he looked at Rhoda with a hungry look...Rhoda introduced them both then Maggie quickly made her exit to the kitchen, her face glowing with pride. Rhoda stood up and poured him some tea. 'You must stay and have some of Maggie's chicken pie with us Hawtin.' Rhoda was trying to talk about anything rather than talk about Molly. She praised Maggie's cooking, talked about the weather and acting. She had waited so long, so eager to meet Hawtin, but now he was here she didn't know quite what to say to him. As she watched him tucking into the buttered scones, she pondered on what to say next. Rhoda held her cup and saucer and sipped her tea slowly. She would have to come out and talk about Molly.

'Your sister was my dearest friend Hawtin. I loved her as if she was my own sister. Molly had so much strength compared to my weakness...I miss her so much.'

Hawtin left the comfort of the armchair and knelt down beside Rhoda. He held her hand and brushed away a tear from Rhoda's cheek.

'Doctor Mackay told me all about you and my sister, how you both had helped him as nurses on board the 'Sea Duchess'. It was tragic the way she died. Can you tell me how it happened? Doctor Mackay told me that she must have fallen over the side of the ship. No one knew she was missing until a search was made. Is that true?'

Rhoda felt a tight lump in her throat. How on earth was she going to be able to tell Hawtin that his sister was murdered? What could she say? Tell him the truth or let him believe that Molly's death was an accident? Her mind was in such turmoil, she didn't know what to say. She took a good sip of her tea.

'Yes it's true that no one knew she was missing until a search of the ship revealed no sign of Molly. I thought she might have been playing some game with me. Molly had such a good sense of humour.' Hawtin looked into her eyes and squeezed her hand. 'I miss her so terribly Hawtin. Every day I think about her.'

Maggie came into the room and as she opened the door an appetizing smell of chicken pie entered the room with her. She flicked a tablecloth onto the table and started to set out the cutlery.

'Oh Maggie I forgot to say, Hawtin will be staying for dinner with us, can you set another place?'

'I already have more cutlery here Miss Rhoda,' said Maggie holding up the set of cutlery to show her. 'I thought there would be another dinner guest.'

Hawtin became flustered. 'Oh I say, I didn't mean to impose on you like this Rhoda. I mean...well...I...err...perhaps I can call again to see you sometime?'

'Hawtin of course you must stay and have dinner with us. I want to hear all about you. Molly thought you might have become an actor. We used to laugh at some of the things she told me…'Friends, Romans and countrymen, lend me your ears…' you must remember acting out your Shakespeare. Didn't you try and collect 'ears' from your audience?'

'Did Molly tell you that?' he laughed. 'Yes I did become an actor. That's why I came here to Van Dieman's Land with Caleb Dunstan's Company. We are appearing at the Theatre Royal here. I thought I could kill two birds with one stone. See you and perform with the Company.'

Rhoda felt a cold shudder for a moment when he mentioned killing two birds with one stone. It brought back the dreadful memory of Gladys. Perhaps this was why she didn't want to tell Hawtin about Molly, not just yet. There would be another time. For now she would enjoy his visit and get to know him more.

'An actor! How wonderful for you Hawtin. Molly would have been so pleased and proud...she was proud of you. We must come and see you in the theatre.'

Hawtin stood up and put his hands on his hips. 'Of course you must come and see me. I can get you tickets. How many would you like?'

'Well there's me, Maggie and Rosswell.' Rhoda turned to Maggie as she carried in a steaming hot, golden, thickly crusted pie and bowls of vegetables. She set the tray down. 'Maggie, Ross would come to the theatre with us wouldn't he?'

Maggie wiped her hands on her white apron. 'I'm sure he would although he might fall asleep if he becomes bored.'

They all laughed as they sat down to eat. Hawtin stared at the pie in wonder.

'I've never seen anything so wonderful. Maggie you're a gem.' Maggie flushed with pleasure as she poured out the gravy.

'Maggie is such a good cook. No one is ever going to take her from me,' said Rhoda. She cast a glance at Hawtin. He was looking at Maggie in adoration as if she were an angel.

'Oh I forgot Lizzie. We must have a ticket for Lizzie. So that will be four tickets. Will that be alright Hawtin? We could pay for them you know.'

'Instead of paying for the tickets, perhaps I might enjoy a few more dinners with you ...as a form of recompense of course. Will that be alright Rhoda?'

They all laughed together. Rhoda looked towards the window. She felt as if Molly was somehow there looking on in approval at the cosy scene. She was glad now that she hadn't told Hawtin....There would be another time.

XXIX

It was the postman that brought Rhoda the letter a few days later. It had come in on the 'Lady Anne.' Rhoda studied the handwriting on the envelope. It looked as if it had been carefully written in a strong script. Rhoda was half afraid to open it. What if they had found out about her murdering her stepfather? It was of no use to ask Lizzie or Molly to read it for her as their knowledge of reading was very poor. She would have to read it when she had finished teaching the children their tracts. Lizzie could take over when they started on their copybooks.

The children were very quiet as they carefully tried their best to copy the alphabet letters Rhoda had written into their books. They were becoming very proud of themselves doing real writing like Miss Rhoda's. She walked softly into the school room. It was a pleasant room now that the Slynes had gone. Pictures of the children's drawings were stuck on-newly painted walls. There were jars of coloured marbles, different coloured stones that the children had picked up on their journey up the hill and in pride of place stood a wooden Noah's Ark with Noah and all the animals given to them by Lady Elizabeth. Several abacuses were propped up on the window sill and a large map of the world set on the wall with painted numbers alongside large dots to help with their counting.

'Lizzie', said Rhoda. Lizzie looked up from her own copybook. 'Lizzie, I've had a letter from England. I'm going to leave you in charge while I go and read it. I think it's of some importance. Will you be able to manage the children?'

Lizzie sat up straight. 'Oh Miss Rhoda, I would love to watch over them. You go and read your letter…I'll ask Maggie to bring you some tea and some hot buttered toast shall I?'

Rhoda nodded and smiled. It was just like Lizzie to think about food for her. No doubt Lizzie would get the same for herself.

She settled herself in the large leather armchair. The fire was banked up high and burned brightly casting shadows across the well polished room. Rhoda opened the thick brown envelope and took out a piece of notepaper and a letter. She looked quickly at the end of the letter and saw Martha's name. Rhoda breathed a sigh of relief. Now she could enjoy reading the letter instead of worrying about who it was from. Then she wondered what if Martha had found out who she was? What if she had found out about the murder of her stepfather?

Maggie quietly came in with her tea and toast while Rhoda sat with the letter in her hand and put the tray down on the side table.

'Eat it while it's hot Miss Rhoda,' Maggie said as she left the room.

Rhoda was mystified about the piece of notepaper. It had obviously been torn from someone's pocketbook. 'Page 54' was written in a strong hand in the top right hand dog eared corner. It was a report of some kind. She carried the letter and piece of notepaper over to the window to see more clearly. It had been written in pencil but had faded over the years. Why on earth would Martha send her a Page 54 from someone's note book? It didn't make any sense to her. As she read the faded page it became more confusing. Who was this Henry Simpson? She couldn't recall anyone by that name. It was a record of this Henry Simpson being a poacher, with many convictions to his name. What had it to do with her?

Page 54

Number 3295

Henry Simpson

Date of committal 10th September 1836

Born: 30th November 1810

Found hiding in the porch of the Parish Church at Frogmore on the night of 3rd September 1836 with intent to commit a felony. He assaulted me while I was apprehending him in the execution of my duty.

Previous convictions:	*Description:*
Riot in a beer house	*Height 6 foot*
10 convictions for poaching	*Hair black*
Sureties for 6 months	*Weight 154 lbs*
Stealing fowls	*Complexion sallow*
Night poaching	*Visage long*
Common assault	*Tattoo of fish on right shoulder*
Sentenced for 2 years	

Rhoda kept staring at the piece of paper though she couldn't understand what it was. She was anxious to read the letter from Martha. Perhaps the letter would tell her more. As she unfolded it she was half afraid that it might contain some dreadful news.

34 Lambay Street

London

My Dear Rhoda

I don't know how to begin this letter there is so much to tell you.

First my dear Doctor Rathlin sends his good wishes to you and he is full of remorse about your predicament caused by Mrs Rathlin. I am writing this account for him as you see Doctor Rathlin has been very ill since his return from abroad.

Some days he is quite sick with the fever and calls out your name in despair. If there is any way to find it in your heart for forgiveness please say it to him. When he recovers, and in his more lucid moments he mentions you and dearly wants to make the journey to Van Dieman's Land to live and see you again.

Now for the rest of my news. I have found out where you used to live Rhoda. Your home was Bellington Hall, Frogmore. It isn't far from London. I made the journey there by fast four. I met Jack. The poor lad is slow in the head and he said something about a secret he was not to tell anyone. Bellington Hall is shut up and the owner has gone away, so Jack said. I wasn't able to rely on anything he told me but fortune found a way. I met Constable Reed's widow in the village. She remembers an Alyce Wilson and asked me to give you this torn piece of paper from Constable Reed's pocket book. Perhaps this will help you to regain some of your lost memory my dear. I met a gentleman in Holborn who was studying the poster I put up asking for inquiries about you. He believes your name to be Alyce Wilson, and just by chance I saw the name Sir Daniel Wilson, Bellington Hall in the label of his hat.

Jack informed me your poor mother drowned by accident in the river. I'm deeply sorry to be the bearer of such distressing news but I feel you should know for your sake. Dear Rhoda do write and tell me how you are faring now. Soon, when Doctor Rathlin improves with his health, we will make the journey. It is my duty to stay and look after his well being until that time arrives.

God bless you dear Rhoda. All our good wishes go with this letter.
Martha Jane Davies.

Rhoda read the letter over and over trying to make sense of the contents. That Owen Rathlin was ill and asking for her made her feel sad and lonely. How she wished she could be with him, to help nurse him back to health. No matter how she tried she couldn't remember her mother. Only her laughter, peals of laughter when she was with Ezra Blackwell. It was as if she didn't exist for them, they were so engrossed with each other. She should have felt sadness at the news of her mother drowned in an accident in the river, but she could only feel numbness, as if Martha had been telling her about a stranger, not her own mother.

The log suddenly shifted in the fire making Rhoda jump. Sparks shot up the chimney like tiny red stars in a miniature world. Rhoda sat and stared into the fire, trying to remember.

'Are you alright Rhoda? You were so quiet I didn't like to disturb you.' Lizzie came into the room carrying a cup of tea.

'Goodness Lizzie, I didn't realise how long I've been here reading this letter. It's so long. I should have left it until later this evening. How are the children?'

'They've gone back Miss Rhoda. It's started to snow very heavy. The guard took them back down the hill early. Have a look how fast it's falling.' Rhoda stood up and stared out of the window. She could barely see anything at all. It was as if a thick, soft, white blanket had been flung softly and silently over the landscape. Lizzie put another log on the fire.

'I should drink your tea Miss Rhoda and go on with your letter. Maggie's getting on with the dinner. It shouldn't be too long.'

Rhoda stretched her feet towards the fire. 'You and Maggie are spoiling me.'

'Well you've treated us well Miss Rhoda. Why, if it wasn't for you I don't know where I'd be, dead more than likely. You saved my life you did. I will always be in you debt I...'

'Nonsense, Lizzie. You would have done the same for me. Now go on. Have a rest with Maggie before dinner.'

Lizzie eyed the letter. It was obvious she wanted to know who it was from. 'It's from Martha, Lizzie. I'll tell you about it later.'

Rhoda picked it up and started to read it again. 'If I can try and fathom out the contents...it's all rather mysterious.'

What intrigued her was Constable Reed's widow insisting that the piece of paper out of his pocket book be given to her. She looked at it again. She didn't know of any Henry Simpson by the description. Whoever he was he was a criminal, a poacher. The whole incident would have happened when she was four years of age. How could she remember anything that far back - to 1836? How could a child be expected to remember? The only thing that had happened then was that her father had died. She tried to rack her mind to remember. What was the date? The date that her father had died? She had to remember. God what was it ? She had to remember - when was it? The day...Then slowly the ice was melting inside her. She felt the coldness of it, standing before the crackling fire. She almost dropped the letter into the fire with shock. The date on the piece of paper! She stared again at the date Henry Simpson was arrested - 3rd September 1836. That was it, the date! Ruth had told her when they were aboard the 'Sea Duchess'. The exact date when they had found her father, strangled. The date she had chosen to be her birthday.

XXX

There had been no time to tell Lizzie about the contents of the letter. Maggie had fallen in the kitchen. It wasn't serious, just a nasty bump on her leg. Maggie was sent to rest while Lizzie finished getting the dinner. All thoughts about the letter were pushed into the background.

It had stopped snowing by the next morning. She was surprised when Hawtin arrived carrying a large parcel. He threw it down on the floor in the kitchen.

'What is it?' Rhoda asked

'Costumes from the theatre. I've heard you ladies are excellent at needle work. Mr. Dunston asks if you would be so kind as to repair some of the tears in the ladies' gowns.' He ripped open the parcel and was about to scatter the gowns onto the stone floor when Rhoda stopped him.

'NO! You can't do that…bring them into the living room. They look beautiful.' Lizzie, Maggie and Rhoda examined the tears.

'Of course we will repair them. When do they have to be ready?'

'By tonight please.'

'TONIGHT?' they all shouted.

'Well it is urgent. There are no more costumes I'm afraid.'

Rhoda put the scarlet taffeta dress against her. 'They are beautifully made. Well, I'm sure we can each take a gown and repair it. Of course it won't be as neat as some of these stitches.'

'It doesn't matter. Things like that aren't noticeable when you're on stage,' Hawtin said. He held a sea green gown up against him.

'What do you think? Is it my colour?'

Maggie laughed, 'It's more like the colour for me.'

'I've just had a thought,' Rhoda said, examining the blue gown with laced flounces. 'We don't have any decent dresses to wear to the theatre.'

They all looked at her in dismay. Hawtin looked unhappy. 'The performance is on Saturday. Can't you make anything up by then?'

'Of course we won't be able to, we're not magicians Hawtin,' Rhoda sighed. They would all look a sorry sight for their visit to the theatre. None of them had given thought to what they were going to wear. Rhoda hit on an idea as the three of them sat sewing the dresses.

'I wonder if Lady Elizabeth might be able to help us. She may have some garments that we might borrow. I'll go and pay her a visit when we've finished our sewing.'

The room seemed to be filled with flowing dresses, reels of cotton and scissors as the three girls continued with the repairs. Rhoda had finished her work and put the sewing needle away safely. 'Two of the settler's children are starting here today with the convict children. Oh dear, what are we going to do?' Rhoda looked out of the window. 'Reverend James gets paid for the settlers. We must take them.' She buttoned her cloak and tied her bonnet ribbons. 'Can you see to them when they arrive Lizzie? I should only be an hour at the most.'

'That's alright Miss Rhoda. The children can get on with their copywriting until you return.' Lizzie looked up and smiled at her. 'They'll be fine with the others Miss.'

As Rhoda made her way up the hill she looked up at the darkening sky. It looked as if it might snow again. She would have to be quick. The weather changed so swiftly in Van Dieman's Land. She gazed up at Lady Elizabeth's Georgian mansion. As she drew closer she was amazed at the high straight tower and the Grecian pillars. It appeared to be enormous at a distance but now, as she got to the drive way, the heavy ornamental gates stood wide open with an avenue of high chestnut trees. The trees appeared to dwarf the house, hiding the grey light of early morning. Rhoda tugged her cloak closer around her as she pulled down on the heavy iron chain that hung at the side of the thick, vaulted doorway. The huge, black door eventually swung open...Albert stared down at her.

'What's wrong Miss Rhoda? This is an early visit.' He looked up at the darkening sky. 'Looks like we'll be having more snow.'

Rhoda waited with one foot on the steps. 'I would like to see Lady Elizabeth if she is available please Albert. No, there is nothing wrong.' She suddenly realised how early it was. She hadn't given it a thought. Lady Elizabeth might still be abed.

'I'm sorry Albert, I should have made my call later but...'

'Come in Miss Rhoda. Wait here and I'll go and tell her Ladyship,' Albert's voice echoed from the corridor, 'although she might still be at breakfast Ma'am.'

While she waited in the cold foyer Rhoda wondered what Lady Elizabeth may think of her having the nerve to ask if they might borrow some dresses. The more she thought about it the more she thought she shouldn't have come at all. She was just about to change her mind about the prospect when Lady Elizabeth came bustling towards her in a beautiful lavender wool gown.

'Rhoda my dear, come along and have some tea with me. You must be frozen. It's lovely to see you.'

145

She led the way to a small morning room and a table laid with porcelain cups and saucers and a silver tea pot. As she poured the tea she asked how everyone was and talked about the changing weather. When they had finished their tea Lady Elizabeth stood up.

'Now Rhoda what do you think of this gown?' She turned around to show Rhoda the back of it. 'Does it fit correctly do you think?'

'It's a beautiful gown Lady Elizabeth. It fits perfectly.'

'Thank you my dear. I'll let you into a secret. I've had this gown for ages.'

Rhoda took a deep breath. Now seemed as good a time as any to mention borrowing gowns for the trip to the theatre.

'Lady Elizabeth, I don't know how to ask you and you may think me most rude, but there is no one else we can turn to...err... Do you have any gowns that we might borrow for a trip to the theatre on Saturday night?'

Lady Elizabeth immediately got excited.

'The theatre? How wonderful. You are going to the theatre Rhoda? Who are you going with? You must tell me everything!'

Rhoda told her about Hawtin, the actor with Caleb Dunston's company and the forthcoming visit to the theatre. Lady Elizabeth's eyes were shining.

'Oh I do love the theatre Rhoda. It's a magical place!'

It was some time later that Lady Elizabeth led Rhoda up to her wardrobe room as she called it, to view her collection of clothes. There was so much to see, capes of all different fabrics, fans, tippets, gloves, bonnets and shoes. Rhoda became anxious that she was spending too much time at Lady Elizabeth's. She had to get back for the children.

'Now then Rhoda, you choose whatever you wish. One for you, one for Lizzie and one for Maggie.'

Rhoda looked at the different array of gowns Lady Elizabeth was setting out for her. It was difficult making a choice but eventually she chose a deep plum velvet for Lizzie, with a tippet of soft grey feathers. She made a quick choice for Maggie, a layered flounced gown in a beautiful shade of pink with a flower and lace trim. She was undecided on what to choose for herself. Then Lady Elizabeth held out a shimmering green flounced gown with a pointed waist, a tissue of fine silk. Tiny flowers were inserted in the décolletage. Never had Rhoda seen anything so beautiful.

'What a wonderful gown.' Rhoda shook her head. 'It's too beautiful for me to wear, Lady Elizabeth I...'

'Nonsense, my dear. There is a story to this gown. But I will tell you that one later. You must wear it Rhoda. It's just the colour for your red-gold hair and green eyes. You really must wear it,' Lady Elizabeth insisted. 'Now, about gloves, bags and shoes.'

She opened up hat boxes, shoe boxes and sorted through beaded evening purses, until at last Rhoda cast her eyes on the pile of clothing and wondered how she was ever going to carry it back down the hill.

'I'll get Albert to carry them down with you...wait...better still.' She looked out from the window. 'Oh goodness it's snowing. You can go in my carriage'.

She left the room to make arrangements, leaving Rhoda to tidy up, folding and putting away shawls, bonnets, bags and gloves.

When she got home she burst through the door with Albert carrying the precious load. Maggie and Lizzie ran to help her, laughing excitedly as they brought everything in to the living room, dumping them all carefully on the armchairs. The gowns for the theatre had been repaired. Hawtin had carried them off unceremoniously back to theatre.

Later they had tried on their gowns and shoes and managed to turn and twist to see a full view of themselves in the small mirror. Lizzie suddenly sat down in the chair. The plum velvet folds of her gown billowing around her.

'Oh Miss Rhoda, I've never seen such a beautiful gown, but I fear I won't be able to wear it to the theatre,' she said tears filling her eyes. She wiped them away with her thin hand. Rhoda knelt down by her side. Her own green silk gown shimmered in the firelight with golden flecks.

'But Lizzie, the gown is perfect for you. I thought you would love the colour.'

'I do love it Miss Rhoda, honestly I do. But Miss, you forget. I'm still a convict. You and Maggie are free women. How can a convict like me be seen dressed like this, going to the theatre?'

In her own excitement Rhoda had forgotten Lizzie's predicament. What could they do? She would have to try and find some way not to disappoint poor Lizzie.

XXXI

Rhoda was angry with herself. How on earth could she have forgotten about Lizzie? She was still a convict and hadn't been given a free pardon like herself. She would ask Lady Elizabeth about it and the Reverend, after all Lizzie was in his employment. She would have to make things right for her. Poor Lizzie, she was so looking forward to her trip to the theatre.

Rhoda became aware that she was being selfish again. How often she had stayed awake at night thinking about her dear friend Molly. If she hadn't had been so selfish just thinking about her own jeopardy, Molly might still be alive. Gladys Slyne had killed Molly because she had thrown away the letter on board the 'Sea Duchess.' Tears stung her eyes like soap bubbles. She brushed them away. She was determined the same thing wouldn't happen again. Her own selfish attitude had to be swept away. She was more determined than ever not to disappoint the hard working Lizzie who had shown her such loyal devotion and in so doing, Rhoda had looked to her for support and strength through the loss of Molly. Lizzie had shown herself to be a dear friend.

Rhoda didn't have to make a visit to see Lady Elizabeth, she had made it her business to call on Rhoda to see if the gowns fitted the girls and secretly, Rhoda guessed she wanted to make a call just to see how she was getting along. After Maggie and Lizzie had thanked her and Lady Elizabeth and herself were seated drinking tea and discussing the forthcoming visit to the theatre, Rhoda mentioned about Lizzie's predicament. Lady Elizabeth became most concerned.

'Oh dear.'

She pursed her lips, took another sip of her tea then smiled.

'But of course, if things come to the worst she can attend the theatre with me as my personal maid.'

Lady Elizabeth had a mischievous twinkle in her eye.

'In fact you can all be my guests, and sit beside me in my box at the theatre.'

Lady Elizabeth leaned forward towards Rhoda.

'Now then what do you say to that?'

Rhoda didn't know what to say. Lady Elizabeth was always full of surprises.

'Lady Elizabeth, you've been so kind letting us borrow the gowns, and now...'

'Don't thank me my dear. You can always repay me with your clever needlework and as for the Reverend what's his name, I can sort it out with him so don't concern yourself. After all it is a morality play we will be seeing and I think I should prepare you that Nellie Frobutt, an enormous woman with a terrible voice, will be giving us a rendition.'

Rhoda started to giggle.

'And giggle you might, but I groan inwardly my dear. She really is quite dreadful. You must try and stifle your laughter or your tears in your handkerchief. Now I really must be off. You must all be ready at 7 o'clock. My coach will pick you up.'

Rhoda thanked her again and saw her off into a biting wind, waving to Albert who waited with the carriage.

When she returned to the parlour Lizzie and Maggie were waiting for her, their eyes shining with happiness.

'Have you two been listening?' she scolded. 'Persons who listen at doors never hear anything good about themselves.'

Maggie wiped floured hands on her white apron, and Lizzie stood with her eyes fixed on the threadbare carpet.

'Does that mean I won't be able to attend the theatre with you then Miss Rhoda?'

Rhoda tried to look sternly at both of them.

'Well it appears that there has been a change of plan.'

Maggie looked horrified.

'A change of plan? I might have guessed...'

Rhoda caught hold of their hands and whirled them round and round.

'A change of plan yes...because we're all attending as guests of Lady Elizabeth and....'

'And we'll be sitting in a box!' Maggie and Lizzie shouted together.

XXXII

The week seemed to fly by. Saturday, the day they had been looking forward to arrived. The weather promised to be fair to them. They were all so excited they could hardly eat a morsel of food. Maggie made sure they had a proper dinner otherwise their stomachs might start to make a dreadful sound whilst they were seated in the theatre. The whole of the afternoon was busy with the preparations and getting ready.

Lizzie's hair was washed, brushed and put in rags. She sat holding one end of the cotton rag on one side of her head as Rhoda wound her brown locks tightly around the piece she was holding.

'Alright, let go Lizzie.' Rhoda took the piece of rag and wound it tightly around the lock of hair. She tied a knot at the bottom. 'There we're almost finished now.'

'Oh my head hurts!' Lizzie wailed. 'What if they don't come out properly Miss Rhoda? I'll look an awful mess.'

'You will look beautiful Lizzie,' Maggie said, polishing her nails with a buffer.

'What about my hands? They look so rough. I suppose I could keep my gloves on. What about my hair Miss Rhoda? Does it suit me like this?'

Maggie picked up the mirror and turned her head from side to side. Dressing for the theatre went on for hours. Rhoda was beginning to despair of both girls with their continual chatter. She was as excited as Maggie and Lizzie, but she tried to calm them down. It was only when they were all seated calmly waiting for Rosswell to arrive could Rhoda finally breathe a sigh of relief, thankful that a visit to the theatre didn't come every week.

She looked at the clock for the umpteenth time. It was only six o'clock and they were ready. Lizzie fidgeted with her beaded purse. She kept opening and closing it, then flicking her fan open and closed.

'Is this how it's done Miss Rhoda?' Lizzie asked, flicking the fan open too quickly so it fell on the floor. They all laughed.

'Well not quite like that Lizzie. Just a gentle flick of the wrist should do it.' Rhoda showed her using her own fan. 'See, just try it again. I'm no expert and if you can't manage it, use your other hand. I'm sure no one will notice in the theatre.'

Maggie got up from her chair and tried to run to the window. She stumbled over the hem of her gown almost tearing one of the pink flounces. Lizzie giggled.

'Be careful Maggie. You don't have to run, just try and saunter slowly.'

Maggie looked down at the hem of her gown. 'Oh whatever would I do if I had torn it?'

'Maggie that's the tenth time you've looked out of the window. It's much too early for Lady Elizabeth's carriage.'

'I'm just wondering what's happened to Rosswell. Surely he should be here by now?'

Maggie stared out of the window. 'Ah here he comes.'

Maggie made a run to the door. Rhoda stopped her. 'For goodness sake Maggie! DON'T RUN in that gown!'

Rosswell seemed taken aback at the sight of the girls in all their finery.

'My eyes deceive me. What a bevy of beauties! I must be in the wrong house.'

Rosswell swirled his cape off his shoulders to reveal his black evening suit. Rhoda stared at him. He looked so handsome. His fair hair gleamed in the firelight, his eyes seemed a deeper blue and his strong tanned face against the fancy white shirt and bow tie made him appear taller and... Rhoda caught her breath, something strange was happening to her. She had felt this before. Someone had opened a secret door deep inside her and let free an unknown butterfly. She just stared and stared at Rosswell as if she was seeing him for the first time. She put a gloved hand quickly to her heart to try and still the fluttering but it would not be stilled. In so doing she dropped her fan, breaking the momentous silence. Rosswell laughed and stooped to pick it up. Rhoda stared at his head, so near to her body she wanted to reach out and touch him.

'My Lady, your fan I believe.' Rosswell handed her the open fan. 'And may I say never have I seen such beauty. You look ravishing. I will have to stay by your side to ward off the young blades who might decide to whisk you away.' Rosswell took her gloved hand and held it to his lips. Rhoda felt her face burning with embarrassment. She flipped her fan over her face, flicking it furiously as Rosswell grinned down at her.

The girls were laughing. 'Rossie you look really handsome,' Maggie said, putting her arm in his. 'Don't you think so Miss Rhoda?'

Rhoda finally found her voice 'Yes Maggie, your brother looks very...'

Rosswell flopped down in an armchair. 'Don't say it Rhoda. I feel like a stuffed bird ready for the oven.' He pulled at his bow tie, pushing his fingers down inside his collar. 'I feel like my neck has been wrung as well.' He jumped up from the chair. 'For God's sake Rhoda, do something with this collar for me.' He stood up close in front of her. 'Something seems to stick just here, see.' He bent his head down even closer towards her. Rhoda tried to step back but he held her tightly gripping her arms. She felt his warmth through the silk of her gown. Avoiding his eyes she pulled his neck towards her, his breath now mingling with her own. She slid her hand into the collar of his shirt.

'I can feel nothing there Rosswell. It must be the collar stud.' She pulled and as she pulled, freeing the bow tie a little, he pulled her close against him holding her even tighter.

'It must be my heart then,' he whispered into her hair. 'My God Rhoda you look so beautiful tonight.' She drew back quickly but not before his lips had brushed hers.

Maggie and Lizzie stood staring at them. Rhoda was embarrassed. She sat down quickly, her gown spreading out around her. Rosswell was still standing looking down at her intently. She tried to avert her gaze away from his eyes but couldn't resist looking at him, still continuing to stare at her, until finally she shouted.

'For goodness sake, stop staring at me Rosswell Hawkes. Whatever will people think?'

XXXIII

The carriage arrived a little before seven. Rhoda gazed out at the starlit sky. It was a beautiful clear night. Rosswell continued to stare as he sat opposite her in the carriage. She listened to Maggie and Lizzie's constant chatter.

'Oh look! We're here. Oh no! I'm so nervous. I think I'm going to be sick.'

'Don't you dare,' said Rhoda as they climbed down from the carriage. 'You will ruin your gown. Whatever would Lady Elizabeth say?'

They walked slowly to the open doors of the theatre. Rosswell started to moan as the crowd thickened. They stopped and read the billboard outside the theatre.

THEATRE ROYAL
Saturday March 10th 1852
LILLIAN'S DREAM
by Caleb Dunston

A Romantic melodrama of an industrious servant girl of good conduct persecuted by a dastardly villain. The defenceless heroine is rescued by an intrepid hero. Set amidst ....Spectacular scenery....in exotic settings.

Dorval Grey.. Caleb Dunston
Lillian, a young girl of great beauty.........Elinor Hambridge
Malin Burns. Hero................................. Hawtin Williams
Lillian's widowed mother.......................Mary Jane Davies

The performance will commence with four charming songs by Mrs Nellie Frobutt.
Doors open at 7.00 pm.   Performance begins at 7.30 pm.

Rhoda laughed lightly. 'I can't wait to see Hawtin as the hero.'

Rosswell muttered, 'What about this Nellie Robust? What's she like I wonder?'

Rhoda couldn't help but laugh out loud. 'It's not Nellie Robust it's FROBUTT.'

The girls were laughing as they were carried forward on a gentle flow of eager theatre-goers. Once inside the foyer a gentleman came forward and ushered them all up a wide, red carpeted staircase where the light from the glittering chandeliers threatened to swallow everyone assembled in their magical radiance. Yet it seemed to Rhoda that the sparkle was reserved for them alone.

Lady Elizabeth greeted them at the door to her own private box. There was a small posy together with a box of chocolates on red plush-covered chairs for each of the girls. When they were all seated Rhoda looked down at the people taking their seats for the performance. The dress circle was almost full. The orchestra started to tune up. The heavy, red velvet curtains edged with huge gold tassels enticed Rhoda. The footlights were turned up as the orchestra begin to play softly.

'We're about to start I think,' Lady Elizabeth murmured. 'Yes this is it.'

Her voice got louder as the music reached a sudden crescendo and heavy curtains pulled apart as if by unseen hands, an audible swishing sound followed by quick intakes of breath. Lizzie gasped. 'Oooh I've never seen anything the like of it. It's magical.'

Mrs Nellie Frobutt was introduced with her accompanist on the piano, a small man with black shiny hair parted in the middle. He sat down at the piano and waited as she came forward to centre stage then walked down towards the footlights, nodding to the audience who applauded politely. There was a sudden surge of spluttering and stifled laughter from Maggie and Lizzie. Even Lady Elizabeth was smiling at the sight of the singer. She appeared to look top-heavy. Her enormous chest was covered with a sea green, long, silk blouse that shimmered and moved up and down with a wave like motion. Her bright auburn hair was an untamed mass of frizz, brought under control with a large blue ostrich feather. Rhoda was intrigued by her. It was only when she opened her large red mouth to sing that she broke her concentration. She stole a glance at Rosswell who sat further back in his chair mimicking Mrs Frobutt. Rhoda tried desperately to compose herself. She gave a small cough to get Rosswell's attention but he was engrossed with his own performance. Just as the music stopped and the applause began, she turned in her chair towards Rosswell.

'Rosswell! Stop it. Whatever will Lady Elizabeth think of you?' Rhoda spoke sternly.

'I told you she was robust, didn't I?' Rosswell whispered. 'God you look more beautiful when you're angry Rhoda. Your eyes remind me of a wild green sea.'

Rhoda ignored him and looked away. Mrs Frobutt was preparing herself for another rendition, folding and flapping her plump arms across her ever increasing enormous bosom.

'Oh God no! Not again please. She looks like a parrot about to take flight...how I wish she would,' Rosswell muttered and shook his head in despair.

'It won't be long now. Just one more song then she's finished,' Lady Elizabeth said.

Her final song finished amongst deafening applause. 'Don't applaud her for heaven's sake,' Rosswell almost shouted. 'She'll take it that we want an encore. Oh my god!'

Mrs Frobutt smiled broadly at the audience with the words. 'Well if you insist on one more rendition.' Rosswell groaned none too quietly as did Lady Elizabeth and various members of the audience who were shifting in their seats and looking around wondering who on earth could possibly find enjoyment in her dreadful singing.

At last she was finished. Rosswell shouted hooray. Mrs Frobutt looked up and waved towards the box...But she shook her head. 'Sadly that must be my last song, goodnight and thank you.' She left the stage wiping her eyes as the curtains closed.

'There you see. Even she couldn't bear her own singing.' Rosswell looked smug. 'Now for the real drama,' he said. He settled back in his chair and winked at Rhoda.

Rhoda watched the curtains swish open, to reveal a woodland setting. As the drama unfolded Rhoda started intently as the evil villain of the piece gave a magnetic performance. Rhoda hated him. The audience hissed and booed whenever he made his overpowering entrance on stage. He was a tall man with shoulder length grey hair and a long pointed beard. There was something about his eyes that made Rhoda give a shudder when he came close to the footlights and turned his head up towards the box with a vicious leer. It was almost as if he were looking especially at her. The poor heroine, Lillian, had charcoaled brows and a pale face that had been powdered white. It contrasted sharply with her dark brown hair, parted in the centre, with long bobbing ringlets that cascaded down each side of her head. Lillian wept when her widowed mother died. She was alone, only to be persecuted by Dorval Grey.

It was when the play got to a sinister part where Dorval was pulling Lillian into the barn. Poor Lillian was on her knees. It was then that Rhoda remembered her own desperate time in the past at the hands of Ezra Blackwell.

'You will marry me Lillian,' Dorval Grey shouted, 'or Malin Burns will meet his end. Come Lillian, come with me. I love you Lillian. You will be mine.'

'Oh save me...my hour is come...who will ever save me now?'

There was a roll of thunder, lightning flashes swept across the stage. Then onto the stage came Malin Burns, the hero. She was saved in the nick of time.

Hawtin played the part of Malin Burns with a toughness that surprised Rhoda. He fought with the wicked Dorval Grey, who produced a revolver. The hushed audience gasped as Malin wrestled with the revolver. It went off with a loud blast that made everyone in the audience jump. Dorval was accidentally killed with his own revolver. Lillian was saved by her admirer, Malin.

As the cast took their final bows in front of the footlights, Rhoda watched as Dorval Grey held up the hands of Lillian and Malin and swept them forward to take their own bows. The whole of the cast stood there smiling at the audience while Dorval Grey stood looking sullen and sinister – the perfect villain.

XXXIV

Rhoda and the girls had laughed and talked for days about the theatre visit.

'Fancy us all going to a real live theatre Miss Rhoda.' Lizzie gazed into the fire and sighed. 'It was just magic. I for one will never forget it.'

Hawtin arrived with some more sewing. They all stared at the grey coat he had thrown over his arm.

'It's just this coat of Caleb's. Looks as if the seam needs some repair to it. Could Lizzie bring it down to the theatre later do you think?'

Rhoda examined the seam. 'It shouldn't take long to do that.' Lizzie volunteered to repair the coat. 'Can I sew it Miss Rhoda…and please can I take it down to the theatre. I'll be quick, I promise…Oh ple..'

Rhoda held up her hands. 'Of course you can. It's obvious that you are quite taken with Caleb Dunston.' Lizzie blushed and went to fetch the sewing basket. When she had finished she held up the coat. 'There, that's strong enough even for you Mr. Dunston.'

When Lizzie had gone to deliver the coat, Rhoda watched her running down the hill to the theatre. Lizzie had blossomed into quite a pretty girl since they had arrived in Van Dieman's Land. Gone was her bony skeletal frame and thin white face. Now she looked alive with vitality. Rhoda looked at her own face in the mirror. Her red gold hair had now grown just below her shoulders and her green eyes shone with a secret sparkle. Something was happening to her but she didn't know what it was. It was as if she was about to be caught up and wrapped snugly in a warm blanket of wonder.

Everything was turning out to be right for each of them. Maggie loved cooking for Rhoda and Lizzie and for the Reverend James and his wife, Mary. The Reverend James had left the religious instruction of the convict children in Rhoda's willing hands. She had loved and nurtured them as if they were her own. Tom was working in the garden, helping to grow all kinds of vegetables that Rosswell had shown him. Letty was looking a lot better after her illness. All the children were looking healthy. Some of the girls were being instructed in needlework, stitching their own samplers as well as learning to cook their own 'pulled up ' vegetables with Maggie in the kitchen. The Reverend James had given his sanction for Rosswell to provide a log and length of timber for a see-saw. Hoops were made with the iron rings from broken barrels. There was plenty of space in the garden under a horse chestnut tree. Rhoda looked at the clock. There was plenty of time before the children arrived.

She reached down and pulled out her letter from Martha which she had placed underneath some small books. She read the letter again then noticed Martha had forgotten to date the letter! Why hadn't Constable Reed put some more information down for her? She had never heard of anyone by the name of Henry Simpson. Who on earth was he? All she could glean from the information was that Henry Simpson was a poacher. The log shifted and spluttered in the grate. The tiny sparks flew upwards at a furious speed. Rhoda watched lost in thought as tiny glimmers of fire slowly flickered new thoughts to filter through the grey tulle of her mind. Could this man Henry Simpson be her father's murderer? He had been found hiding in the porch of the Parish Church at Frogmore. Hiding from what? The words leaped out at her 'with the intent to commit a felony.' Suppose he had already committed the felony? Suppose the felony had been the murder of her father? Did Constable Reed suspect this Henry Simpson as being guilty of the crime? He must have suspected him. Why keep the paper from his notebook all this time?

There was a loud knocking at the door. Rhoda pushed the letter safely back inside the drawer, and closed it quickly. She opened the door and there on the threshold stood Martha and Doctor Rathlin.

XXXV

After the initial shock, surprise burned slowly. Rhoda, Martha and Owen Rathlin sat beside a glowing fire sipping hot tea. It had been such a thrill to see them. Rhoda was at first confused as to what to say after such a long time. She was overawed by it all. They talked about the delay in the voyage.

'I had just finished reading your letter again Martha, and then you both turned up as if by providence.'

She poured some more tea and became flustered as Owen watched her every move, almost dropping the plate of cakes Maggie had made.

'You look in good health Rhoda...I don't know what to say about... err ... He looked uncomfortable, his pale face drawn. His eyes were sunk back into their sockets. He gazed down at his long fingers and clenched his hands. 'Dear Rhoda, I don't know where to begin to say how sorry I am about....' he stopped. He could say no more. Rhoda could see his distress. She knew what he wanted to say to her, but couldn't find the right words. Kneeling down beside his chair she took his hands. How ill he looked. This wasn't the Owen she remembered. She had tried to carry a picture image of him in her mind, but now staring up at him, she was looking at a frail old man. She looked quickly at Martha. Martha shook her head and busied herself collecting the tray of cups and saucers and quietly left the room leaving them alone.

'Owen, please! I know what you want to say to me. I would not want you to take pity on me any longer. You must rid yourself of any guilt you may have for me.'

She stood up and towered over his frail frame. 'Look at me Owen... I'm a free woman now. I'm happy here. I've made some wonderful friends. Life is good to me Owen. I want you to be happy for me.' She bent down as he took her hand and pressed it. She was surprised at the strong hold on her. His eyes glistened.

'Oh my god! Rhoda. How I've longed for this moment. I suffered Hell's torment at what you might say to me.' He pulled her closer and kissed her gently on the cheek. He pulled back changing as he realised what he had done. He put his head in his hands. 'I'm sorry. Can you ever forgive me Rhoda?'

'I have nothing to forgive you for Owen. But I ask you to make me one promise.'

'Ask it. I will promise anything for your forgiveness.'

She looked into his sad eyes. Where once she had seen deep pools, there were now dead, empty eyes without a soul.

'Promise me Owen, promise that you will bury your guilt and make a new life for yourself. Will you promise me that? It would give me great peace of mind.'

'Dear Rhoda. I made you a promise. I will try to do what you ask. It will be difficult but…' Rhoda pressed a finger over his lips to stop him saying anything further. She shook her head. 'Don't break your promise to me,' she whispered.

He kissed her hand. They sat down again as Martha came into the room coughing slightly.

'Now tell me. What do you plan to do in Van Dieman's Land?'

Maggie brought in more tea and some hot buttered scones she had freshly baked. Lizzie said she would take care of the children while Rhoda attended to her visitors. The next hour was taken up with constant chatter. Owen was going to visit a doctor friend who was doing some medical studies. He might take up an offer of helping him at the hospital and dear Martha would continue to be his housekeeper. He fell asleep in the armchair.

'The poor dear,' Martha whispered. 'How he's longed for this moment to see you again Rhoda. Or should I call you Alyce?'

'NO…no I continue to be Rhoda Lambay, the name Owen christened me.'

Martha smiled broadly. 'Oh! It's Owen now is it?'

Rhoda blushed and gazed down at him sleeping. 'Martha he looks quite frail. I wonder if the voyage was too much for him. How he's changed.'

'He will soon pick up again. This is just what he needs, a new home and new surroundings. I must admit the wonderful scenery is so much like England.'

They talked some more about Van Dieman's Land and then Rhoda had to ask her about the letter and the note from Constable Reed's pocket book. Martha carefully picked up the scattered crumbs that had fallen onto her woollen dress.

'There's not much more I can tell you dear.' Martha went over her journey again to Frogmore.

'The house was closed up then and the owner had gone away? That's what you wrote in your letter. I wonder what happened to them?'

'Yes it was all shuttered up. Do you remember any of it Rhoda? I was hoping it would help you to remember your home.'

Rhoda gave a small shudder. How could she tell Martha about Ezra Blackwell and what she had done? 'No, I can't remember anything at all.'

'What about Jack? The poor lad seemed to talk in riddles.'

'Jack?'

'Yes. Don't you recall in my letter he had a secret or something that he mustn't tell anyone? Can you remember anything about Jack and his secret?'

Rhoda poured some more tea for Martha, trying to stop her hand from shaking. The secret Jack kept... Could it be that he had found out she had murdered Ezra Blackwell? Was that the secret he couldn't tell anyone? Was he protecting her? Rhoda shook her head and quickly steered away from that part of the conversation. It was bringing back too many terrible memories. Memories that had to stay locked up forever in the darkest recess of her mind.

She changed the subject to the gentleman Martha had met in London. Martha settled back and sipped her tea slowly. 'Oh you mean the gentleman I met in the George and Bear? He appeared to know of an Alyce Wilson. He looked very important and well dressed I can tell you, quite handsome looking, with a grey beard. I had the impression he was someone of the nobility, a Lord or someone of importance.'

'You said he had a label in his hat that said 'Daniel Wilson, Bellington Hall.'

Martha frowned. 'Yes that was strange. I wondered if he was some relation to you. Or he may have come by the hat by some other means. Sir Daniel Wilson it said.'

Rhoda tried to remember anyone who was a 'Sir' in her family.

'Could it have been your father's hat or your Grandfather's perhaps?' Martha put her cup and saucer on the lace tablecloth. 'Well he could have got it from a second-hand shop. People in the gentry often give clothing away to the poor. Could it have been your Grandfather I met?'

Rhoda sat upright in her chair. Of course that was it. It could have been her Grandfather's hat. She told Martha all about the missionary girl, Ruth, and about her father being found strangled. 'I suppose my Grandfather could have been a Daniel Wilson but I....'

Martha clutched at the ebony beads about her neck. 'Oh my God, you poor dear.' Martha went and put her arms around her. 'How you have suffered.' Martha's eyes were filled with tears. Rhoda stiffened in the chair. She could hardly say the words.

'He could have been my Grandfather Wilson but supposing…' Rhoda stopped.

Martha looked concerned. 'What is it dear? Supposing what?'

Rhoda got up quickly and fetched Martha's letter from the drawer.

'Look,' she said, unfolding the letter. 'What if this Henry Simpson was the man you saw in the George and Bear? Why else would Constable Reed want me to see this? Why did he keep it all this time? He might have had cause to believe this was the man who had killed my father. The dates fit exactly. What do you think Martha? Could it be the same man you met in Holborn?'

Martha looked stunned. Her mouth opened and closed like a fish gasping for air.

'Why I never gave it a thought.' Martha became flustered.

'Of course you couldn't have because you never knew about my father's murder until now. It's only at this moment reading the letter again, and thinking about the label in his hat. The one you saw that said 'Bellington Hall' It could be one and the same.'

Rhoda became excited at what she had discovered. Only now did it dawn on her that she would never, ever find out. Henry Simpson had disappeared long ago. Martha put her arm around Rhoda's shoulders.

'You may be right in what you say my dear.' She gave a deep sigh. 'Suppose this man was Henry Simpson. He's long gone now. I could make some enquiries for you in London. I know many of the cabbies and coach drivers. What if I write to some of them? They could ask around. Something may come of it. What do you think?'

Rhoda flung her arms around Martha.

'Martha you are the best friend in the whole world. It's worth a try. Anything is worth a try. All is not lost.'

Owen stirred and sat up in the chair rubbing his eyes.

'What's not lost?' he said sleepily. He stretched out his long legs and sat up.

Rhoda didn't want Owen to know anything about what Martha and she had been talking about. She didn't think it would be appropriate for Owen to be concerned about the elusive Henry Simpson, after all, the man was long gone now. The less Owen knew the better at this time. Rhoda looked at Martha and shook her head quickly and at the same time pressed her finger to her lips, indicating secrecy. Martha smiled and changed the subject.

'Rhoda was just saying about repairing one of her gowns...err...'

Martha stopped and looked at Rhoda.

'Yes I was just saying to Martha all is not lost. I can easily sew a frill on to conceal it. After all anything is worth a try isn't it Martha?'

When they were ready to leave Martha gave her a warm hug and a kiss on the cheek.

'I'll do all I can,' she whispered, 'but it will take time.'

Owen took hold of her hand. He seemed loathe to let it go.

'Dear Rhoda. I must see you again and soon. There is so much we must talk about. Do say we will meet again soon, promise me.'

There was such an urgency in his tone and the pleading look in his eyes almost made her rush into his arms and beg him not to leave. Instead she did the next best thing. She kissed him lightly on the cheek. He appeared taken aback at her swift action, but took her hand and pressed it gently to his lips. She wanted to feel the touch of his lips on her hand. She wanted to treasure the pressure of it. To hold her hand against her cheek when he had gone to feel the warmth of it, but there was no warmth. The pressure of his lips against her hand had been light as a whisper. It had been the same when she had kissed his cheek. He had been startled at her action. There had been a coldness in his movement. It had lasted only for a brief moment, but Rhoda had sensed his mood.

She recovered herself saying 'But of course you must come to dinner, when you are settled. You didn't say where you are staying. Is it in Hobart?' Owen fastened his cape. The weather outside had become thick with fog. Owen glared at the fog.

'I am taking a house outside Hobart near the River Derwent. My friend is leaving to take up another position. We are lucky the house is already furnished. You will have to come and see it Rhoda.' He turned away and stepped out into the greyness.

'This damned fog - it's a curse. It's just like London,' he muttered.

Rhoda watched them disappear. She heard the carriage leaving and remembered his last words to her as he left – 'this damned fog.' He had said the same words long ago, when she was tucked up in a warm bed in his house after her accident. He had blamed the 'damned fog' for her accident with the hansom cab. Her heart ached with the memory of it. How she had nurtured every moment he had been with her, taking care of her after her fall. She had kept her memories of him with her throughout the long voyage. They had given her hope in her blackest moments. Yet now seeing him again, looking into his veiled eyes, there was nothing she could see to give her any hope now. 'A curse' – was that how he saw her now? He was carrying a burden of guilt for Isabella Rathlin. Had the burden of guilt become heavier since they now met again…Yet he had pulled her to him and kissed her gently, she had felt the warmth of his kiss.

She stood and stared out of the window at the swirling fog. It was as if she was looking into her mind. Everything seemed distorted. It seemed as if Owen had to make his own peace of mind by seeing her again, to release the guilt he carried. But now she had made him promise to bury his guilt and make a new life. He could see she had made a new start. She had been pardoned and set free.

She drew her shawl closer around her shoulders. The fog had thinned out into long soft spirals. They looked liked grey waves rising, trying to peer close in at the window. She kept thinking of the guilt Owen was carrying, but she sensed he would never be free of it. Just as she would never be free of the guilt she carried deep inside her, tapping behind the secret door deep down in her soul, trying to free itself.

It was wonderful to see Martha again. She had helped her so much. She just prayed Owen and Martha would never find out about the terrible guilt she carried within herself - the guilt of murder. Somehow she knew it would always rise up within her at unexpected moments. She would have to make herself deal with it. Try and make it heal within her.

XXXVI

Rosswell Hawkes came into the room, his face flushed with excitement. He caught hold of Rhoda around her waist and waltzed her round the room, until she shouted out to him to stop his nonsense. The children were laughing as Rhoda straightened her apron.

'Whatever is the matter with you Mr. Hawkes?' she shouted. 'Get on with your work children.' The children bent their heads as they continued to giggle quietly, turning their heads to glance up at Rhoda and Mr. Hawkes.

'I wish you would behave yourself in front of the children Rosswell,' she whispered. 'I want them to concentrate on their work. Have you gone mad or something?'

Rosswell pulled at her hands. 'I have to talk to you Rhoda. I've got something important to tell you. Can't you leave the children with Lizzie for a while?'

She left Lizzie in the school room with the children and closed the door of the living room behind them.

'Now what is it Ross. What do you want to say?'

Rosswell pulled Rhoda down into the chair while he knelt at her feet. For one moment Rhoda thought he was going to propose to her. She made to get up from her chair but he stopped her.

'Promise me you won't breathe a word woman. I must have your promise before I tell you. It's a secret.' Rosswell got up swiftly and opened the door, then closed it again quietly. 'Now Rhoda, don't get excited will you?'

Rhoda was losing her patience. 'For goodness sake what is it?'

'Promise you...'

'Won't say a word... I promise. Now what is it this secret?'

Rosswell whispered it so quietly that she didn't hear it at first then he repeated it.

'Gold...'

'GOLD what?' She almost shouted it out. Rosswell put a hand over her mouth to silence her.

'Be quiet and just listen to me.' Rosswell breathed the words into her ear. He held on to her tightly until she wriggled free of him.

'No one can hear us. Just tell me what you are talking about.' She stopped and mouthed the word 'gold'.

'No one knows about it yet. I'm going to Bendigo with my team of

Demons.'

'DEMONS? Who are they?'

'They're free convict men now. They'll be my team. We'll cross the Bass Straits to Melbourne and then make our way to Bendigo.' Rosswell's eyes were shining. 'Demons from Van Dieman's Land, good strong men'

'Bendigo…with convicts? And you call them demons?'

'They're free convict men now Rhoda. Just like you they earned their freedom. They can be trusted. They're a bunch of good men. When we find gold I'll come back here for you.'

Rhoda put her hands on her hips defiantly. 'What do you mean 'come back here for me'?

He wiped his brown hand across his forehead. 'I didn't say that right did I woman?'

'Don't call me woman.' Rhoda snarled the words at him. He annoyed her.

'Well what I mean to say is…well this is difficult finding the right words, I mean.'

He caught hold of her hands roughly and pulled her to him. She could smell the grass, hay and heady mix of wild flowers. She closed her eyes for a moment.

'Well I was hoping we could get married or something, Rhoda my love.'

Rhoda opened her eyes and stared at him as if he were a stranger. She pushed herself away from him.

'HOW DARE YOU! We could get married OR SOMETHING! I'm completely affronted by your words Rosswell Hawkes.' Rhoda glared at him.

'Does that mean you will say 'Yes my beloved'? Does affronted mean yes?' He caught hold of her again.

'How dare you propose to me in this manner. You are an arrogant…..'

'I'm sorry but I thought there was something between us, you remember the night we went to the theatre, you looked so beautiful and I could see it in your eyes that you loved me.'

Rhoda felt as if she were about to burst wide open in anger. The sheer insolence of the man. Whatever had possessed him? It must be the madness of going to search for gold. He had caught her unawares. He stared down at her making her feel quite nervous. She was sure he could hear her heart erratically pumping warm rivulets of blood. She pulled at her apron and patted her hair, trying to assume some form of composure.

'Rosswell, I think I can forgive you your haste. You are in a state of excitement about this gold find. I suggest you try and calm yourself and set about making preparations for when you leave for Bendigo with your demons.'

Rosswell smiled at her then laughed out loud. He picked up his wide bush hat, pushed it on his dusty head, picked her up again and whirled her around before putting her down and kissing her unexpectedly on the mouth. She tried to heave herself away from him but he continued to clasp her tightly until she was afraid she was going to faint away in his arms. Something she didn't want to experience. When he let her go she swung out at him with her fist and caught him a blow against his solid chin. He doubled up in the pretence that she had hit him too hard. Then he straightened up and put his face close up to hers and whispered, 'You'll keep what I said a secret won't you woman?'

He stopped as he opened the door. Frowning he turned to her. 'Is that a YES?'

Rhoda found her voice at last. 'GET OUT ROSSWELL HAWKES,' she yelled. She grabbed an empty inkwell and threw it at his swift retreating figure.

XXXVII

Doctor Owen Rathlin pushed himself further into the corner of the travelling coach and thought about Rhoda. She had looked more beautiful than ever. He admired the way in which she had coped and survived her harsh treatment. Now, as he made his journey to the Derwent Asylum to meet his fellow student from his medical days, he pondered on the possibility of one day asking Rhoda to be his wife. He needed a wife, someone to comfort him after all the weary years of attending to Isabella and her long list of wants. Rhoda appeared to be strong and confident in herself. She would make a fine doctor's wife.

The horses clattered to a stop. He had hardly paid much attention to the passing scenery. He was tired and didn't like the countryside much. The invitation from Thomas Watkins to come and view the asylum was a chance not to be missed. He had wanted to see the forms of treatment the lunatics were given. The chance to compare and view some case notes would be of interest to him. He hadn't made up his mind yet to work in the hospital or in practice. Thomas had written to him about a possible vacancy arising at the hospital. It was the prospect of practising in a new area of medicine that appealed to him.

Doctor Thomas waited on the steps, his large hand shielding his eyes against the bright sunlight. When he realised it was his old friend he hurried forward to greet him his arm outstretched.

'My dear fellow, it's wonderful to see you after so long. How many years is it? God knows. Come on in.' He pushed open the heavy door. 'Come in, we've got so much to talk about, then I'll show you round. I thought you might have come here by boat. It's a beautiful river the Derwent.'

'I've had more than enough of boats to last me a life time, what with sea sickness. The voyage was terrible. When we reached Cape Town, I thought of turning back to England. But even that prospect was daunting enough.'

They sat and talked about old times. Owen had made himself comfortable in a leather wing backed armchair. He studied Thomas as he drank his tea. He was a giant of a man, with large strong hands. Owen thought he looked more like a farmer than a doctor. They finished their tea. On their way through the old dingy building, Thomas talked about the Asylum.

'There used to be about sixty convict invalids here and ten lunatics years ago. There's more now of course.' Thomas stopped and stroked his cheek. 'Well there's sixty lunatics or more now and less invalids. What does that tell you Owen?'

'Probably the cause being convicts who become insane when locked up. It's replacing one form of incarceration with another, poor devils.' Owen muttered, 'I'd like to see some case notes Thomas if I may,' as he crossed the quadrangle.

'Case notes? I'm afraid we don't keep any of those here Owen.'

'But you must have some form of records kept on your patients, surely?'

'They're not patients Owen, they're inmates. Nothing can be done for them. The noisy ones are kept away from the quiet ones, which makes life easier for us all.'

They walked by vegetable gardens and exercise yards of various sizes. They passed what seemed to be a house and privies. The yards and grounds were divided by high walls. They reached the far building across the courtyard.

'The lunatics are kept in this back section. The women are separated from the men. I can let you talk with one of them if you like and you can make your own notes. Remember we get fees paid for some of the inmates.'

The corridors were dingy. There was a ward with a few females who stood and stared at him as they passed through.

'There are sixteen cells here, a kitchen and the Superintendent's quarters. These are the quiet ones.' He opened a door to reveal an elderly, thin, scrawny woman seated at a well scrubbed table reading a heavy leather bible. She was muttering to herself, flicking the pages over and clapping her hands as each page was turned. She looked up at him with small bird like eyes. Her mass of frizzy hair was fastened on top of her head. She reached out to him with a claw like hand and grasped his, almost pulling him down on to the hard wooden chair beside her.

'Have you come to read the bible? But I don't know your name dear.' she smiled.

'Good day to you, madam. I'm Doctor Owen Rathlin.'

'Owen? That's a good name doctor. A Welsh name. Are you from Wales?'

'I'm from London. Do you mind if I talk with you for a while?'

'Of course not. My name is Gladys Slyne. Gladys is a Welsh name, so we are both good. Names are very important to a person. Some names have a wicked sound to them. The devil names his own, the wicked and the evil. My husband is the Reverend Arthur Slyne. We live near the church overlooking Cockle Creek and Recherche Bay. A lovely place.' Gladys smiled and hummed a little tune to herself. Owen resisted writing notes twisting the pencil in his hands – hesitating.

'You can write your notes Doctor. Arthur was always scribbling notes for his sermons. We tried hard to give the convicts a good Christian household.'

'Why did you come to Van Dieman's Land Gladys?'

Gladys clasped her hands together in her lap and stared at him. She smiled sweetly.

'Me and dear Arthur came to Van Dieman's Land to save so many souls. You do understand that don't you Doctor? We sailed on the 'Sea Duchess' from London.'

Owen nodded in approval. This was interesting as Rhoda was on the same ship.

'The Sea Duchess'? Why I know of someone who was on that ship, you might remember her. Her name was Rhoda Lambay.'

'Rhoda Lambay was a convict girl.'

'She was a convict at the time, but now she has a free pardon for her crimes.'

'A free pardon? A free pardon? She was guilty of MURDER Doctor.'

'No, Rhoda was wrongly convicted of stealing a white petticoat.'

'Was she indeed? But not wrongly convicted of murder Doctor?'

'No Gladys.' Owen shook his head. 'You have the wrong person Rhoda is...'

'Rhoda Lambay is Alyce Wilson isn't she?' Gladys rocked in her chair.

Owen stared at her. How did she know Rhoda's real name? 'Yes she is Alyce Wilson. She had lost her memory and was given the name Rhoda….'

'Lost her memory? Well she remembered it very well on board the 'Sea Duchess.' She remembered killing her stepfather, Ezra Blackwell, in the barn with a pitch-fork.' Gladys laughed. 'Oh yes. She confessed it to her friend Molly Williams. And do you know what Doctor Owen? Soon after, her friend Molly went missing from the ship, pushed over the side so they said. Now say she's not a murderer.'

Owen recoiled in horror at what Gladys was saying. This talk about murder, the woman was mad. She would say anything. This couldn't be true. Rhoda had lost her memory after the accident with his hansom cab, surely she couldn't have been pretending to have lost her memory. No, this just wasn't true. Owen looked across at Thomas standing near the door way. Thomas shrugged his shoulders. 'The woman is suffering from delusions Owen, you mustn't believe all…'

Gladys stared at the bible. 'It's in here the name Rhoda. It's here. I know it's written.'

Owen gave a short laugh. 'Gladys you are getting confused with names.'

'I'm not confused Doctor. The world is confused if they can't see a murderer with their own eyes. But I know.' She pulled him closer and whispered hoarsely. 'Rhoda Lambay isn't her real name. It's Alyce Wilson and I heard her confess to murder on the 'Duchess'. They think I'm mad doctor but I know what I heard and saw that night of the storm. I swear on this bible I heard her confession Doctor Owen Rathlin.'

Owen gasped in horror at what the woman was saying. She was right about Alyce Wilson being Rhoda's real name, but MURDER? Well that was madness. But he had to find out more. He heard Thomas let out a long sigh of boredom. Owen gave him a quick glance. 'Just a few more questions please Tom, it's very important.'

Owen sat back in his chair and rubbed his hand over his forehead. Spittle started to run from the corners of Gladys' mouth. Her breath smelled putrid as she pulled him close, whispering so that no one could hear her words except Owen.

'It was Alyce Wilson who murdered her stepfather, Ezra Blackwell, with a pitchfork in the barn, but it was Rhoda Lambay who made me confess to the murder of her friend so that she could put me away in here so no one would ever find out the truth. Who would believe the ranting of a mad woman?'

Owen stood up. He had to get away from her. She was poisoning his mind against Rhoda. His mind was reeling with terrible thoughts.

'May the Lord strike me dead if this is a lie sir. You must believe me. She confessed to her friend Molly on the night of the storm. They were together in the surgery on the 'Sea Duchess'. I overheard her confession to Molly. It was only me and Molly, her dear friend who knew about it. Molly went overboard. So she was safe. No one knew she was a murderer. She would have hanged if she had been found out.'

Owen walked towards the door.

'Before you leave Doctor Owen Rathlin, I can see that you don't believe me but look I am going to swear an oath on this bible that what I have told you is true.'

Gladys put both hands on the bible and swore she was telling the truth. As he turned to leave she caught hold of him again.

'There is only one way to find out if I tell the truth', she implored.

'And what may that be Gladys?'

'It's quite simple. Ask Rhoda Lambay or Alyce Wilson or whatever she calls herself. Ask her if I tell you the truth. There is no one but me who knows the truth.'

XXXVIII

Rhoda was sitting mending a tear in her dress. As she sewed she thought about Rosswell Hawkes and his unusual behaviour towards her. She could understand his excitement at the prospect of finding gold in Bendigo, but what perturbed her was his thinking that she would be prepared to marry him, as if it had already been planned. Rhoda had always thought of him in brotherly terms, remembering the night when he had looked so handsome when they attended the theatre. Their eyes had met and she did feel something happen to her. Her face flushed at the thought of that mysterious moment. Rosswell had mistaken her coy glances for something more. Why burst out his love for her without any warning? AND, he had even been more excited at the prospect of finding gold with his 'band of demons.' How dare he speak to her that way. AND he still continued to call her 'woman'. He must know how it infuriated her.

'Rosswell Hawkes, you have a lot to learn about women, me in particular,' she muttered. Lizzie came into the parlour with a cup of tea, and several rounds of hot buttered toast.

After they had eaten the toast and drank the tea Rhoda put the cup and saucer down. The cup clattered.

'Are you alright Miss Rhoda? I mean I don't want to pry but you look upset about something.' Lizzie looked concerned as she cleared the table.

'No I'm alright Lizzie, nothing to worry about I'll ....'

There was a loud knocking on the door. They both looked at one another in surprise.

'Are we expecting anyone this morning?' Rhoda asked.

Lizzie made her way to the door. 'Not that I know of,' she called over her shoulder.

Rhoda put down her sewing and folded the dress placing the needle and cotton in the work basket, then looked up to see Owen Rathlin standing there, gazing down at her with an anxious look. Lizzie hovered behind him looking flustered, waving her hands about and shaking her head. Owen had obviously pushed past Lizzie before poor Lizzie had time to announce him properly. Rhoda frowned at him. She was puzzled, but tried to speak lightly. She smiled at him...

'Owen. How nice to see you so soon. Have you settled in alright?'

Owen didn't answer. There was a long silence. Lizzie continued to hover in the doorway. Still there was this heavy silence in the room.

Something was wrong. Rhoda could sense it.

'Lizzie will you bring in some tea please and….,' Rhoda stopped in mid sentence.

'I've no time for tea thank you.' He turned to Lizzie then back again to Rhoda. 'I have something important to ask of you,' turning again to the waiting Lizzie. 'I would prefer it if we could talk with some privacy Miss Lambay.'

Rhoda felt as if she had been hit. 'Miss Lambay!' What he had to say must indeed be serious. Rhoda recovered herself. 'Thank you Lizzie.' Lizzie closed the door quietly. Owen still stood never moving from his position.

Rhoda stood up. 'Well at least sit down Owen for goodness sake.' Rhoda was beginning to feel uncomfortable about the situation. She had already endured Rosswell's clumsy advances and now she had to endure Owen Rathlin and his mysterious performance. He perched himself on the edge of the old leather armchair and stared at her as if she were a stranger. Again the long silence.

'What's happened Owen? What did you want to ask of me?'

Rhoda had a fleeting thought of…no surely he was not going to ask her to marry him. Then she remembered the kiss she had given him on his cheek, the warmth of his lips as he tenderly kissed her hand. Such a feeling of warmth had flooded through her in tiny waves. But this was a different Owen that remained sitting almost rigid before her.

'It's no use,' he said abruptly, standing up. 'I can't sit down Rhoda. I have to ask you this standing up.' Rhoda made to stand up herself. 'No,' he pressed his hand to still her movements. 'No I'd prefer it if you remain seated Miss Lambay, or Miss Alyce Wilson, whatever you wish to call yourself.'

Rhoda suddenly became angry. How dare he speak to her in such a manner. Why was he so rude to her? Rhoda was in two minds about asking him to leave. She stood up.

'I can stand up in my own house if I wish to Doctor Rathlin,' she retorted swiftly. 'How dare you speak to me in such a manner. I demand to know what this is about!'

Owen studied her face as he came closer to her. His icy stare unnerved her and he spoke his words slowly and deliberately, as if every word had to be said with a cautious clarity. Rhoda became afraid of this stranger before her. Whatever was wrong?

'Tell me Miss Wilson, do you know of a Gladys Slyne?'

174

Rhoda was almost put off her guard but her subtle knowledge of handling Gladys Slyne and her questioning playing the 'deadly game' had made Rhoda more resolute.

'But of course I do. I used to work for her here, when we arrived in Van Dieman's Land. Her husband was the Reverend Arthur Slyne. Why, I met them on 'Sea Duchess'.

Owen clenched his hands behind his back and paced up and down the small parlour.

'And is it true then that Gladys Slyne was incarcerated in the Derwent Asylum?'

'Yes she was, and is still there as far as I know.' Rhoda said defiantly.

He stopped pacing the room and came and stood before her.

'Now tell me Alyce Wilson, did you murder your stepfather?' His voice had become hardly a whisper. His eyes held hers. She buckled under the strain. She had to sit down. Rhoda collapsed into the rocking chair. She rocked to and fro trying to find the words to tell him. How did he find out? Only Molly knew, but Molly was dead. Rosswell knew, she had told him when they had sat together under the tree. There was only Gladys Slyne but ……..

'You haven't answered me. Did you kill your stepfather in the barn with a pitchfork?' Owen shot the deadly words at her. Words she wanted dearly to forget.

'Yes, YES! YES! I did! It's true!'

Owen sat down again in the leather armchair. His face paled like death. He held his head in his hand and didn't look up at her.

'Oh God! I was hoping it was the ramblings of a mad woman. So all she told me was true. Oh my god! You killed your stepfather?'

'Yes, but you don't know why. I was abused. I suffered years of abuse at his evil hands. I was stupid and I went into the barn to see the kittens. I knew I would be violated by him so I tried to escape up the ladder to the loft in the barn…he grabbed me and I picked up the pitchfork and plunged it into his chest. I was petrified. There was no one to help me I……'

Rhoda stopped. The look of sheer horror on Owen's face! Then she told him everything. The last flimsy swathes that veiled her past had been ripped from her by the man who had meant everything to her. The man she trusted, the man who had christened her with a new name. Owen stared at her almost as if he were afraid to know any more. He held up his hand. Rhoda felt her heartbeats almost choking her.

'Wait…your friend Molly. Gladys said she fell overboard on the 'Sea

Duchess'.

'Yes she did. But Molly didn't fall Owen, she was pushed to her death by Gladys Slyne. The day we were all on deck watching the whale I....'

'Was it only Molly who knew about you killing your stepfather?'

Rhoda nodded her head. He still persisted in his harsh questioning.

'You confessed your sin to Molly. And then Molly was murdered by Gladys. It doesn't make sense. If she had overheard your conversation why would she push Molly to her death? What reason would Gladys have for killing your friend?'

Rhoda felt her face flush with anger. Did he imply it might be herself?

'Why indeed? You might well ask me. Gladys confessed to killing Molly.'

'Confessed when? Was it in a court of law?'

'Gladys confessed when I showed her the strip of white bloodstained cloth I had bound around Molly's arm. I found it up on the deck after Molly went missing.'

'You used that to get a confession from Gladys Slyne? It could have been a piece of cloth that belonged to anyone couldn't it?' Owen's tone was sarcastic.

Rhoda was almost at a loss for words. Owen was questioning her as if she were the guilty person, not Gladys Slyne. He held his chin in his hand and stared at her.

'Gladys Slyne confessed to killing Molly. Everyone heard her confess...'

'But the woman is supposed to be insane....isn't she ?'

'Yes she is. Did Gladys tell you she also killed young Ethan Davies?'

'Who in heaven's name is Ethan Davies?' Owen's voice shook with anger.

'Ethan was a shipmate on board the 'Sea Duchess'. He was going to tell me who he had seen talking to Molly before she disappeared. But before he could tell me Ethan suffered the same fate as Molly. Gladys pushed him to his death.'

Owen stood up and paced around the room, shaking his head in disbelief.

'So it appears that another person suffered the same fate as your friend Molly. Could he have heard your own confession to murder when you told Molly?'

'No he wasn't there?'

'How do you know he wasn't listening somewhere?' Owen gave her a sly look.

'No, I'm sure he wasn't. It was Gladys. Don't you see it was Gladys who murdered Molly…She was the one who overheard my confession.'

'How do you know she heard you? There doesn't seem to me any reason for her doing such a terrible crime. What would have been her purpose? You had a reason, so you say, for murdering your stepfather. If he had been abusing you why didn't you tell your mother or confide in someone? Someone could have helped you.'

Rhoda shook her head in despair. Tears welled up threatening to disclose her weakness when all along she had fought to be in control of her emotions. Owen Rathlin avoided her eyes.

'Rhoda I will not denounce you of that you can be certain.' He stopped and held out his hands as if pleading his case. 'How could I after all you have suffered. You had to pay the penalty of my own wife's accusations against you. I can't condemn you but there is so much evidence weighed against you. I don't know what to believe.'

In that moment Rhoda made a move towards him. Why didn't he believe her? Didn't he feel anything for her at all? Not even pity? Whatever had been between them had been snuffed out like a candle flickering in its last spurts of life. Rhoda could feel it deep down within her. The secret door that was kept ajar with hope and a possible love, closed firmly with a thud.

Owen picked up his hat as if to leave. But how could she let him go like this, there was still so much more to be said? He looked at her, sighed and looked stern.

'I'm sorry Rhoda.' He turned his hat round and round with his long, firm hands, gazing down at it, unable to decide what to say next. It was as if he was waiting for her to speak. So much silence between them. She wanted to call his name and run to the protection of his arms. Just one small gesture would be enough. Rhoda felt the anger rise within her. She had already been subjected to Rosswell and his uncaring feelings towards her and now she had to try and compose herself with the one man who she had cared for. He didn't believe her and never ever would, of that she was now certain.

Rhoda straightened herself up, clenching her hands together by her side.

'Doctor Rathlin, there is just one other thing before you take your leave. I would appreciate it if nothing was said to dear Martha about meeting Gladys Slyne, and, well, you know, about my terrible crime. Martha has been so kind helping to find out my real name and trying to help me remember my past.'

'You can rest assured Martha will never hear any of this from my lips.' Owen's tone was very serious. 'One more thing that intrigues me is how you can remember killing your stepfather and yet you cannot remember anything else in your past?'

'Of course there is so much more I could tell you, but I doubt it would be of any use to my case. I have been charged accordingly, by you, no matter what I say. Now if you will excuse me I have work to do. Good morning.'

Rhoda started to shake with anger, her voice didn't sound like her own. Owen stared at her, his mouth wide open. 'Is that all you have to say? Am I to be dismissed?'

'There is no more to be said. Now if you will excuse me,' Rhoda swept towards the door and held it wide open. She called for Maggie.

'Maggie, will you please bring me a cup of the delicious coffee Lady Elizabeth kindly sent down for us.'

Maggie paused in the doorway. 'Will that be coffee for two Miss Rhoda?'

'No. Just the one cup please, Doctor Rathlin is just leaving.'

Owen turned in the doorway putting his hat on his head as he mumbled, 'Good morning Miss Lambay. Just one more thing, it's just possible that Molly and Ethan did fall overboard. These tragic accidents happen all too often on board ship, it would be wise to remember that.' He hammered the final nail into her secret door, sealing it forever.

'Goodbye Doctor Rathlin.'

She watched him as he walked down the path, a strong wind had blown up. The 'roaring forties' had started to blow in. He held on to his hat, turned to look at her one last time. Something caught in her throat. Salty tears stung her cheeks with the force of the wind. She wanted to run after him, shake the truth into him. Instead anger again took hold of her and she yelled after him.

'I hate you Owen Rathlin…Do you hear me? I'LL HATE YOU FOREVER!'

But he never heard her. The sound of the horses, the clatter of the carriage and he was gone. She knew she would never see him again. He had become the judge and jury. He had condemned her without pity.

XXXIX

In the days that followed Owen Rathlin's departure Rhoda kept herself busy around the house. She prepared work for the children, scrubbed the kitchen table with such a force Maggie declared that they wouldn't need any plates they could all eat off the pristine table. She fussed over her because she wouldn't touch even a small morsel of food. She tried to coax her with cups of tea, some special little cakes that were a favourite.

When Rhoda had finished cleaning away her anger Maggie made a large pot of tea and toast and carried it into the parlour with Lizzie. She put it down on the table and started to pour the tea. Rhoda looked up and took the tea cup from Lizzie.

'Miss Rhoda shall I take Mr. Dunston's shirt back to him today?'

Rhoda sipped her tea. 'What shirt? I didn't know we had a shirt here of Mr. Dunston's.'

'Yes Hawtin brought it yesterday. He wanted it as soon as possible Miss.'

'Deliver it? Yes, you can Lizzie, and take this bill with you. Hawtin will bring the money they owe us for all our sewing. It's quite a bit. In fact, bring me the account book Lizzie please.' They were making a small sum of money between them with their sewing. Rhoda studied the account book as Lizzie put a plate of toast next to Rhoda's cup of tea. She winked knowingly at Maggie.

'I can bring the money back with me if you like Miss Rhoda,' Lizzie suggested.

Rhoda took a bite of her toast. 'I'm starving,' she said gulping down another piece of the thickly spread buttered toast. 'No, that's not a good idea Lizzie, there are thieves about.' Maggie and Lizzie laughed. 'As we are getting more sewing coming in from the Settlers I'll ask Reverend James if we can use the small schoolroom when the children have finished their lessons. We'll have more space to work in there, with the big tables for cutting out garments. Then we'll just have to carry the unfinished work into my own room.'

Rhoda wondered how they would manage to complete all the work they had to do, but she was glad they were all busy. She didn't have time to stop and think about Rosswell or Owen Rathlin. MEN, she considered, were selfish and inconsiderate.

Just as Lizzie was about to leave there was a sudden storm. The rain washed down the window panes looking as if the tide had reached up the hill and was trying to enter in desperation.

'You can't go in this Lizzie; you'll have to wait until it stops.' Rhoda said, frowning at the sight outside the windows.

'But I have to go Miss Rhoda. Caleb said I had to deliver the shirt myself...'

Lizzie broke off and her face went very red. Rhoda stared at her.

'What do you mean...CALEB said that you have to deliver his shirt? Are you on first name terms then with Mr. Dunston?'

'Oh God now what 'ave I said? I mean Mr. Dunston of course. But he did insist that I deliver his shirt personally. Only me, no one else.'

Rhoda didn't like the sound of Lizzie calling Mr. Dunston 'Caleb' and insisting that she and no one else was to deliver his shirt. It seemed very suspicious. She threw Maggie a glance. Maggie was frowning at Lizzie.

'I don't like the sound of this one bit Lizzie.' Maggie shook her head. 'No it don't seem right to me. It doesn't matter surely who delivers the shirt does it?'

'It's got to be me,' Lizzie said defiantly. 'Please let me go now Miss, please.'

What Maggie had just said seemed to confirm Rhoda's suspicions. Lizzie had always appeared eager to deliver the completed sewing repairs to the theatre. Rhoda had always let her go. She became excited at the prospect of going into the theatre.

'Lizzie, did Mr. Dunston insist it had to be you to take this shirt to the theatre?'

'Well he did say that when the other actors had finished their rehearsal, he would give me an audition as a supernumerary.' Lizzie folded her arms.

'A super-what-ary?' Maggie gawped at Lizzie. She started to laugh.

Lizzie started to cry and flopped down in the leather chair like a spoilt child.

'Don't tease her Maggie.' Rhoda looked down at Lizzie and stroked her hair. 'Don't cry Lizzie, I know what a supernumerary is.'

Lizzie looked up, brushing away her tears. 'What is it Miss Rhoda? I don't know what it is but it must be something to do with the stage.'

'Yes it is. A supernumerary is a walk on part. You simply walk on. You don't have to say anything. If this was a stage set it would be like Maggie just walking in here and putting down the tea tray. I might say 'Thank you Maggie' but Maggie wouldn't say anything, just leave through the door, see?' Rhoda smiled. 'It's easy but it's an important job especially for the actors on the stage.'

'Oh Miss! However do you know all that?'

Rhoda thought about it. However did she know? She must have picked it up from the past somewhere. She shrugged. 'Well, I must have heard it somewhere but you don't have to speak any lines.' Lizzie recovered quickly. 'Well that's good because I can't read properly yet can I and I didn't want to tell him I couldn't read.' Lizzie's eyes were glowing. Rhoda noticed how pretty she looked. Her figure was getting more rounded. The thin scrawny look had vanished. Lizzie was glowing with health.

'Lizzie, Mr. Dunston must know that you won't be available for some time yet. But in the meantime of course, if you continue with your reading perhaps in the future we could have a talk with Hawtin and well...'

'Oh you mean that I might be able to be super what's it in the future?' Lizzie's eyes shone with happiness.

'Of course, Lizzie. You can do whatever you want in this life if you really want it?'

Rhoda thought she sounded a bit too philosophical but she needed to assure Lizzie without hurting her feelings. She didn't mention the fact that Lizzie was still a convict and still had some time yet to finish her sentence unless she got a ticket of leave.

The rain had stopped. Lizzie jumped up. 'Now can I go Miss Rhoda?'

'I think we'll go together Lizzie, I can do with a walk. Fetch our thick coats. We might yet have more rain.' Rhoda watched as Lizzie almost fell over herself, anxious to get the coats and be off to the theatre.

'A good idea to go with her, Miss Rhoda. I'll make a nice dinner for your return,' said Maggie.

As Rhoda put on her coat she was thinking about what she was going to say to Caleb Dunston. What were his intentions with Lizzie? Although she had to be careful how she approached her questioning. The man could be genuine in wanting to help Lizzie further her ambition, but it wouldn't do any harm to find out more with some gentle probing. She would have to watch that she didn't say anything inappropriate. After all they were getting a fair amount of sewing from Caleb Dunston's Company of Actors. She had never met the man face to face. On the stage he looked like a kind old gentleman, probably in his sixties. She mentioned this to Lizzie on the way to the theatre and Lizzie roared with laughter.

'IN HIS SIXTIES? Why Miss Rhoda, he's much younger than that. More like his late forties. Dark and handsome Miss. No doubt he will be pleased to meet you after all this time. He always talks about you Miss Rhoda. Says you're a real beauty.'

'But I've never met the man, face to face that is,' Rhoda protested.

'Well he's seen you around the market shopping sometimes he said.'

Rhoda wondered what kind of conversations Lizzie had with Mr. Dunston, especially as they appeared to include her.

XL

Rhoda looked up at the sky as they neared the Theatre. The rain had stopped but there was a chilly wind and a few threatening clouds that appeared to hover over them. Lizzie pushed open the small brown painted door which read 'Stage Door'.

'You won't say anything about me not being able to read will you Miss Rhoda?'

'Of course I won't. We're only here to deliver this shirt for goodness sake Lizzie. Mr. Dunston is most probably rehearsing. We might not even get to see him.'

Rhoda followed Lizzie into the dimly lit passageway shutting the door behind her. A bald head, wearing spectacles appeared behind an opening in the wall as if by magic. Rhoda gave a stare. Lizzie laughed.

'Hello Billy, it's only me, Lizzie. I've brought Miss Rhoda with me today...err...to deliver Cal...I mean Mr. Dunston's shirt.'

'That's fine Lizzie. Good day to you Miss Rhoda. I've got a shirt of my own that needs a bit of mending. Think you could do it for me Lizzie?'

'Course we will Billy. Shall we go through then?'

Lizzie pointed towards the end of a dimly lit corridor. Billy nodded and went back to reading his crumpled newspaper.

'Billy's a nice old man. He's the doorman. Looks after us all he does.'

Rhoda smiled to herself. It was as if Lizzie had taken the theatre to her heart, as if she already belonged to Caleb Dunston's Company.

'Here we are, Mr. Dunston's dressing room.'

Lizzie rapped her knuckles against the polished wood of the door. Rhoda noticed the emblem of what had once been a star shape. It was ingrained in the wood almost as if it shouldn't be there at all. No one answered. A young girl brushed past them in a sparkling dress. Her long blonde curls swept down each side of her painted face. 'He's not in there. He's up on the stage if you want to see him.'

'If he's rehearsing we'd better leave his shirt in here in his dressing room. I'm sure that will be alright.' Rhoda was speaking to the young girl and to Lizzie, who already looked as if she was disappointed at not meeting Caleb.

'No you can't leave it in there,' said the girl, almost melting away into the gloom of the corridor. 'Go through here.' They heard her open a door. 'It leads into the auditorium.'

Rhoda and Lizzie made their way through the doorway. Except for a few lamps burning it was almost in darkness as they moved along the second row of seats with their eyes on the stage. The young girl in the star spangled dress whispered something to a man dressed all in green, who looked like a giant elf, and pointed towards the stalls.

'Oh dear, they're in the middle of rehearsals Lizzie. We can't interrupt them.' Hawtin waved to them in his green elf costume.

'Hello Lizzie and Rhoda,' the elf called to them. 'We're just trying on our costumes to see how they look ready for the pantomime.'

Lizzie laughed! 'Look at the spangles on her dress. She looks like a real fairy.' Someone attached a pair of gossamer wings to the back of the fairy, and handed her a long wand that sparkled as she waved it to and fro through the air.

Lizzie couldn't take her eyes off the young girl. She danced with gentle flowing movements. When she finally finished her dance she sank down onto the floor and crossed her arms. Lizzie clapped her hands, forgetting it was only a rehearsal. As she did someone came on to the stage and bowed towards the direction of Lizzie and Rhoda. A tall man dressed in a red and black costume, a close fitting black cap over his head with large red shiny horns on either side. Rhoda knew instantly that this tall man who seemed to command the stage was Caleb Dunston. He pointed the red glittering three pronged trident towards them.

'I am the fearful Demon King. You mortals heed my warning bell. You can't escape me here in Hell. For I, the Demon King....With Devils Dwell.'

Caleb Dunston's deep and powerful voice penetrated every part of the theatre. He swirled his flowing red satin cape around him and bowed towards them. Lizzie clapped her hands again but this time more quietly.

'Thank you dear Lizzie. Come on up to the stage. I believe you have my shirt with you...' Lizzie hesitated. 'Come on.' Caleb bent closer towards the auditorium. 'Come on, don't take all day. I need to try my shirt on.' Lizzie made her way up the wooden steps at the side of the wings on to the stage. 'Who's that with you?' he asked her as she took the centre stage with him. He shielded his hand across his eyes to peer out into the dimly lit theatre. Rhoda stood up and walked down the centre aisle towards the stage.

'It's me Mr. Dunston. Rhoda Lambay.' Rhoda felt her face go as red as the Demon's face. He crouched down and held out a gloved black hand towards her.

'Pleased to meet you, Miss Lambay. You are an excellent seamstress and also a person of great beauty. You should consider becoming an actress. We're all pleased with the amount of work you have done for us.'

His dark eyes glittered behind his red painted face. 'Well Lizzie, how does it feel to be on the centre of the stage? This is the spotlight position you know. Every actor fights his way to be centre stage.' Lizzie just clasped her hands together in front of her and murmured, 'Wonderful… it's wonderful Mr. Dunston.' He rested his arm across her shoulders 'One day Lizzie you'll be standing here as a great actress.'

Rhoda watched the spectacle on the stage. The young girl in the star spangled dress threw down her wand and strutted off the stage. No one noticed only Rhoda. Everyone was listening to Caleb Dunston, each one hanging on every word. 'Now then, I'll just take this confounded thing off.'

Caleb pulled the red and black demon shirt off his back and handed it down to Rhoda. 'Can you do something with this please Miss Lambay? It needs to be cut a bit lower. It's almost killing me.' He bent forward to show her.

'See here.' He showed her the neck part of the shirt. 'If you could cut it down say six inches it would be more comfortable to wear.' Caleb was pointing and showing her the costume.

She was aware of the smell of tobacco on his breath and an intoxicating aroma of cologne from the heat of his body. His eyes stared into hers as he smiled showing perfect white teeth. When she went to take the shirt from him she tried not to look too closely at his body. He held the shirt close against his chest then handing it to her quickly he stood up, in one quick movement looking down at her laughing, reaching for the white shirt Lizzie held out for him. He slipped it on, still continuing to laugh down at her. But not before Rhoda had seen something. Something she never thought she would ever see. Had she imagined it? She had only glimpsed it in that moment. She couldn't be sure but it looked as if there was a tattoo of a small fish on Caleb Dunston's right shoulder. Rhoda strained her eyes to see more, but he had fastened the shirt. He bent down towards her.

'What's the matter Miss Lambay? Have you never seen a man's chest before?'

He unbuttoned the shirt and pulled it apart revealing his strong chest.

'There you are, now you see me, now you don't.' He laughed and turned away walking towards the wings. 'Thank you Miss Lambay.' he called over his shoulder.

'No, thank you Mr. Dunston,' Rhoda called out to him.

Rhoda thought about the tattoo on Caleb Dunstan's shoulder. She was sure it was a small fish although she doubted herself seeing it in the half light of the theatre. And another thing, had it been on the right shoulder or the left? She had become so flustered when he came close to her that she couldn't be sure.

XLI

After they left the theatre Rhoda looked up at the sky. A storm was on the way.

'Come on Lizzie, I think we'll make it up the hill before this storm breaks.'

As they hurried along the street Rhoda asked Lizzie is she had noticed a fish tattoo on Caleb Dunston's right shoulder.

'Why yes Miss, I did. I tried not to stare at him too much. It wasn't a big fish though was it Miss Rhoda? It looked quite neat I thought and hardly noticeable.'

They had to almost run up the hill. The storm decided to break when they were half way up and there was no shelter. They arrived at the open cottage door with Maggie waiting anxiously in the porch for them. Rhoda threw her old battered umbrella down in the porch in desperation. She was drenched right through to her underwear.

'Get out of them clothes right away. You'll catch your deaths, both of you.'

They discarded their sodden clothing in the warm kitchen and eagerly wrapped themselves in warm blankets that Maggie had prepared for them.

Warming themselves before the fire in the parlour Maggie brought in hot lemon tea.

'Come on, drink this down both of you,' Maggie fussed, making sure they were comfortable. Rhoda told Maggie about their trip to the theatre and the wonderful costumes the actors were wearing. They laughed when she mentioned Hawtin all in green like a giant elf and Caleb Dunston's demon costume and his fish tattoo.

'It seemed strange to me for a man in his position to have a tattoo on his person,' Rhoda said, staring into darting flames as if she was entranced with them.

'Oh I don't think so Miss. My dear father had a tattoo of an anchor on his forearm,' said Lizzie pulling her blanket closer around her. 'Lots of men have a tattoo!'

'What did your father do Lizzie?'

'He was a sailor at one time Miss. That's why he had an anchor tattoo. It had special memories for him I suppose,' Lizzie murmured sleepily. 'Like a trademark Miss.'

'A trademark? I would never have thought of that.' Rhoda shivered and sipped the scalding drink Maggie had made. 'I wonder what trademark a fish could be?'

Lizzie yawned. 'I don't know Miss. Something to do with fish I suppose. A fisherman maybe or a fish monger. Isn't the sign of a fish a Christian symbol as well?'

They both laughed out loud. 'I can't see Caleb Dunston as a fishmonger.' Lizzie almost choked on her drink. 'He's too posh...I can't imagine him gutting a fish or chopping off their heads. Oooh! And imagine him looking at them fish eyes Miss...dead eyes like this.'

Lizzie opened her eyes wide, her mouth gaped open as she looked at Rhoda. For an instant Lizzie reminded her of the Reverend Slyne and his dead fish eyes, how they used to terrify her. She wondered in that moment what had happened to him.

'It seems strange doesn't it for such a gentleman to sport a tattoo?' Rhoda put down her empty cup and moved closer to the fire. She couldn't stop shivering.

'I think perhaps our Mr. Caleb Dunston probably liked to fish for sport. What do you think Lizzie?' Rhoda looked across at Lizzie for her answer but she was fast asleep.

Later that night Rhoda woke in terrible fear. Her face was burning, her head ached. She felt around her bed to make sure she was safe. A terrifying dream had awoken her. She had been almost drowning in live, wet fish. And Caleb Dunston was standing over her holding out more wriggling fish to throw to her. The wetness she felt was real enough. Her nightgown was damp and she had to remove it quickly. As she pulled it from her shivering body, her hands trembling, she remembered the past. The memories had come to her silently and as furtive as a nightmare. Was she fully awake? She was back in her old room at home, the pale moon pointing accusing fingers at her from the window.

Rhoda fumbled in the heavy drawer for a clean nightgown. She pulled at it sobbing, afraid of her nakedness. Someone was watching her, someone was in the room with her pulling, wrenching, clawing at her cotton nightgown. Threatening hands, a heaving sweating force ripping it from her thin childlike body. She found her breath, whimpered at first then let out a choking scream. It wouldn't leave her throat while hands that gripped like iron held her fast. The sheer terror shook her whole body. Why couldn't her scream pierce the room, shake the whole house, even the whole universe? They must hear it.

The massive hand that covered her mouth imprisoned the fear within her. She was going to die, she knew it. Death was caressing her, acting as a friend, then just as she was about to surrender to its soft murmurings, she twisted her head and in that desperate second, with all the little breath left within her, she screamed. And as she screamed she saw the moon hide her face and look away disinterested. Rhoda screamed again and called for help. She fell onto the floor sobbing, still looking for the terrible hands that had gripped her body. Someone was in the room again with her. Soft gentle hands pulled her nightgown over her head and pulled her down into warm clean bed clothes, murmuring soothing words of comfort.

'You are safe now Rhoda. It's just a bad dream. Shhh! Rest now.'

Someone was wiping her hot face with cool water, holding her head up to make her take sips of water. Resting, exhausted, her head throbbing with memories, strange people and thoughts that were tangled up in her mind. She couldn't shake them free.

'Where am I? What's happening to me?' she breathed. Then more voices softly whispering. She had to strain to catch what these voices were saying. Waking and sleeping, small bits of conversation floated down upon her like soft dandelion clocks. She was in a meadow, she was safe. There were buttercups, clover leaves, tiny daisies made into daisy chains for her red gold hair. 'You are a daisy princess.' Her body was spinning out of control. There were more soft murmurings. She knew it was death again claiming to be a friend. She called out to Molly. Molly, where was she? Why didn't she come to her? 'Molly for God's sake, help me,' she shouted again and again. Ezra Blackwell's face taunted her. 'Whore,' he whispered, 'you murdered me...' His blackened hands reached out for her. 'Jezebel. Whore of Babylon, come to me.'

She jerked up in bed her eyes wide open wildly searching the room. 'NO...NO don't let him take me. Don't let him take me.'

'No one will take you, Rhoda. I won't let him take you.' Strong firm hands held on to her and pressed her gently back onto the pillow. For a moment she saw his face.

'Rosswell Hawkes.' Her hands reached up to touch his face. 'Please stay with me. I need you to protect me Rosswell.' She gripped tightly on to his rough shirt. 'Hold on to me. For God's sake, he's trying to take me. Oh God what can I do?'

She knew she was shouting the words at him trying to scream out the terrible fear that was rooted inside her. How could she make them listen to her? It was as if every word she shouted was like an echo, mocking her, mimicking her and wallowing in her terror.

'Rhoda my darling, I'm not going. I'll stay with you for as long as you want me. No one or anything is going to take you. Do you hear me Rhoda? You are safe now.'

Her chest was hurting her, her head ached. As her hot hands dropped weakly onto the bedcovers, she let out a long sigh as warm tears caressed her hot cheeks. Rhoda sobbed as each salted tear became the liquid fear that she tried to drive from her mind. How she wished the salt would cleanse her body and soul of the terrors that she knew would be her clinging companion, hers forever.

Rosswell's cool strong hands became her fortress. 'I will hold you forever. I love you. Stay with me Rhoda.'

Rosswell bent down close to her face. She couldn't see him but she could feel the warm breath from his mouth. She could smell the life in him like dried heather, crisp bracken and well worn hardened leather. But there was something else she had to cling on to that appeared as silk-strong as a spider's web. He loved her.

XLII

It took six weeks for Rhoda to be born to a new life. She knew that Lizzie, Maggie and Rosswell had nursed her back to them with their love and devotion. Lady Elizabeth had sent her own eminent Doctor Sheridan Beese to attend her. Lady Elizabeth had fussed around the house making sure that everything that was in her power would make Rhoda well again.

She stood at the window and brushed her hair. It had grown almost to her waist until Lizzie had cut a few inches off it when she was getting her strength back. Maggie came into the room carrying a tray with hot chicken soup and freshly baked bread. She placed it on the table by the window and pulled a padded blue chair ready for Rhoda.

'Come on Miss Rhoda. You have to eat all of this and I've instructions to stay and make sure you eat every last bit.' Maggie stood behind the chair with one hand on her hip.

'Well you don't have to stand there as if you're some prison warder Maggie. Come and sit down with me and eat.'

Rhoda looked out at the bluest sky she had seen for ages. One or two light clouds hovered in the distance. Cockle Creek sparkled in the sunlight and out across Recherche Bay waves were strung out like frills on a green silk dress. Rhoda smiled at the scene before her. She was a little afraid of the happiness she was feeling. Deep inside her a warm feeling had spread itself like a coverlet over her secret door every time that Rosswell Hawkes appeared or if she even thought about him. Or if someone mentioned his name, the little secret door would open and gently ruffle the softness. Then the warmth of it would surge upwards trying to find a way to escape, finally brushing her cheeks into delicate pink tea-rose petals. Try as she may to hide the soft blush, she couldn't keep it solely to herself. Everyone knew. Maggie, Lizzie, Hawtin and even Lady Elizabeth seemed to know the secret.

Maggie came in and put her dinner on the table.

'Oh Miss Rhoda you haven't touched a scrap. I shall have to tell Rossie when he returns from Port Arthur.' Maggie stared at her, shook her head and smiled. Rhoda turned away from the window at the mention of 'Rossie'. She sat down quickly and started to eat the soup. Maggie smiled at her.

'Hawtin called a few times when you were so ill. He left flowers and messages for you. Oh and Mr. Caleb Dunston sent his apologies for not calling on you when you were ill but he sent his good wishes for your speedy recovery.'

Rhoda broke off a small piece of bread and idly dropped it into the hot soup.

'Did he send a letter then?' Rhoda asked.

Maggie carried her bowl of soup to the table and sat down opposite Rhoda.

'No he didn't. It was Hawtin who brought his message and.....' Maggie jumped up from the table. 'Oh dear! I forgot all about it. Whatever will he think?' Maggie left the parlour for a few minutes and returned in a fluster. 'There, Hawtin brought you this when you were so ill. I'm sorry Rhoda, I forgot all about giving it to you.'

Maggie put a small box on the white lace tablecloth. Rhoda stared at it puzzled.

'Whatever can it be?' She held the box in her hand.

'Well you'll only find out if you open it. Sorry Rhoda I put it in the kitchen drawer and forgot about it.' Rhoda opened the wooden box and took out a silver chain. She held it up to the light. A tiny silver fish dangled from the chain. It was held by a very fine small piece of silver thread coming from the open mouth of the fish. Rhoda stared at it.

'It's beautiful but very strange. I don't know if I like it or not.' Rhoda held it out to Maggie.

'It's very sweet, but I must say I feel sorry for the poor fish.' Maggie held it against her own neck as she looked into the mirror.

There was knock on the door. Maggie dropped the fish down on to the table and went to answer it. Rhoda looked up as Lizzie came into the room with a basket from the market. On the top was a small bunch of flowers. Hawtin followed her in pulling off his cape and throwing it on to a chair.

'Rhoda you have some colour in your cheeks at last.' Hawtin bent down and kissed Rhoda on the cheek. Then he looked concerned. 'Are you sure you feel stronger? I must admit you look better than last week.' He sat down and sniffed the air. 'Do I smell some delectable chicken soup, or am I too late?' Everyone laughed. How much Hawtin loved to eat, yet his waist line always seemed to be the same size. Maggie went out to the kitchen. 'It's a good thing I make extra what with you and Rosswell to feed.' she muttered and shook her head.

Lizzie gave Rhoda the flowers. 'I met Lady Elizabeth down in the market. She asked me to give you these and to tell you she is going to Port Arthur this Friday and she wants you to accompany her in her coach.'

'These flowers are lovely. Why does she want me to go with her to Port Arthur? Did she say?' Rhoda buried her face in perfume of the flowers.

Lizzie had already taken off her coat and was seated at the table with Hawtin.

'I'm starving,' Lizzie sighed. 'What?…umm... Port Arthur, she said something about going to collect some fabric for clothing or something, but she did say the sea air will do you a power of good. I agree with her. It will be good for you to take some of the clean sea air Rhoda.'

Maggie carried a large tray with two steaming hot bowls of chicken soup and a plate of warm fresh bread rolls. Hawtin rolled his eyes upwards.

'Maggie you are a saint. I think I will have to marry you one day. I can't let you go to anyone else.'

Maggie blushed. Lizzie moved her bowl and picked up the silver chain.

'Why what's this then? I haven't seen this before. Whose is it?'

Rhoda took it from her. 'It's mine. It's a gift from Hawtin.' She turned towards Hawtin.

'I'm sorry I forgot to thank you for it Hawtin.' She fastened it around her neck.

'There what do you think? It is an unusual pendant but thank you for being kind.'

Hawtin gulped down a chunk of bread almost choking.

'Hey hang on a minute. I didn't give you any gift Rhoda.' He saw the frown on Rhoda's face. 'But wait on. That doesn't mean to say that I wouldn't give you any gift of course, but what I mean to say is, it's not from me Rhoda. I brought it here when you were ill. It's from Caleb Dunston.'

'WHAT! Caleb Dunston sent me this silver fish...I wonder why.'

'I don't know. When I told him you were almost at death's door, he asked me to give you this. You were so ill at the time Maggie took it and kept it until you were well.'

Rhoda felt herself trembling as she looked in the mirror at the fish dangling from her neck. There was something about it that didn't seem to be right.

'Don't you like it then Rhoda?' Hawtin asked. He seemed unconcerned by it. He caught Maggie's eye and puffed. 'That was delicious Maggie. I'm full up to here now,' pointing to his neck.

'No room for apple pie then Hawtin?' Maggie said whisking away the empty bowls. Lizzie walked over to Rhoda and looked in the mirror at her studying the fish.

'Well isn't that strange Miss Rhoda. We wondered about Caleb Dunston's fish tattoo didn't we. It's like as if he knew we were talking about it. Don't you like it then?'

Rhoda unclasped the chain. 'Yes it's very strange Lizzie and no I don't like it. I don't think I will ever wear it.' She put it back into the small wooden box. It was only then that she noticed the shape of the wooden box. It was crudely carved and resembled a miniature coffin. It seemed such a strange gift to give someone.

'If you like it Lizzie...here, it's yours to keep.'

XLIII

Rhoda didn't have much time to dwell upon why Caleb Dunston had sent her the silver fish. She thought it a very strange gift and for it to be given to her from someone she hardly knew was equally strange. It wasn't as if he was a friend, after all she had hardly spoken to the man. Lizzie had told her that perhaps Mr Dunston was interested in Rhoda more than she imagined.

'I think he has taken quite a fancy to you Miss Rhoda,' Lizzie chuckled.

Rhoda's thoughts were now filled with the prospect of a journey with Lady Elizabeth to Port Arthur. Lady Elizabeth had arranged for her coach, driven by Albert, to pick Rhoda up at nine o'clock Thursday morning. Rhoda was so excited. This visit to Port Arthur would be so different from the last time, eighteen months ago. It was then she had arrived as a convict girl, terrified of what lay ahead of her. But now today she would be arriving as a free person and accompanying a real lady, Lady Elizabeth.

Lizzie and Maggie insisted on helping her dress as if she were a fragile china doll, all the time warning her about keeping herself well wrapped up for fear of any change in the weather.

'We don't want you taking ill again do we?' said Maggie putting a clean white handkerchief inside Rhoda's green velvet muff. She tucked a matching tippet around Rhoda's shoulders. She felt quite stifled. She was sure she would faint. They were muffling her up, not considering the bright sunshine outside. Rhoda let them persist in their wrapping, after all she could shed the outer clothing when she was in the coach. Rhoda made a skirt from six yards of soft grey wool and a frilled blouse of white cotton and lace. And she wore a green tartan coat kindly given to her by Lady Elizabeth. She looked at herself in the mirror as she tied the wide grey ribbons on her green velvet bonnet. She had trimmed it herself, with grey rouched ribbon and bavolets edged the back of the bonnet. Her hair had been brushed and curled until it shimmered in the morning sunlight.

'Oooh you look beautiful Miss Rhoda,' Maggie said, wiping a tear away with the corner of her apron. Lizzie closed her small valise. Rhoda twirled around and gave a deep curtsy to herself in the mirror. Thoughts of Molly came flooding back to her.

'You look like a lady or something.' Rhoda said the words to her image in the mirror. Molly had said them to her so long ago, when they were in prison together. Her heart ached a little. How she wished she could be here to see her now. She raised her skirts to reveal her white frilled petticoat and kicked out the frills with her Italian soft leather boots.

'It was a white frilled petticoat just like this one that brought me here to Van Dieman's Land. Just think, I would never have met any of you if it hadn't been for a certain white cotton petticoat.'

'And I would never have met anyone as beautiful as you Rhoda Lambay if it hadn't been for a white petticoat.' Rosswell lolled in the doorway gazing at her. Rhoda whirled towards him, her face flushed with hearing his voice.

'YOU Rosswell Hawkes. What are you doing here? I thought you would be on your way to Bendigo by now.' Rhoda looked away from him and stared in the mirror.

Rosswell came further into the room. 'I wanted to make sure you were completely recovered before I left. Besides I have to go to Port Arthur today.'

'You're going to Port Arthur as well….. Why?'

Rosswell stood beside Rhoda and looked at himself in the mirror.

'We look a pretty good looking couple, don't you think so Maggie?'

Maggie laughed at him. 'You look real handsome Rossie.'

'And you look real handsome, WOMAN.' Rosswell spun Rhoda round to look at him. 'What do you think, do you think I…' Rhoda became impatient and picked up her tasselled bag.

'Are you going to Port Arthur because I'm going Rosswell? Albert will be here to pick me up in Lady Elizabeth's coach soon. How are you getting there?'

Rosswell pushed his wide brimmed hat back off his face and stared at her. She felt her heart thumping so loudly she wondered if everyone could hear it in the stillness of the room.

'I'm going with my 'Band of Demons' in a covered wagon. We have to pick up equipment, like pick axes, pans for panning GOLD. Shh! Shhhh! And shovels, tents and food supplies for a few months. AND NO I am not going because you're going Rhoda.'

Rhoda felt defeated. She had wanted him to say that he was going because she was and that he wanted to see her. His eyes were mocking her. Rhoda became angry. 'GOOD,' she almost shouted. 'Well I hope you have an enjoyable time with your shovels and pans.' She flounced past him pushing him out of the way.

'You're forgetting the tents and pick axes and food, very important for me and my Demons.' Rosswell stuck his hands up either side of his head and made a face at her.

'Oh yes. I was forgetting your DEMONS Rosswell Hawkes. Convict men aren't they?' Rhoda tossed her head. Rosswell glared down at her. 'EX-CONVICTS my dear, misinformed woman. They are now FREE MEN. Free to do what they want with their lives. Like you Rhoda Lambay, surely you must remember you were a convict once. Or have you so quickly forgotten?' Rosswell tugged his hat straight and made for the door.

'Goodbye Rhoda. I may see you in Port Arthur....but then again I may not.'

He swept through the door without waiting for a reply from her. Rhoda bit her bottom lip to stop the flow of tears. Maggie and Lizzie were watching for her reaction. She stared at her pale face in the mirror. Why had they quarrelled again? Maggie put her arms around Rhoda. 'That's my own fault. I asked for that Maggie. I shouldn't have called them convicts. They're free men now, like myself.'

'I'm sure he didn't mean to be so horrid to you Rhoda. Don't cry, please don't cry, the coach will be here any minute.' Maggie looked out of the window.

'I'm not going to cry Maggie, whatever makes you think that I am.' Rhoda sniffed and looked again in the long mirror. 'I don't think it's right, the clothes I mean. I don't know what the fashion is these days. I should have waited for the paper patterns to arrive from England. Lady Elizabeth said they would be here soon.' Rhoda smoothed her hand across the sloping shoulders and the tight sleeves of her jacket. 'Do you really think these clothes are suitable?'

'Of course they are. This is your own style Rhoda. Why do you worry about fashion?'

Lizzie folded her arms and sighed. 'I heard that Fanny Burney in 1801 had her own style. She wore whatever she wanted so I was told.'

'You're quite right Lizzie, I shouldn't be fussing like this.'

Maggie called to her from the window. 'The coach is here!'

They heard the clatter of hooves. Rhoda picked up her valise and stopped at the door to kiss them both on their cheeks.

'Be good both of you and don't feed Hawtin too much food Maggie,' she laughed.

Albert took her valise and put it in the coach. Lady Elizabeth waved to them from the open window. Rhoda looked up at the sky. It held the promise of a warm early May day. She felt happier as she stepped up into the coach. She was determined that the quarrel between herself and Rosswell wasn't going to spoil her excursion to Port Arthur. Lady Elizabeth had been extremely kind to her, treating her like a daughter.

'It's going to be beautiful day Lady Elizabeth!' she called out to her.

XLIV

'Are you sure you're feeling well enough my dear?' Lady Elizabeth enquired.

Albert had set off leading the two horses in a steady canter across the top of the hill. They looked down at Cockle Creek and Recerche Bay in the distance. She could see a sailing ship making its way towards the port, the sails full and billowing as it caught the wind. Rhoda gasped at the sight of it.

'Oh yes Lady Elizabeth, I'm getting stronger every day.'

'Well we mustn't over exert you. We'll stop for lunch and then continue our journey stopping for dinner at 'The Ship's Lantern.' It's a charming little inn and the food is excellent. After a good night's rest we can go on to Port Arthur. I stay there several times a year.'

'That sounds wonderful Lady Elizabeth. The proprietor must know you very well indeed.'

'Yes. Polly Davies and her husband own the Ship. She used to be my cook years ago, when my daughter was alive and...' Lady Elizabeth left the sentence unfinished... 'Oh dear me and my tongue. I'm sorry I didn't mean to tell you that.' Lady Elizabeth looked away from Rhoda.

Rhoda touched Lady Elizabeth's hand. 'Don't be sorry about it. Would you like to tell me about your daughter? I mean I don't want to pry or anything.' Rhoda became flustered. 'What I mean is, well I really would like to hear about your daughter.'

Lady Elizabeth's eyes brimmed with tears but she smiled at Rhoda.

'You are such a dear girl Rhoda. You remind me of her, the same green sparkling eyes. Her hair was beautiful, though a shade darker than yours.'

Lady Elizabeth slipped out of her jacket. Rhoda did the same. She was beginning to get stifled in all the clothing Maggie and Lizzie had made her put on for warmth. She was much more comfortable now but Lady Elizabeth insisted she draped her paisley shawl around Rhoda's shoulders. Then she settled back in the padded cushions and folded her hands in her lap.

'Alzenia, my daughter, was eighteen when she died. It was a tragic accident. It happened in Port Arthur. Sir John and I had brought her here to recuperate from her illness. Alzenia loved the sea. She would watch the sailing ships for hours.'

'She was like me then. I love the sea, the ships and the boats. I don't know why as I don't remember living near the sea. I think I lived in the countryside.' Rhoda smiled.

'You love the sea Rhoda? Now isn't that strange and you both have green eyes like the sea itself. It was the sea that took her away from us. Alzenia had difficulty in walking. She used to love to sit in the boat and help row it in the harbour. One day she tried to stand up in the boat. The sea had suddenly changed from being calm. The waves chopped and churned like angry lions. I tried to call out but she was too far from the shoreline. She toppled over and fell into the sea. One of the convicts jumped in to save her, but they were both drowned. His head came to the surface then he went under again. Their bodies were washed ashore.'

'How terrible that such a tragic accident happened and you were witness to it all.'

'They said it was the callipers on her legs that weighed her down. John Leyshon was the name of the convict and a brave man to have risked his life. He was a trusted kind man and was due to get his ticket of leave the next day. Sir John never got over it. That's why his work takes him from here for long periods at a time.'

Rhoda didn't know quite what to say next. 'I'm so sorry Lady Elizabeth I….'

'Don't be sorry my dear. The sea brought you to Van Dieman's Land. I believe you were sent to me for a reason.'

Rhoda suddenly remembered the green dress she had worn to the theatre.

'The green dress I wore to the theatre that night. That was Alzenia's wasn't it? You wanted me to wear it.'

'Yes I did. I hope you're not offended Rhoda. You see it was such a pity I had clung on to it for so long, Then when you came to the house looking for dresses to wear to the theatre, I knew Alzenia would have wished for you to wear it my dear.'

'Of course I'm not offended. I'm flattered that you thought of me.'

'I'm glad. It suited you perfectly. You looked radiant in it, and that young man Rosswell Hawkes looked so handsome. He appears to have taken quite a fancy to you. He's got a rugged strong look about him, someone who would take care of you. If I was only younger…' Lady Elizabeth stopped and looked out of the window. 'Why, we're almost at our stopping place for luncheon. I must admit the journey has made me famished.'

When they had finished their lunch and rested awhile, they started their journey towards Port Arthur. Lady Elizabeth soon fell asleep. Rhoda covered her with a soft blanket and stared out of the window at the passing scenery. Albert had whipped the horses up into a gallop as the coach rumbled along a straight road, then she felt the coach slowing up as it lugged up a hill and across the high road. She looked down and could see the tall masts of sailing ships in the distance. She opened the window a little and breathed in the clear crystal sea air. It was powerful and brought back so many memories of the voyage on the 'Sea Duchess'. She wished she could see the ship again. White clouds puffed their way out to the horizon. The view was wonderful and she wondered for a moment if she should wake Lady Elizabeth to see it, then realising that she had probably watched this scenery so many times before she let her sleep.

It was later when the horses had clattered into ' The Ship's Lantern' and been welcomed by a large Polly Davies in an enormous white apron. She had insisted on kissing Lady Elizabeth and Rhoda. She was a happy, bustling, busy lady with her dark hair swept up into a large bun that sat atop of her head with a small muslin frilled cap starched and perched firmly in its place.

She brought some tiny almond cakes and coffee into the parlour. Rhoda didn't feel very hungry but ate some of the delicious cakes as Polly and Lady Elizabeth talked together.

When they were shown up to their rooms Lady Elizabeth rested. Rhoda sat by the gabled window and watched the gulls swooping and gliding. She thought about the tragic accident that had happened to Alzenia and the brave convict who had tried desperately to save her. She sat for a long while deep in thought about Van Dieman's Land and how lucky she was to be a free woman and have the friendship of Lady Elizabeth. Small wonder then, that Lady Elizabeth showed kindness to the convicts who worked for her. Albert had told her that all the convicts she employed would be prepared to do anything that was asked of them, she was held in such high esteem.

Rhoda didn't intend to fall asleep. She wanted to make the most of every moment. She woke with a start wondering where she was then remembered. She washed and dressed herself in her lavender striped cotton dress that Maggie had wrapped carefully for her in her valise. When she had brushed her hair she found a hair-band with tiny white flowers and beads on either side that had been tucked inside the dress. She put it on and smiled to herself. Lizzie or Maggie must have made it for her to wear with her dress for dinner. How fortunate she was to have such dear friends. They were like sisters to her.

At dinner Rhoda and Lady Elizabeth talked about dresses, fashions and Mrs Amelia Bloomer with her design for 'bloomers excellent for cycling' but they laughed at the thought of wearing them as a fashion statement. Rhoda had fillets of mutton with mushrooms and vegetables followed by Polly's surprise 'Crystal Palace Pudding'. As Rhoda sipped her wine Lady Elizabeth asked if she would go with her to see Alzenia's resting place.

'Why of course I will go with you. Where is she buried?'

'In the green sea that she loved...on the Isle of the Dead.'

XLV

Rhoda woke refreshed the next morning, excited about seeing Port Arthur. She had saved a little money from her dressmaking and looked forward to buying something special for Maggie and Lizzie and looking at some of the shops. Rhoda put on her grey skirt and green jacket. She looked out of the window. The day was fine but way out over the sea wisps of grey cloud threatened the horizon like clouds of dust. Over a breakfast of creamy porridge, 'fairy' toast, marmalade and coffee with swirls of delicious cream, Lady Elizabeth planned the day.

'I've a surprise for you Rhoda. I have to pick up some containers of fabric and things from England later, but I didn't tell you the name of the ship carrying it.' Lady Elizabeth paused with a twinkle in her eye. 'Can you guess Rhoda?'

'Not the 'Sea Duchess' is it?'

'Yes my dear, the old 'Sea Duchess' that brought you here. I know the Captain very well. He's arranged for us to go on board whilst my cargo is being unloaded.'

'Oh to see the ship again would be wonderful. Thank you Lady Elizabeth. I've often thought about the voyage and my friend Molly.'

Lady Elizabeth took her arm. 'Well of course you must miss your dear friend Molly, like I miss my dear Alzenia; we have both lost someone who was very dear to us. But my dear, Rhoda life is full of surprises, some are good, others bad but we have to accept it all. And you have such loyal friends in Lizzie, Maggie and Roswell Hawkes.'

Polly came to see them off. She had written down the recipe for the 'Crystal Palace Pudding' to give to Maggie. Then they were off. The horses, refreshed after their night's rest, seemed to gallop like the wind.

'Look there it is, Port Arthur', Lady Elizabeth called out.

The view from the top of the hill spread before them like a painting. Below them was Caernarvon Bay. Rhoda could see Point Puer, the place that had once housed the 'bad boys' as Maggie had called them. She wondered at the isolation of the place when it had been open. As they came further down the coastal road Rhoda could see the tall masts of the waiting ships. Which one was the 'Sea Duchess'?

'There used to be a thriving whaling industry here,' Lady Elizabeth said shaking her head, 'but not any longer. Everything is changing. Most of the businesses went bankrupt.' There was the old flour mill and the granary warehouses. Convicts in their yellow uniforms went to and fro wheeling heavily laden crates and boxes either to unload or load the waiting ships. As they drew nearer Lady Elizabeth pointed out to her the penitentiary that used to be a flour mill. Onward past the hospital and the convict church with its gothic structure. Finally the coach drew to a halt and Albert put the steps down for them to get out.

'Thank you Albert. You made good time.' Lady Elizabeth dropped some coins into Albert's hand. 'Off you go now, rest up the horses and have a few hours for your own time. You've earned it Albert.'

'Thank you very much your Ladyship. I will be here as you arranged at 3 o'clock.'

He touched his hat. 'Goodbye Rhoda.'

They watched as he took the horses and coach over to the stabling yard. Lady Elizabeth sighed. 'Now then my dear, before we do anything else we will take the boat over to Possum Island to visit Alzenia. Shall we do that first?'

'Possum Island! I thought you said Alzenia was on the Isle of the Dead.'

'Yes I did and it is called that now, but originally it was Possum Island'.'

'Why did they change the name then? Possum Island sounds so much nicer?'

They wandered down to the quay where a small boat was waiting.

'Ah here we are. Peter and James will row us out to the island.'

One of the oarsmen helped them down into the boat then when they were safely seated pushed away from the side with his oar.

'You will soon see why they now call it 'The Isle of the Dead' Rhoda.'

Rhoda watched as the oars clipped the waves easily. When she looked ahead she could see the small island. It wasn't far from Mason Cove. Further out she could see Point Peur on the right. It enthralled her to be on the sea again. She looked back at the tall masts of the sailing ships. One of them would be the 'Sea Duchess'. 'This is really wonderful Lady Elizabeth, to be here on a boat back on the sea again'. She caught one of the oarsmen smiling at her. Then she turned her attention back to the island. It looked a bit sinister. The very name of it, 'The Isle of the Dead', sounded Gothic and eerie. As they drew nearer the gentle swell heaved the boat upwards. Rhoda wondered at the size of the island. It looked quite big close up. There was a wooden jetty ahead and clumps of trees.

When they had tied up the boat and stepped onto dry land one of the oarsmen handed Lady Elizabeth a posy of small pink and blue flowers.

'Thank you for remembering to get them for me Peter. You are kind.'

'It's the least I can do for you your Ladyship. I knew you was coming today same as last time.' Peter stepped back into the boat. 'We'll be back in an hour if that's alright by you my lady.'

'Yes, I think the weather will hold out for us...won't it Peter?'

'It should do but if things change, as they sometimes do, we will be back sooner.'

Lady Elizabeth waved them off. 'Such good boys.' She said softly 'They were convicts once you know, but such nice boys now.' Rhoda didn't know but she guessed that Lady Elizabeth had no doubt helped them in the past.

'Now then, up we go. I'll show you Alzenia's tombstone then you can wander around a bit and see the rest of the island while I sit and talk with her. I can tell her all about you.'

They passed several headstones and family vaults as they walked upwards. Rhoda was amazed at how many there were. 'How many people are buried here?' Rhoda asked.

'I think it's about a thousand. You will find tall headstones with their backs turned away from the convicts unmarked graves on the lowest part of the island. Ah here we are. This is Alzenia's spot. You see we put her here overlooking the sea. It's a lovely spot. I usually sit here on this wooden bench. Do you mind Rhoda if I sit here on my own for a while?' Lady Elizabeth placed the posy resting against the stone. There were only a few words written on it.

OUR DEAREST DAUGHTER
A L Z E N I A

Someone had carved small fish leaping over tiny waves underneath her name. Rhoda felt something cold sweep over her at the sight of them. Lady Elizabeth was sitting quietly as Rhoda decided to slip away and explore the rest of the strange island where convicts, even in death, were not only looked down upon but had to face a different way. She spent the time wandering alone looking at the misspelt names and broken headstones. She started to count them then gave up as it seemed a macabre thing to do.

She reached the lower part of the Island. Lady Elizabeth was right. The graves in this part were just mounds of earth with no markers to say who they were. As she stepped back her footing slipped. She looked down and was amazed to see a freshly dug open grave. It startled her and she looked around. Perhaps the burial party would be arriving soon. Something caught her eye. It was just a flash, sunlight flashing on a shiny object though she couldn't be sure. She looked up towards the high carved headstones. The height of some overpowered her as they leaned forward. She wished now that she had stayed nearer to Lady Elizabeth. Hearing of the tragic death of Alzenia had unnerved her. She had to get back to Lady Elizabeth.

Without her hardly noticing tiny tendrils of mist beckoned with childish fingers around her grey woollen skirt. Rhoda looked quickly out to sea. The darkened waves reminded her of bobbing black bears. It was only as she decided to make a move that she noticed the mist had become like clawing damp and sweating hands. Her instant idea was to move quickly or she would be trapped in the mist unable to move for fear of stepping off the island into the sea. Rhoda tried to push down the fear and looked around her for her best way up, but she could no longer see the headstones clearly. They looked as if they were closing in on her.

She wanted to call out for help and was just about to but in the same instant she saw what looked like a shrouded figure approaching slowly, as if with care.

'Thank God,' she breathed. 'Hello there.' She waved her hand then the figure disappeared again. 'Wait,' she called in desperation. 'Please wait. I'm lost in this mist.'

'Lost are you? Well stay where you are. I can just about see you.' It was a man's voice that reached her over the damp air. She started to breathe heavily. Thank goodness someone was here. She was sure she recognised the voice.

'I know you. I know your voice. It's Mr Dunston from the theatre isn't it?' Rhoda waited for an answer.

'Yes it's me dear Rhoda. Did you like the little silver fish I sent you?' The silver fish! She felt relief from her fear. Whatever must he think of her? She had never bothered to thank him for it.

'Yes I did and thank you for sending it to me. I should have thanked you before. It was very rude of me not to…' Rhoda stopped talking. It was as if she were having a conversation with the fog. She couldn't see the shrouded figure at all. He had vanished like a magician's sleight of hand. The dampness was seeping into her clothes, crawling along her spine. Memories of her accident in the London fog came back to her. It was so long ago. The mist cleared a little. She was startled as a face peered down at her. It was Caleb Dunston.

'It's alright Rhoda, you're quite safe now.' Caleb reached out to touch her. 'Give me your hand.' He took hold of her hand in a strong grip, almost hurting her. Then the voice and the strong grip of his hand worried her. Doubts invaded her body. Why was Caleb Dunston here on the Isle of the Dead? Had he been following her? Lizzie had said about Caleb fancying her, was this some kind of ploy to make himself more known to her? She uttered a cry. 'My hand, you're hurting my hand.'

He released the pressure on her hand but still continued to grip it.

'I'm sorry Alyce, I didn't mean to hurt you. It was careless of me, forgive me.'

ALYCE…he had called her Alyce! How did he know her name?

'You called me Alyce. Why?'

'That's your real name isn't it? Alyce Wilson of Frogmore, England?' He swept off his hat and gave her a deep bow. 'Daughter of Sir Daniel Wilson…err...now deceased.'

He had swept off his hat and inside it was a wig of grey hair. He pulled off his beard.

She should have known from the bear like hands, but his voice had changed.

'EZRA BLACKWELL!…Oh my God! I thought you were dead I….'

'Go on, don't be afraid to say it Alyce. You…killed me. But I'm very much alive. You should have made sure I was dead, before you left the barn. It was Jack who found me. Now it's your turn for a tragic accident. After all, no-one knows I was once Ezra Blackwell. I am now Caleb Dunston, respected Thespian, a great actor. All the world's a stage my dear and we are merely the players. We have our exits and our entrances, and play many parts. It's now time for your exit Alyce Wilson.'

There were so many things she wanted to ask but this game looked as if it was going to be her last one of the 'deadly games'. She had to play for her life. If she could manage to keep him talking someone was sure to come looking for her. She tried to calculate the time she had been on the Island. Peter and James said they would return if the weather changed. They were probably on their way by now.

'How did you know I was here?' Rhoda asked, looking around his large frame to see if anyone was coming to find her.

'Don't try and trick me Alyce.' He raised his cane as if to strike her.

'Wait, wait a moment. I must know why you sent me the silver fish. Please tell me why?' Rhoda was desperate in her pleading. She watched and held her breath as he brought down the black ebony silver topped cane and rested it lightly on her shoulders.

'Please Ezra, tell me why you sent me the fish pendant. I must know?'

Rhoda knew there wasn't much time left. She wanted to know why he had sent it to her, especially when she was so ill. She had to keep playing for time.

'Dear Alyce. If only you had let me love you.' He pulled her closer to him. She held on to him tightly. As long as he held her close he wouldn't be able to strike her with the cane. But then he pushed her away and caught hold of her. She was sure that she could see a flicker of light in the thick mist, just a flicker but it was coming towards them. Rhoda had to keep him facing her, if he turned and saw whoever it was, he could kill her and get away from the scene.

She reached towards him as if to touch his face. 'The silver fish Ezra. Why the fish?'

He pulled back his cane and laughed out loud. She could see his teeth almost like the snarl of a bear and then to her right she saw the lantern sway a little and stop. She could make out several people through the clearing mist.

'The fish, my dear Alyce, was my sign. I was a poacher at one time before I strangled your father, so I could marry your mother…'

Rhoda almost fell back. Her head was reeling. 'YOU strangled my father?' And then it all seemed to make sense. That was why he sent her the silver fish.

'That's why you sent me the silver fish wasn't it? You wanted me to know?'

He held her closer, his hands about her neck. 'Yes, I wanted you, my little fish.'

He was tightening his grip. There was just one more card to play to win the game. She reached up and scratched at his face. He released his hold on her.

She shouted the words out so that everyone could hear.

'But it wasn't YOU! It was HENRY SIMPSON who killed my father.'

She could hear Ezra gasp in astonishment. He almost let go of her then held her even tighter. 'Yes it was him, Henry Simpson who…'

They were his last words. Ezra was struck from behind. Rhoda saw a long handled spade slicing the damp air with a tremendous thud. Ezra fell across her as the force of his body pushed her backward into the open grave. She could smell the wet earth as she screamed, landing with little breath left in her body. A row of faces looked down at her, Rosswell's DEMONS. They looked concerned, except one face that was grinning down at her.

'Not thinking of staying down there are you woman?' Rosswell called down.

'Pull me up you beast. Get me out of here.' Rhoda held up her arms as they pulled her out of the open grave.

Ezra was lying on the ground. 'Is he alive?' she breathed.

The mist had lifted. Everything was clear. Lady Elizabeth was calling out to her as she made her way down towards her. 'Rhoda my dear, what's happened?' Rosswell held on to her.

'Wait a minute, I must find out, just to have peace of mind.' Rhoda knelt beside Ezra and fumbled with his outer clothing.

'What are you doing Rhoda, for God's sake?' Rosswell whispered hoarsely.

Rhoda pulled down the coat and shirt, almost tearing the buttons and there it was. Her hands trembled and then she saw it. The fish tattoo.

'That's it - the fish tattoo. This proves he was Henry Simpson.'

'Who in hell is Henry Simpson?' Rosswell shouted.

'Who in HELL is Henry Simpson, alias Ezra Blackwell, alias Caleb Dunston…? You've met your nemesis at last.'

THE END

Bibliography

Convict Women - Deidre Beddoe
Sailing Ships - Patrick Brophy
Sailing Ships - Cedric Rogers
The Story of Australia - A.G.L Shaw
Criminal Ancestors - David T. Hawkings

About the Author

Anne Reeve was born in Barry, in 1935 and grew up in Malpas, Newport. After working in various jobs, she met her future husband John when they both worked at 603 Regiment T.A. Malpas. From there they moved to Margate and Islington taking on tenancies at The Walmer Castle and later The White Lion at Islington.

She now lives in Cwmbran, Gwent, has four children, six grandchildren and two great grandchildren.

Anne gained a degree with the Open University (Drama, Social Science and Education) and became a teacher until she retired. She now devotes her time to her love of writing stories.

She is Chairman of Cwmbran Writer's Group where members all work together, in a close friendly atmosphere, holding workshops, writing poems, stories and plays. Anything that acts as a springboard to develop writing is used. Between them the group have produced several magazines and books.

Acknowledgements
Source photograph Tasmanian Devil –Wikipedia
Sue Moulton – Editor (with grateful thanks for her wonderful help and guidance)
Cwmbran Library Staff (for research)

When Alyce Wilson suffers a blow to her head with Doctor Owen Rathlin's hansom cab, she is taken inside his house to recover. She is unable to remember anything. Owen decides to 'christen' her with a new name, Rhoda Lambay, 'Lambay Street so you won't forget where I live will you Rhoda Lambay?' With his departure Rhoda becomes aware of something sinister in the house. Her decision to leave early next morning puts Rhoda's life in jeopardy. She has been caught like a fish in a net, with no way of escape. Danger, terror and fear of not knowing her past produces a dread of the future. Her only friend is Molly a convict girl. It is with Molly's help she has to learn to play the 'deadly games' that will test her own sanity and strength. Can she capture the 'devil serpent' in its own trap and set free the elusive butterfly which remains deeply hidden within the 'tangled terrors' securely locked behind her own 'secret door'?